LAIRD OF GLEN LAGGAN

LAIRD OF GLEN LAGGAN

A SENTIMENTAL COMEDY

BY

J. J. BELL

LONDON
CHAPMAN AND HALL, LTD.
MCMXXXI

Published by CHAPMAN & HALL, LTD.,
11 Henrietta Street, LONDON, W.C. 2. Printed in Great Britain
at the BURLEIGH PRESS, Lewin's Mead, BRISTOL, and bound by
A. W. BAIN & CO., LTD., LONDON

To

MR. AND MRS. ARTHUR AITKEN

LAIRD OF GLEN LAGGAN

I

TO the departing holiday-maker the Dundas Street entrance to Queen Street Station, the L. & N.E. Railway terminus in the City of Glasgow, may well appear as a golden gateway to a thousand and one delights, though to the everyday traveller it is a not very inviting passage to a small dingy courtyard of uninspired design, around which the grime of past generations appears to have been preserved, and wherein reigns an all but perpetual gloom.

We are not, however, here concerned with the psychological influence of railway station architecture upon the travelling public, nor yet with its effect upon those whose daily work is done in its lights and shades. No doubt, a man's mentality is affected by his environment ; and, as our little tale proceeds, we shall discover in the make-up of Colin Maclaggan small things that would not have been there had he been, say, a doctor, a banker, or an artist, instead of what he was, a railway porter. And though we are meeting Colin Maclaggan for the first time, in the garb of a porter and on duty as such, we shall probably find it more interesting to regard him as an ordinary member of Humanity.

It was a chilly, drizzling afternoon towards the end of February—" Glasgow at its worst," said citizens, forgetting what their city could be like under fog, or after snow. There was a lull at the Dundas Street entrance. An express for the North was due to depart and apparently the last of its passengers had already reached the platform. But at a railway station, as Colin Maclaggan would have told you, the minute that matters most is the last minute.

Colin stood on the pavement, under the clock—as it chanced, the only porter there just then—a man of medium height, fairly broad, turning grey, with rather a fine cast of countenance, his mouth under the short moustache suggesting humour of the kindlier sort. A bit of a dreamer, you might have guessed from a glimpse of the brown eyes ; but for the moment, at any rate, you would have been wrong. Nor did his slack figure, lounging attitude, left hand playing idly with the small change in his pocket, betoken lack of alertness. The last minute is, indeed, the minute that matters, often to the porter, as well as to the passenger—financially.

A taxi took the awkward curve from the steep thoroughfare and rolled into the courtyard. Colin was at the door, as it flew open, and caught the rug and two suit-cases thrust at him, glancing swiftly at a label on one of them. A big, heavy man, his frantic eye on the clock, stumbled out and would have fallen but for the porter's ready support.

" Can I catch it ? "

" Got your ticket ? "

" Yes ! "

" Number 3 platform—front portion—run ! "

The train was moving when the passenger, from a " first smoker," in the secretive way of so many travellers, handed Colin his reward, with a " Many thanks, Porter," and drew up the window.

Colin's hand went to his pocket, came back and opened.

A halfpenny !

A fellow porter saw, and let out a short, dry chuckle. For a moment Colin's expression was glum ; then he said—

" Ach, well ! I daresay he meant it for a bob."

From these words of his you may learn something of the nature of Colin Maclaggan. Which, indeed, is the only purpose in recording this and another incident, both quite trifling in themselves.

His day's duty now ended, Colin went to the porters' room for his raincoat. Time was when he would have scorned, as well as grudged, the price of such a garment ; but, two winters ago, a chill induced by a drenching had meant three weeks' absence from work, and he had accepted the warning and made the purchase. It was Maggie, his wife, however, who saw that he donned the coat, these doubtful mornings.

He was a few minutes later than usual, and of the little army of porters going off duty at that hour, only one was left in the room when Colin entered. The man's way of looking up suggested that he had been waiting for Colin. A lanky, morose-looking fellow, ten years Colin's junior, he was moving about in a restless, nervous fashion. He did not speak till Colin was about to go. Then he said abruptly, huskily—

" Man, Colin, I wish ye would lend us a couple o' bob. Ye'll get it back on Friday, sure ! We havena a penny in the house."

Colin shook his head, but his hand moved to his pocket. " The greyhounds again ? " he asked.

" Ay—blast them ! But I'm done wi' them. I ken I've said that afore, but it's gospel this time. Friday, sure ! "

Colin handed over the money, shaking his head again—now at himself, for he was already aware of his folly. This borrower's Friday was a day that never, never came. " Mind, Hugh," he said, with an attempt at firmness, " I'm lending for the last time. If you were a single man . . . " With a motion of his hand against the other's thanks, he went out.

He left the precincts of the station, calling himself a " damn fool." He had had no right to lend—or, rather, give away—the two bob. Maggie could have done with the money. It was a dashed shame, the way he treated Maggie, the best and hardest-working woman in the world—a dashed shame !

A confectioner's window, brilliant in a drab row of shops, caught his eye. The very thing ! He would take home some sweeties to Maggie ! It was Colin's way, when conscience was troublesome, to buy something for his wife. He fancied the method as entirely original. So, having paid eighteenpence for a pretty box of chocolates, he proceeded towards his home in the regions of Parliamentary Road, a thoroughfare not quite so dull as the name implies, though nearly as long as it suggests. Glasgow, however, with its economy of pronunciation, gets over the word in four syllables.

As he climbed the stairs, he removed the wrapping from his purchase and brought from a pocket a couple of newspapers, with many pictures, selected from his gleanings in the compartments of a morning train, which Maggie would enjoy during her evening leisure, if any. He entered a house on the third landing, hung up his raincoat and cap in a dim passage, and strolled into the kitchen.

" Well, you've got home ! "

" You're busy ! "

The remarks were uttered simultaneously, as they had been uttered about five thousand times in the past, without their obviousness ever once having occurred to the speakers. Colin was home, and Maggie was busy, and that was that !

This afternoon, as it chanced, Maggie was busy at the task of ironing. She was a more than comely, fair-haired, blue-eyed woman, still in her early forties—flushed at the moment—on whom domestic exercise had failed to have much of a " slimming " effect. Neither she nor her man were Glasgow born. She was of the North-East, with, perhaps, a drop of the old Norsk in her blood—a good mate for Colin, of the softer, easier-going West Highlands. Nearly all their years had been lived in the City, and there their girl and boy had been born. Had you told Colin that his wife was above him in certain ways, he would have agreed gladly and cordially ; had you hinted that she had real claims to beauty, he would have been amazed.

He laid the papers and pretty box on the table, and winked blithely.

" What a man ! " she said, with a quiet smile, and he noticed neither the sigh in her words nor the shadow in her eyes. Nor could he have imagined her saying to herself : " Well, well ; Colin's Colin, and he'll never have any sense about money."

Suddenly, as one struck by a recollection, she turned, pointing to the high mantelshelf.

" There's a wire for you—came half an hour back."

" A wire—for me ! " Colin about to sit, straightened himself, staring. " What's in it ? "

" I didn't open it. It's addressed to yourself—

' Colin Maclaggan.' " With a swift change of tone—
" Colin, don't tell me you've been betting on horses ! "

" Me ! " He laughed and went over the hearth.
" Fine you ken I got my cure for that, twenty years
back."

" Then I'm not much heeding what the news is. Open
it—quick ! "

" Who would be sending a wire to me ? " He tore the
envelope and took out the message. " Gosh ! . . .
Maggie, it's from Bob ! "

" Bob ? . . . Oh, Bob Maclaggan, your cousin that
went abroad, dear knows how long ago—just after he
had borrowed three pounds off you ? "

" Ay, that's him ! I wonder when he came home—
good old Bob ! "

" If he can afford to send you a wire, he can pay back
the three pounds ! "

" Oh, never heed about that now, Maggie. Listen to
what he says :—*Coming to see you nine to-night. Important.*"

" Is that all ? ' Important ! ' Well, if he's wanting
another three pounds—"

" Maggie, this wire was handed in at Fort William !
What can Bob be doing up there ? "

" Trying to borrow, maybe, and now—"

" Aw, whisht, woman ! It's many a year since I heard
news of Bob, but he was beginning to do not so badly in
—I forget the name of the place—somewhere in South
America, anyway."

" If he was doing not so badly, he should have sent
you the three—"

" Maybe he's coming now to pay it back. Anyway,
it'll be great to see Bob again !—Are you not for a
sweetie ? " He slid the box towards her, and sat down.

" Later on, maybe. I'm too hot for sweeties. Will your cousin be seeking his supper, when he comes ? Mind you, I wouldn't grudge him a bite of supper, the three pounds and all, but it's the half-holiday and——"

" I expect he'll have a feed in the train—there's a restaurant ; but don't fash yourself about a supper ; he can get a cup o' tea, if he wants it. D'ye ken, Maggie, I've got it into my head that Bob has piled up a big fortune, and now he's been making a grand tour o' the West Highlands. Though he's got no friends there, as far as I ken, he was always keen on the places. I mind he used to be wild at me for not caring where my forebears belonged."

" He wouldn't be making a tour at this time o' year, surely ! "

" H'm ! I hadn't thought o' that. Still, what for has he been at Fort William ? " Colin paused and sighed. " He might have let me ken he was home. It wasn't very like a cousin, that—was it, Maggie ? "

" Now don't be starting to vex yourself about nothing, Colin. Your cousin'll be here at nine, and then you'll get all his news. I'll allow he wasn't a bad chap, except for the three pounds ; and I would forget about the three pounds, only I can't bear to see you diddled."

" But maybe, at long last, he's coming to pay up ! "

" Well, well," she said, fetching a hot iron from the range, " smoke your cig and read your paper, and let me get through with this job. Ronnie'll be in in no time, wanting his tea in a hurry. He's got some ploy on to-night—something about motor-cars. He's getting awful discontented wi' the wholesale provision trade— says he wishes all the bacon in the world was at blazes—"

" Poor Ronnie—he's but a lad—"

" Now, Colin, I'm warning you, you're not to be soft wi' Ronnie. He's lucky to have the job. Many a boy would be glad o' it. He's got plenty nonsense in his head already—like his sister."

" What has Peggy been doing now ? " Colin lit a cigarette.

" Oh, she seems happy enough wi' her job at the cash desk, but I whiles think her being among the iron-mongery at Lawtons' is sort o' hardening her—and you mind what a soft-hearted wee thing she used to be—eh ? "

" How hardening her ? "

" Well, I don't like the way she's treating that nice young fellow, Charlie Fortune. I suppose she's at the pictures wi' him this afternoon, like on every other half-holiday."

" No harm in that, woman ! "

" No—but Charlie wants her, and if she doesn't want Charlie, she should let him go. She's old enough to ken her own mind, and to see that Charlie's in dead earnest."

" She's but twenty—give her a chance ! Love's not such a solemn business as it was in our time ! "

" You're right there ! I suppose it's the fashion, but I whiles wonder if girls are in earnest about anything nowadays, except their looks and their legs."

" Toots, Maggie ! " Colin smiled. " Peggy's fine ! Anyway, Charlie Fortune's not ready to keep a wife."

" I wouldn't wonder if he's not far from ready ! He's high up in Lawtons', and his folk are well off, though his father did begin on the railway."

" Is that one to me ? "

" Don't be silly, man ! Old Fortune had great luck when that uncle o' his left him the garage, just when the motoring was beginning to get popular. He and Mrs. Fortune are welcome to their fine house in Cathcart ! As for you, Colin, you would never be content away from the railway. If you was a millionaire, you would be setting up a private railway station and paying passengers to let you handle their luggage ! " Mrs. Maclaggan laughed, set down the iron and drew her hand across her brow.

" It's you for the comical, but there's maybe a grain o' truth, as they say, in your fun," he admitted. " I've been overlong on the railway to fancy myself at anything else. Gosh, I wonder what's the news that Bob's bringing wi' him."

" See if you can wonder, wi' your mouth shut, till I get through wi' this." She spread out a piece of pretty, silky flimsiness. " My, that Peggy of ours is daft for the dainties ! A body would think her daddy was a duke ! "

About the same hour, the daughter, along with the young man whose earnestness was troubling Mrs. Maclaggan, came out of a picture house in Sauchiehall Street.

" Well, what about it, Peggy ? " he was asking, his hand at her elbow, as they reached the pavement.

Peggy was frowning slightly ; the lines between her brows betokened indecision. She was a tall girl, with her mother's fine features and colouring, except that her eyes were more grey than blue, while her mouth betrayed less tenderness than the woman's. To the casual eye she was undeniably pretty ; to Charlie, who had studied it, her face was beautiful. No doubt, he was right—sometimes, at any rate. She carried herself as though she owned the world, and the pride of a young girl is a beauty in itself,

" Say you'll come to the Palais to-night," pleaded Charlie, who was rather an ordinary-looking young man, dark-haired, not short but thickset, as are so many capable young men to-day, with wide apart, honest hazel eyes. " Or don't you want to come with me, Peggy ? "

" Oh, I'd like it fine, but—but—oh, well, I'll come ! " she finished. She could not have told just then whether she was giving in to please Charlie, or herself.

" That's good ! I'll be up for you at the back of seven."

" Righto—but you're not to come home with me now. I've got something to do."

" If it's shopping, I can wait outside for you."

" Charlie "—not unkindly—" if you don't do as you're told, I'll change my mind about the dance. See, there's your yellow car coming—unless you're going to the train, and that's not my way."

Having dismissed him—he lived with his people on the South side of the River—she crossed the street, and presently came to a window devoted to hosiery, where she halted. She knew to a ha'penny how much was in her purse ; she knew she could not afford a new pair of stockings ; and she knew she ought not to have said she would go to the dance. So, having considered all the reasons against the purchase, she went in and made it. Nearer home, she called at another shop, where she was known, and made another purchase ; after which she felt uplifted, rather than otherwise.

She entered the kitchen as Mrs. Maclaggan was clearing the table, preparatory to laying it for the evening meal.

" Hullo, Daddy ! Hullo, Mother ! "

The response of Daddy was more enthusiastic than that of Mother, whose eye had been caught by the two parcels in her daughter's hand.

Peggy felt, rather than saw, the glance, and said—
perhaps a little shame-facedly—

" Slippers and a pair of stockings, Mother—I just had
to buy them. Charlie's taking me to the Palais, and I'm
at the limit—really ! And I had to get the slippers on
tick till Saturday. You won't mind if I don't give you
my bit next week, will you ? " She referred to her
fortnightly contribution to the household exchequer.

Maggie was tired ; she was often tired at this time
of the day ; and her thoughts might have been put into
the angry question, " How on earth do they all expect
me to carry on ? " But the gleam passed from the blue
eyes, and she said quietly : " All right, lassie, all right.
But do try and be cannier wi' your money."

" Righto ! " said Peggy, relieved, and turning to her
father, spied the bright box on the table. " Chocs ! "
she cried, and proceeded to help herself, chaffing her
father about his extravagance.

Ronnie came in—a good-looking lad of seventeen,
with his father's brown eyes.

" How's ham ? " Mr. Maclaggan jocularly inquired.

" Rotten ! " the son answered, with a grin.

" Ronnie," said his mother, " is that something you've
been buying ? "

" Just a book—a book about motor-cars," he replied,
with a frank look. " When'll tea be ready ? "

" That's the third book you've got about motor-cars.
A body would think you was expecting to own a car ! "

" Well, maybe I will—some day."

" You'll never, never own anything if you spend your
money the way you're doing ! And you haven't given me
your bit for last week ! "

" I'm terrible hard up, but you'll get it next week,

B

sure." He moved near to her. " Sure, Mother ! " His tone was affectionate, not wheedling.

Again the blue eyes lost the gleam. " All right, laddie, all right," she said, and turned to her preparation of the meal.

Peggy went away to get off her out-door things, and Ronnie, helping himself to a chocolate on the way, joined his father.

" It's a rare book," he said, undoing the parcel. " If I can't drive a car, I could take it to pieces and put them together again."

" Great ! " said Colin, but absently. He had been watching his wife, and though not quick to see things, he was not blind. He cleared his throat.

" Look here, Ronnie ; after this you've got to pay your bit to your mother, before you buy books, or anything else. See ? "

It was so very seldom that Colin asserted his paternal authority, that the son looked blank, while the wife, at the hearth, half-turned her head. But neither was quite so astonished as Colin himself. He blushed.

Meanwhile, in the first-class section of a restaurant-car on the West Highland Railway, a passenger sat in solitude, nibbling at water biscuits, sipping very weak tea, and studying by turns a number of typewritten letters, an architect's plan, and a photograph. He was elderly, small, thin, clean-shaven and, despite a bronzed countenance and keen eyes, had a delicate look. And he was on his way to Glasgow, to cast a bombshell into one of that city's most peaceful little homes.

II

"A TAXI!" exclaimed Colin, who had been watching the clock. "Gosh, it must be Bob!" "Run down and fetch him up, afore the neighbours get round him," said Maggie. "A taxi! Looks like as if he was flourishing!"

"Maggie," anxiously said her husband from the door, "you'll not be mentioning the three pounds to him?"

"Away, man! What d'you take me for?"

As he went out her smile faded. Her hand went to the mantel, as if for support. That fine bloom of hers was a deception. She had been wearied before she started, immediately after tea, to "shine up" the kitchen. It had not occurred to her to ask the help of her daughter, and it had not occurred to Peggy to offer it. Girls who were out all day were not supposed to work after they came home. Mrs. Maclaggan had laboured at the "shining up," not because of any particular regard for Bob, who had been a frequent guest in the old days, nor because she expected him to return as a prosperous person. At the back of her mind, as she toiled, was the thought, "I've never affronted Colin, and I'm not going to do it now."

But the smile revived, and she stood very erect, a blithe and bonnie woman in a freshly laundered old blouse of faded blue, when Colin led in his cousin, who appeared to have got lost in a monstrous overcoat.

" Here's Bob, Maggie ! "

" He's welcome ! "

You might have suspected that the visitor came in anxious, if not nervous, and found relief and encouragement in the sight of his hostess.

" Maggie," he said, gravely, holding her hand, " you are handsomer than ever."

" Bob ! " she cried, shocked, then laughed—and it may be that she felt less fagged than a minute previously.

Colin took his cousin's coat and put him into the armchair.

" When did you come home, Bob ? "

" I landed at Liverpool, yesterday."

" Yesterday ! Then you must have travelled by night to Glasgow, and to Fort William on the early morning train ! You've had a big day."

" You must be tired," said Maggie. " What about a bite o' supper ? "

" Thanks, Maggie ; but I had all I wanted on the train—and I've a good many things to say to you and Colin."

" Tell us one thing, now," Colin put in. " How did you get the address ? We've had a few changes since you went abroad."

" That was easy. This morning, I arranged with one of your railway officials to find it for me and wire it to Fort William. But tell me about yourselves.—I ought to have written, but the months and years slip away, and —well, there's no use in going back on that.—How's the world been using you ? "

" Oh, not so bad," said Colin.

" Might have been worse," said Maggie. " You'll see the family—just the two—later on. Peggy—she's twenty—is out, dancing, and Ronnie—he's getting on for eighteen—is at some ploy wi' one o' his companions. Though I say it, Bob, they're good bairns."

"Take after their mother," Colin gaily remarked. "Are you still T.T., Bob ? "

"Got to be, for my health's sake. But don't let me—"

"Colin's not keen," said Mrs. Maclaggan. "He got in a half-mutchkin, just in case you would take a drop."

"I can be a terrible hard drinker—when I get the chance," said Colin.

"Behave yourself ! " said his wife.

"But the chance never comes ! Bob, what about yourself ? You're not a single man, are you ? "

"I was married—for a year," Bob slowly answered. "She died—the little one, too."

"Well, well ! " muttered Colin, and a much longer speech might have conveyed less kindly sympathy.

Maggie's lips came together and her head gave a little wag.

"Since when," Bob continued, "I've done nothing but work and, I don't mind telling you, make money."

"And now, maybe," said Colin, after a short pause, during which he and Maggie avoided each other's glance, "you'll be thinking o' retiring."

His cousin smiled. "No ; I'm not thinking of that. I'll carry on as long as I'm allowed."

"So this is just a wee holiday," Maggie ventured.

"Yes ; I think it's going to be a sort of holiday, for two or three months ; but I must be back in the Argentine in the summer. I came over in rather a hurry—and now I'm going to tell you why. Colin, put your hand in my coat, and you'll find a big envelope."

Colin did as requested, and passed over the envelope.

"Thanks." Bob drew out a photograph and handed it to his cousin. "Ever see that before?"

Colin seemed to be looking across a narrow sheet of calm water at a wood under the shadow of a great rugged mountain. Sheltered by trees on three sides was a large white mansion, with a tower over the doorway and turrets at the corners. At a little distance to the left of it was the ruin of an ancient castle.

Colin's gaze narrowed; then suddenly he smiled.

"Gosh, it brings back lang syne!" he said. "You and I were but laddies when our granny took us to see that place—Glen Laggan Castle, where the Maclaggans lived, about the year One."

"Not so far back as that, man! Not quite two hundred years ago," said Bob. "Let Maggie see it."

While she looked at it, he watched her.

"Lovely!" she murmured at last.

"You like it?" he asked quickly.

"Surely! I think it must be the bonniest place in the world!"

"Well, then"—he took a breath—"it's yours, Maggie—yours and Colin's."

"Thank you, Bob. We'll get a frame for it, and be proud to have it on the wall."

"I don't mean the photo; I mean everything that's in it—the loch and the mountain, the house and the estate, and the old castle—they're yours and Colin's—and your children's." He took another breath. "I bought Glen Laggan, to-day!"

His glance passed from the one to the other. It was evident that they did not comprehend.

"Listen, and I'll explain," he said. "I've always been interested in the old place and the history of the

Maclaggans. Many a book I've read, many a dream I've had, out yonder in the Argentine, about the West Highlands of Scotland. Many an inquiry I've made by correspondence; and for some years, now, I've been aware that of the Maclaggans who last owned Glen Laggan, only two direct descendants were alive—you, Colin, and myself."

Again he looked at his host and hostess, but their eyes were upon each other, questioning, apprehensive.

" Let me assure you that I'm quite sane," he resumed, with a smile, " and, please, give me your attention. Since the Maclaggans lost their estate, after the ' Forty-five,' it has had a good many different owners. One of them built the modern castle, as they call it up there, about 1860. Last year, I read in the papers of the death of the proprietor, an English millionaire; but then I was still dreaming. But, last month, I read that Glen Laggan was to be sold by auction on the 17th of February —to-morrow —and that wakened me up ! I saw, no longer in imagination, but in reality, Maclaggans in Glen Laggan once more ! I set the cables working, and took the first steamer for home. The auction was cancelled, and I acquired Glen Laggan by private bargain. . . . Now, is that not clear enough ? "

" It's clear," said Colin, taking out a packet of cigarettes, " that you must be a millionaire, Bob, and I'm sure Maggie's as pleased as I am."

" I'm all that," agreed Maggie, whose blue eyes held a puzzled expression.

" No ; I'm not quite a millionaire," Bob replied, shaking his head at the proffered cigarette, " but I have enough to see the thing through comfortably for everybody. I propose for the present, Colin, to settle on you investments yielding ten thousand pounds a year, tax free ; but if we find that insufficient, then—"

The packet fell from Colin's fingers. "Stop it, man, stop it!" he cried. "We can take a joke, Maggie and me, but—"

"I believe Bob's serious," Maggie put in—

"Thanks, Maggie!" said Bob.

"But, all the same," she added, "it's just pure nonsense. In the first place, why does Bob come to us when he's got himself?"

"That, too, is easily answered! I'm a childless man ; I've got my work out yonder ; and even if I had the will, I haven't the health for this old country, all the year round. But I want, more than anything in this world, to see a Maclaggan back at Glen Laggan—and, Colin, you're that Maclaggan."

"I never heard the like!" said Colin, recovering the packet and awkwardly lighting a cigarette. "You're a fair wonder, Bob, but you've let your imagination get the better o' your common sense. I'm willing to take your kind words for gospel, but—but—oh, man!—I think I see myself a braw Heilan' Laird, and Maggie, there, a lairdess—or whatever they call it! Haw, haw!"

"Maggie," said Bob, quietly, "would be referred to as the Laird's Lady, or Leddy, as they pronounce it up there."

"Me!" Mrs. Maclaggan went into fits, sobered abruptly, and blushed beautifully.

"Colin, my friend," his cousin proceeded firmly, "get this into your head, to begin with :—You have a far older name and better blood than any man who has owned Glen Laggan in the last hundred and eighty years!"

" God help us ! " muttered Colin. " Is that a fact ? "

" And as for you, Maggie, I'll say only this :—If you haven't got the blood of a Norwegian Princess—and I suspect you have—you are a woman who can be whatever she wants to be ! "

After a little silence he continued : " Mind you, I'm not saying it will be easy—it will be very difficult, at first —but I'll do all a man can do to smooth the way, and I have not a doubt of your winning through. I thought it all out on the voyage over. I'm not asking you two to move straight away from here to Glen Laggan—to plunge into the unknown, as it were. Glen Laggan, with some alterations I'm making, won't be ready for you till May. Meanwhile, I'm going to ask you to move to a biggish house, in a secluded spot, some miles out of Glasgow— Maggie will catch the idea—"

" Bob," she said, " you mean more than kindly, but it —it just couldn't be done ! "

" And it will help you, Colin," he went on, as though she had not spoken, " to get used to the change. That, however, is only one of the plans I've made to ease things for you both."

" Thanks, thanks," said Colin ; " but, as Maggie says, it just couldn't—"

" Wait a moment ! " Bob's next words came slowly, impressively. " What can't be done for our own sake may be done for the sake of others. What seems impossible for to-day, may be feasible for to-morrow. Though you don't want Glen Laggan for yourselves— though for a thousand reasons you don't want it—will you refuse it for your boy and girl ? "

" God ! " said Colin softly, and Maggie put her hands to her face.

III

ELEVEN o'clock. What changes within two hours! Mrs. Maclaggan had made tea, which they were drinking almost in silence. The electric tension, so to speak, had gone out of the atmosphere; there was that subdued, relaxed feeling that sometimes succeeds the making of a tremendous decision. Bob Maclaggan was experiencing the reaction no less than were his host and hostess.

" I daren't touch it," he remarked, " but I think Colin ought to have a dram."

Colin grinned feebly. " I feel as if I'd had a few extra already."

" Go on, Colin! " said his wife. " It'll maybe bring back the use o' your tongue. I don't seem to have a word to say."

" There's time enough for the details, Maggie," Bob said hastily: " but maybe, Colin, if he had a tonic, would find some questions to ask before I go." He drew his hand across his eyes. " I seem to be completely used up."

" No wonder! You've had a day of it," she returned sympathisingly. " Hurry up, Colin! And afterwards you'll fetch a taxi for Bob."

" There's two questions," said Colin, helping himself modestly, " that don't need a tonic. They've been tormenting me near all the time. The first is: Do you expect me to wear the kilt up yonder? For, if so, I doubt I'll have to go back on my word."

" I expect you'll come to the kilt in time, but it's not a condition," Bob replied. " You'd carry it all right—wouldn't he, Maggie ? "

" Oh, my goodness, Bob, don't give me any more bad dreams for to-night ! " she cried. " What's the other question, Colin ? "

" Is there a railway station ? I mind there wasn't one when our granny took us there."

" Yes ; there's a little L.N.E.R. station, less than a mile away—two trains a day, I believe, each way."

Colin heaved a sigh. " That's one homely touch, as they call it, anyway ! Well, here's to ye, Bob, and if I don't seem as grateful as I ought for myself, believe me, I can say 'God bless ye' for what you're doing for Peggy and Ronnie."

A little later, the taxi being below, Bob rose to go.

" After all, it'll be just as well for your young people not to meet me to-night," he said, getting lost once more in his coat. " I'd rather they got used to the idea. Tell them I'm not looking for thanks. I'm getting more than I'm giving—my dearest wish ! To-morrow I'll be seeing lawyers, and so forth, but in the evening we can have another talk. Meanwhile, Colin, I want to pay a very old debt. I confess that I forgot—for a time. You can assume that the money you lent me, all those years ago, has been used ever since in my business in Buenos Aires ; so that you're entitled to a small proportion of the profits." He laid an envelope on the table, beside the photograph. " Good-night, Maggie—and don't be afraid. You and Colin are going to win ! "

Colin went downstairs with him, and on his return found Maggie at the table, gazing at the photograph.

" Is it true ? " she said, laying it down and going back to her seat at the fireside.

" Is an earthquake true ? " said her man, taking up the envelope. " Bob's the limit for freehandedness. It'll be a fiver, anyway." He took out and unfolded a green-tinted oblong of paper, a banker's draft—and drew a sharp breath.

Presently he stepped over the hearth and held the paper, fluttering slightly, before his wife's eyes.

" Maggie," he said thickly, " did ever ye think to see in this world—a thousand pounds ? "

For a while she stared, comprehending, if only in a vague fashion, how that piece of paper, with its printing, figures and signatures, represented rare and pleasant things, of which she had never dared even to dream. A sob escaped her.

He let the paper drop into her lap, laid his hand on her shoulder, and cleared his throat.

" You've been a good woman to me, and you've never got anything for yourself," he said. " But, by God, you're going to get it now ! "

Emotion was checked by a sound from the outer door.

" That's Ronnie," she whispered, and thrust the draft into Colin's hand. " Quick ! Fold it and put it under the picture. It'll be easier if he starts to ask questions."

Ronnie came in to find his parents in their accustomed places, his father lighting a cigarette ; but he sensed something unusual.

" What's up ? " He turned from one to the other.

Then his glance was caught by the photograph. " What's this ? Where did you get it ? My ! I could do wi' living in a place like that ! Grand for motoring."

" That's a mercy," said his father, accepting the

opening, " for it just so happens that we're all going to live in that place, before very long."

" Come, Daddy, none of your codding ! " Ronnie laughed, dropping the card and picking up the draft. . . . " Help ! " he shouted ; then—" Oh, I see ! You've won a cross words puzzle at last ! Good for you ! I never thought you could have done it ! A thousand pounds —great—and a grand house into the bargain ! That's a proper prize ! But, of course, you were joking about us ones living in the house. You should get a lump of money for it—shouldn't he, Mother ? " He turned back to his father, whispering confidentially ; " What about a wee two-seater—eh ? "

" Colin," Maggie put in, " tell him the whole truth." Which Colin did, avoiding elaboration.

" But that's splendid ! " cried his son, when he had got a grasp of it all. " That cousin of yours must be a white man—pure ! Daddy, does it mean that you'll not have to work on the railway any more, and Mother'll have a servant and as many good clothes as she likes ? "

" I suppose it means something like that," replied Colin, whose vision of the future had not developed quite so far.

" Anyway, it means that we'll have a fine big car, and I'll drive it ! "

Peggy came in, slipping off her coat. In her pale green frock—her mother's handiwork—she looked as alluring a damsel as ever confounded an honest young man. Her eyes were ashine, her manner was a little strange. She had something to tell her parents, but it would have to keep till Ronnie was out of the way.

" Ronnie, what on earth's wrong with you ? " she exclaimed at the sight of her prancing brother, who was flourishing the photograph and banker's draft in **front** of her face.

If outwardly she received the news less wildly than he had done, the spirit in her was all aquiver. If she asked few questions about the future, her quick brain was busy imagining it, and in ways that would have astonished her parents. Yet while her heart thrilled to her imaginings, she was striving to ignore a problem that had come to her as suddenly as the news—with the news, in fact—a problem that became more insistent as the visions grew wider and clearer.

It was very late when Mrs. Maclaggan, practical once more, reminded them all that the morrow would bring its day's work, as usual; for, as she pointed out, there was to be no throwing up of jobs till she gave the word.

For a while after Ronnie's departure to bed, Peggy lingered, dreamy and distrait; then rather abruptly she retired, without having told her parents that, in answer to his pleading at the dance, she had promised to marry Charlie Fortune.

IV

A MINOR philosopher has observed that the important events of our lives never happen at the right moments, meaning, of course, that were the arranging of the programme in our own hands, we should order the items in a sequence more convenient to ourselves.

Peggy Maclaggan, without putting it into words, may have thought as much during the wakeful night which followed the sudden and tremendous upheaval in the family existence. If only, for instance, the visit of her father's cousin had happened before her going to the dance with Charlie Fortune ; if only she had hesitated another twenty-four hours, as she had felt like doing, before giving Charlie her promise to marry him ; if only—

But if we in our haste conclude that Peggy was merely a coldly calculating, self-centred young person, we shall be unjust. Peggy was a product of a generation which takes its guiding lights, not from the wisdom, but from the evidences of the unwisdom of the older. Born into a world in which age was busy stultifying itself, she knew now what she wanted to avoid in the course that lay before her.

A kindlier, happier upbringing than that of very many of her youthful neighbours had been hers ; yet, quite early in her 'teens, she concluded that her parents ought to have done better—not necessarily for her and Ronnie, but for themselves. She was constantly informed by little things that they had had a better education, or had made a better use of it, than many of the people closely around them, and that their ideas of things generally, while not " superior," were larger and finer. Nevertheless they appeared to be content, sometimes aggravatingly so, with their circumstances ; at any rate, her father never grumbled, while her mother seldom betrayed impatience.

At seventeen, though never had she entered a home with its husband and wife on easier, pleasanter terms, Peggy had decided that she would never marry a man like her father, or submit to a life like her mother's. The world was full of bright and beautiful things. The fault would be her own, if she did not obtain her share of them. And if that be heartlessness, then is all modern youth condemned.

Before leaving her 'teens, Peggy had attracted a goodly number of " boys," and none of them did she like nearly so well as Charlie Fortune. Of two things about Charlie she was certain : he would be good to her, and he would get on in the world. Daddy was good to Mother, in his way ; but Charlie would never be so easy-going with himself, nor so careless with money, as Daddy was. Yes, she would be safe with Charlie, and happy, too, if she could love him enough—for she was not so modern as to regard love as immaterial.

In her waking dreams of that night, however, Charlie was an intruder ; for those dreams were not of the sort that might have been suggested by love stories, printed or pictured, which end, seemingly for good and all, in neat little scenes of peace and plenty. Peggy had read or witnessed, had enjoyed and been moved by lots of such love stories, but they would have seemed insipid enough had she remembered them now. Vague as her visions of the future were bound to be, they held more than scenes of dancing to the pipes of pleasure and lounging among the rose-leaves of luxury. She saw herself not merely taking what money had given, but doing what money had made possible —and the deeds were not all petty, or wholly selfish. "Give me a chance," says Youth, "and I'll show the world something!" For while Peggy had ideas of her own for the future, it need not be assumed that she had no ideals.

Despite doubts concerning her engagement to Charlie, she had no thought of breaking it. For one thing, she could not have brought herself deliberately to hurt Charlie; for another, a bargain was a bargain—a rule of conduct which, without being aware, she had learned of her parents; and maybe, after all, everything would come right in the end.

So she got up in the morning, a little late, wondering less what she should say to Charlie than what Charlie would say to her, when he learned about Glen Laggan.

Her father had left for his work before the arrival of the postman. Allowing, no doubt, for that possibility, Cousin Bob, at the North British Hotel, had directed the letter to her mother—an invitation to the family to dine with him at 7 o'clock in his private sitting-room; no reply expected; he would be awaiting them at the main entrance.

Though she had told herself that she was prepared for anything after last night, Mrs. Maclaggan was all dismay.

"It'll be all right," her daughter assured her. "It's not as if we were going to be among the crowd, and

c

you'll have time to spend some of Daddy's thousand pounds on glad rags before—"

" What about yourself, Peggy ? "

" The frock I had on last night will have to do. There's a room at the Stores, where I can change. No time to come home. Anyway—"

It was on her tongue to explain that having promised to spend the evening with Charlie, she would have to give half-an-hour to telling him the news ; but she left the sentence unspoken and, shortly afterwards, went from the house, feeling, somehow, ashamed of herself. She was not given to shirking things, and the realisation that she had been a coward was not pleasant. As a matter of fact, she had refrained from mentioning Charlie, lest her mother should ask a question which she would have been bound to answer, and which, for an indefinable reason, she did not want to answer just then.

Though employed in the same building, she and Charlie seldom met during the day. He was upstairs, she on the ground floor, and their midday meal hours did not coincide. It was after six o'clock when the opportunity arrived.

The moment they met on the pavement, she said : " Charlie, I've got something to tell you." She spoke, abruptly, gravely, and saw his colour rise, then ebb almost to pallor, the light in his eyes go out.

" Peggy, don't tell me you've changed your mind ! "

She shook her head, faintly smiling. " But it's a—a serious thing and will take a while to tell."

" Well "—a laugh of relief —" we've got the whole evening before us."

" No, Charlie, that's just what we haven't —but you'll understand in a minute."

Uneasy, he took her to a neighbouring tea-room.

"Now, Peggy dear, what is it? Were you too late getting home, last night? Was your mother—?"

"No, no—but an awful lot has happened since last night. When I got home, I found that a cousin of Daddy's, just back from abroad—"

She told her story coherently enough, if rather baldly, and without interruption other than an occasional half-suppressed exclamation from the listener.

"Isn't it wonderful, Charlie?"

"Ay, Peggy—wonderful—splendid."

"Like a fairy tale—isn't it?"

"Just like a fairy tale."

A pause.

"Charlie, aren't you pleased?"

"Pleased? Of course I am! Why should I not be pleased, when you are?" He smiled. "Now, what will you have to eat?" The waitress had already brought cups of tea. "Surely you've time for a bite."

"That's another thing I've got to explain, Charlie." She told him of the invitation to the North British Hotel.

"I see." He brought out a packet of cigarettes.

She drank some tea, reflecting that he was taking it all pretty coolly.

"I wish I had thought of fetching along the photo," she said presently. "It's a real lovely place —a dream! I'll fetch it with me to-morrow—but you'll be seeing the place itself before long—only four hours or so in the train from Glasgow."

"I'll be glad to see the photo. I suppose you're all very happy about it."

"I never imagined our family could be so lucky. Oh,

yes, of course I'm happy—though I can see a good deal of trouble ahead."

" Trouble, Peggy ? "

" Well, it'll be a big change for folk like us—won't it ? Dear knows how long we'll be like fish out of water. Yes, I can see that part of it, clear enough! Still, I expect, we'll get used to it and enjoy it—in time. I believe it'll be easier for Ronnie and me than for Daddy and Mother. All the same, Daddy's folk owned the place long, long ago. Maybe there's something in that."

" A lot ! " he said kindly. " Is it a big house ? "

" Oh, pretty big ! I don't know how many rooms, but Ronnie and I counted thirty-three windows in the front."

" Then it's a—a castle ! "

" You might call it that, but the real old castle, close by, where Daddy's folk used to live, is all in ruins. It's lovely, too. If there had been a roof on it, I'd sooner have had it than the fine house."

" Not so comfy, though," he said, with something like a smile.

" I dare say ! But think of living where your folk had lived for hundreds of years ! "

" I expect," he said slowly, " you'll get used to it all very soon—you, anyway. I've always fancied there was a bit of the lady in you, Peggy."

" Charlie, don't be getting delirious ! "

" Well, you'll find it out for yourself. I doubt, Peggy dear,"—a short laugh—" I'll never manage to—to live up to you."

" Now you've fairly taken leave of your senses ! " She gave him a glimpse of her smiling grey eyes before turning again to her teacup.

He appeared to make up his mind. His hand went into his jacket-pocket, the fingers closing on a small, square, velvet case. Yet there it hesitated.

Abruptly she said : " I was just thinking how wonderful it must be for Mother and Daddy—I don't mean the grand new home and all that, but the never having to look twice at a pound any more."

" Is it as good as that ? " he asked. " There's not many folk nowadays, even the best off, that can forget about a pound-note ! "

" Oh, but I should have told you that bit of it, Charlie ! You must have been thinking it pretty poor fun, us getting that big house, and no money to go with it. But—"

" I guessed your father would get rents from the estate."

" Maybe he will ; I don't know anything about that ; but Daddy's cousin is making it so that Daddy will get ten thousand pounds every year—"

" Ten thousand pounds ! " said Charlie, mainly to himself.

" For always—sure ! I wonder now that Mother hasn't lost her head—but maybe she hasn't taken it all in yet. It's like a sort of miracle—isn't it ? "

" Yes."

After a little while his hand came from his pocket—empty —and travelled to his vest. He looked at his watch.

" Is it time I was going ? " she asked.

" Just about it. I'll walk up to the Square with you."

" You haven't touched your tea."

He drank if off and signed to the waitress.

It was barely five minutes' walk to the Square. There was a short cut through a lane —a busy passage, an hour ago, but now, the homeward rush over, deserted. In its half-darkness —

"Stop, Peggy!" he said, softly; "let me kiss you."

"Charlie! Here? Why, what's the matter?" But, after a swift glance this way and that, she gave him her lips.

"Sweetie," he said, under his breath, "God bless you!"

They went on and came into the Square, the Municipal Buildings, mountainous and dim, ahead; the North British Hotel, with its many lights, gay and warm, on the left.

"You never thought you would ever escort me to such a swell place—did you, Charlie?"

"No, Peggy, I never thought it. . . . It's just the hour."

"Daddy must have passed yon shining door thousands of times—and now he's going to see what's inside. What a queer world it is!"

"Are you just going to walk in?"

"Not much! I'm not the bold-as-brass sort—you ought to know that by this time! I've to meet Daddy and the others at yon statue—don't know its name— and his cousin will be waiting for us at the big door. That man thinks of everything; he's pure white, as Ronnie says."

"That's good." Charlie halted and held out his hand. "Well, I'll be leaving you here," he said steadily. "See you to-morrow night—maybe."

"Sure! I'll be at work as usual, every day, till Mother says the word. Mother's soft enough sometimes, but not all the time." She broke off in her laugh to regard him keenly. "Charlie, you're not sorry, are you?"

" Me ? I'd be a pretty rotten blighter if I was sorry—
would I not ? " He smiled. " But it's a big story you've
told me, and I need time to get used to it. Good-night,
Peggy dear. See and enjoy yourself."

She left him, her heart warm, telling herself that he
was " the best ever " ; vowing that were a chance to
come before the evening was over, she would let them
all know of her engagement. . . . As it happened, no
chance came.

Cousin Bob's entertainment, though by no means
intended to impress his shy guests, gave her a glimpse
of what money could do in the way of refinement.
Cousin Bob himself, as Ronnie afterwards expressed it,
" fell for our Peggy, right away." It may have been
that the little man saw in the girl a helper in his scheme ;
at any rate, he declared at once that she must be freed
from her present occupation as soon as possible ; in the
morning he would introduce himself to her employers,
with a thumping order in ironmongery for Glen Laggan.
" Call me ' cousin,' " he said, " and I'll try to deserve it."

Peggy liked him, though she wondered how so puny
a person could ever have found the energy to become so
wealthy, and she enjoyed the evening very much—
better, indeed, than did her parents. As for Ronnie, he
accepted the grandeurs and luxuries pretty much as a
matter of course, and was, if anything, disappointed
in his host, who, as he had early discovered, knew nothing
whatever about motor-cars, except their prices.

Ronnie was the only member who had any conversation
for the way home. Peggy was wondering about many
things. Colin and Maggie were tired, and oppressed by
gathering apprehensions of the future. The thousand
pounds would surely have lost less of its glitter in those

twenty-four hours, had it been the sum total of Cousin Bob's beneficence.

"Oh, woman," said Colin, as they were going to bed, "I feel as if I was play-acting in the movies."

"I hope you may never feel worse than that," she replied. "But play-acting won't help us, anyway, for we're up against the real thing. I wish we was ten years younger, Colin. We've got a terrible lot to learn."

"It's a good job we ken our ignorance," he remarked sagaciously.

"May we never forget it!" she sighed. "All the same, Bob was right when he bade you remember you were a Maclaggan. You never had any conceit, but maybe you'll want some pride before you're through! Ay, Bob was right!"

"Well, pride or no pride, I'm depending on you, Maggie."

Her smile was sweet. "And when, my man, have you ever done anything else?"

With the morning, before she was up, came a letter for Peggy. Eyeing the envelope, she wondered what Charlie could have written about, seeing that they were going to meet again so soon. All her guesses were wrong.

"DEAR PEGGY,

After we parted to-night, I walked round a goodish part of Glasgow, and did a bit of thinking. Peggy, you and I have made a mistake, but it is not too late to put it right. Your father's good fortune (I don't grudge him a penny of it) has changed everything, and nothing can be the same again. So I am writing now to give you back your word.

Don't think twice about taking it back, Peggy. I know you would have held by it, whatever happened—not just for love, but out of kindness to me and honour to yourself. But we have got to try to be wise, Peggy, and the promise that seemed wise yesterday is foolish to-day. You are going into a different world, where everything will be so different that I cannot follow you, and you will have new duties, as well as new pleasures. Our little plans have got to go overboard, and if you do not see that now, you would see it soon enough. Better break it now than have it broken later.

Don't think it's easy to write all this. It has just got to be written. You are free, but all my life I'll be proud to remember that you once promised to marry me. And now we can be good friends, as before, though I suppose our meetings will be coming to an end very soon. That's all, Peggy dear.

CHARLIE."

She had a cry over the letter. She would never, never take back her word! There was nobody in the world like Charlie—never would be anybody. . . .

It was another drearily wet morning. Running to board the tram, she felt a cold splash of mud on her stocking—what a beginning for a new day. The tram was overcrowded. A polite young man, or one susceptible to a pretty face, rose and offered her his seat, and in the act trod so heavily on her foot that her eyes filled. Everything in Glasgow was horrid!

Sitting in that stuffy, steamy atmosphere, she suddenly remembered that before long she would, if she wanted it, have a lovely car of her own, even for the clean soil of the Highland roads, and her thoughts became focussed on Glen Laggan and all the comfort and protection it represented. . . .

Towards the end of the short journey her thoughts went back to Charlie. She felt like crying again—there was a lump in her throat ; yet maybe—maybe—after all, Charlie was wise—more wise than he knew. For now she was almost certain that she did not want him enough. She wanted the future of her visions more.

V

SOON it became apparent that Cousin Bob had, to use his own words, thought things out on the voyage from South America; also that, for a man of so poor physique, his energy was remarkable.

Within the week he had the Maclaggans out of their modest home and into a Victorian mansion, some twenty miles from the City, in the Drymen district, with a glimpse of Loch Lomond afar—a half-way house, as he called it, between the Glasgow tenement and Glen Laggan. The phrase was apt enough, the idea behind it reasonable, if optimistic. Three months of residence in that secluded place, safe from outside influences and distractions, would, he argued, serve at least as an introduction to the new mode of living, and give his friends a chance to find themselves in their altered circumstances. His consideration was mainly, of course, on Maggie's account, for he had the imagination to foresee that the greatest difficulties would be hers.

The old home was deserted without any manifestation of joy. On that morning, indeed, Maggie wept a little, and Colin, who had been on night duty, wished the departure could have been made about 5 a.m. There were neighbours whom Maggie was sorry to leave, and to whom she had confided, discreetly, that Colin, though still working, had come into " a bit o' money." Colin, who, for a good many years, had not gone out of an evening, except, with his wife, to the pictures, realised that he cut a mighty poor figure of a prospective Highland Laird, as he exchanged awkward handshakes with grinning men and garrulous women, whom he hardly knew. Peggy and Ronnie, having already gone to their work— Peggy to hers for the last time—escaped what, to them, would probably have been a mere annoyance.

The simple household possessions, save a few having associations, with which Maggie could not part, had been distributed among her friends, and the taxi held all that she wanted to take with her.

She and Colin, after a wave or two of farewell, sat back in the cab, silent and downcast, till it was close to George Square, where they were to transfer themselves and belongings to Cousin Bob's big " Sunbeam," in which they had stoutly refused to be seen by their late neighbours. " Swank ! " Colin had muttered, meaning " bad taste," when Bob had suggested its calling for them.

Now Colin raised his head and spoke. " Never heed, Maggie ! Keep up your heart ! It's an earthquake, but we've just got to try and find our feet again. There's only one thing I couldn't get over, and that would be if you was ever to turn on me to upbraid me."

" I'll never do that," she replied, sitting erect and blowing her nose. " If there's any blame, it's mine more than yours, for I ken I could have put a stopper on the whole affair, if I had wanted."

" Ah, but your first thought was for Peggy and Ronnie."

" My first thought—well, I dare say it was. But let's be honest, Colin. We're, neither of us, so old that there's no pleasures left in life, and I'm willing to allow that as soon as I jaloused exactly what your cousin was after,

I had thoughts for myself—thoughts o' easiness and softness and—and prettiness, and so on."

" I'll not deny, woman, that I had notions, too — especially after I read the words ' Pay Mr. Colin Maclaggan One Thousand Pounds '." He smiled, then became grave. " Still, I doubt I'll miss the Railway."

" You and your Railway ! " she said, laughing in spite of herself. " You'll soon forget about that ! "

" Maybe ay, maybe no ! As I've said to you before now, Maggie, a porter's life is maybe not what you could call a noble one, but it's got variety, especially at a station like Queen Street. The King himself doesn't get the variety that I get betwixt my breakfast and my supper ! The different kinds o' folk that a porter meets would have filled Noah's Ark—"

" Whisht, man ! Yonder's the Hotel, and I think I see Bob waiting for us at the door." She heaved a great sigh. " Oh dear, I'm not looking forward to that big, grand house, and the servants, and all the rest of it ! I'm fair terrified ! "

" If ye've any trouble wi' the servants—if they hand you any back-chat—just you give me a call ! "

" I'll die first ! Colin, I've told you before, and I'm telling you again, the last thing you're to do is to go into the kitchen. If you love me at all, keep mind o' that ! And you're not to speak to the servants—"

" You said last night, I could say it was a fine day, and the like."

" Well, maybe I did. But you're to say it as if—as if you had made it a fine day—not, of course, as if you was conceited about it, but just as if you had done it without any trouble. You see what I mean ? "

" I wish to God I did ! "

" Mind your tongue, man ! I'll try and explain another time. Here's the Hotel!—But don't ever forget about not going into the kitchen—not if the boiler bursts."

Poor Maggie! All her worst fears were to be proved as nothing to the realities. Cousin Bob had done his best. He had engaged—at Heaven knows the wage!—an elderly, genteel woman, to show Maggie " the ropes " and keep the cook and three young maids in their places. She, too, did her best, succeeding at any rate, where " the ropes " were concerned ; and had Maggie been an ordinary, brazen " new rich," all might have been well enough. But Maggie, honest, sensitive woman, was to learn that there is a snobbery in every grade of society, and that a table-maid, origin unknown, may droop her lashes contemptuously while handing the potatoes to her employer, and address her mistress in accents refined to the point of impertinence.

It hurt Maggie dreadfully ; it enraged Colin.

" I wish you would leave the hussies to me," he said, one night, in the privacy of their bedroom; "I would soon give them the fright o' their lives."

" No, you wouldn't ! " she returned. " You would get the fright of your own. There's only the one thing for it ; carry on and pretend you don't notice anything. I can thole, if you don't interfere, and—and if you don't call me ' Maggie woman,' in front o' them, and don't use bad language, and don't—"

" When do I ever use bad language ? "

" Well, language that folk accustomed to a house like this wouldn't use—oh, you ken what I mean ! It's for your own sake, man, as well as Peggy's and Ronnie's."

" Have they been complaining ? " he asked, quickly.

She shook her head. " Ronnie's too pleased with

everything to complain about anything. Everything here is 'champion' to Ronnie." She smiled, faintly. "Of course, Peggy sees what's wrong, though she doesn't make a song about it. She seems to ken—I suppose it's her reading—how folk in a house like this would behave themselves. We could both learn a lot from Peggy."

"Ay, Peggy's clever! Bob says she's a wonder. I wouldn't like to let her down—nor you either, Maggie. I'll ask her about things, and I'll try to mind what you've said, though dear knows there's a hell o' a lot—I mean, a terrible lot—o' things to mind. What is it, woman," he demanded, suddenly, "that makes folk in a big house behave different from folk in a wee house?"

"That's just what we've got to learn," she said, a little sadly.

"Seems to me there's more room to—to live, in a wee house."

"We haven't been that long in this big one, Colin—just ten days. Have patience. Give yourself a chance, and me, too. It'll be a while yet before you hear me say I'm beat."

"You're plucky," he said, "but I just can't stick the cheek of these damned hussies!"

"Well, I'm going to stick it!" she returned, with a toss of the head, which, somehow, reminded him of his courting days.

She "stuck it." Her native dignity began to assert itself; her blue eyes acquired a gaze that wavered not till the be-powdered face of impudence turned red under it; her tone of voice, quiet and steady, without harshness, gained an authority that grammatical lapses could not weaken. At first it was acting, more or less, but the acting became a second nature. By the end of the month the cook and housemaid, having agreed that she was " the right stuff, anyway," amended their manners so patently that she knew she was winning ; whereupon in cool words, though with a rapid heart, she astounded the two other girls by " sacking " them, with wages instead of notice. She felt like fainting immediately after the deed, but the moral effect of having done it was to serve her well in the future.

" Good for you, Maggie ! " said Colin, when he heard of it. " Just what I would have done, myself, three weeks back, if you had let me."

Cousin Bob congratulated her, adding : " Carry on ! I'm going to get you a man—call him a butler, if you like—"

" A butler ?—Oh help ! " cried Colin.

"—to help you to boss things at Glen Laggan. I've been visiting some friends—business friends—lately, and from what I can gather, the modern home-wrecker seems to be the domestic servant."

" Oh, I wouldn't say that, Bob," said Maggie, who was no enemy of her sex. " I think half the trouble in the world—betwixt men, as well as women—comes from forgetting that a bargain's a bargain."

" I hope you're not serious about the butler, Bob," Colin put in. " I don't think I could stand up to that."

" He'll give you support, should you require it," said Bob, with unwonted jocularity ; and Colin guffawed in a fashion that made his wife think once more of the servants.

It is not to be assumed that Maggie's heavy bucket of anxieties, apprehensions and annoyances, had lost more than a drop through her little domestic victory. There were days when she came near to letting go. Colin, too, was often far from being helpful. While frankly admitting his dire need of education for the new life, he waxed impatient over many of the lessons. For instance, he constantly and crossly declared his inability to see the sense in having his morning meal in one room, his cup of tea, on his return from work, in another, and his dinner in a third. " Pure damned nonsense," he called it. And why couldn't he sit in his shirt sleeves, without a blasted collar, at the fireside ? Most of all, he objected to dinner in the evening. Probably the formality displeased him more than the dinner itself, for now and then he was pleased to compliment Maggie on one or other of the dishes, forgetting that she had not cooked it. Even the cheerful sight of his son joyously tucking in, while expressing approval of nearly every course in the word " champion," failed to mollify him.

In the end it was Peggy who improved the situation and saved her mother a good many heartaches—and all with one little word. Nearly all Peggy's days were now spent in going about with Cousin Bob, making purchases for Glen Laggan, taking driving lessons, acting as his secretary, meeting his business friends, and enjoying dainty meals in the Station Hotel, while he nibbled at the plainest dish on the menu. Her young eyes saw, her quick brain registered, many things likely to be useful —many things, too, that promised difficulties—in the future. But the knowledge she most greatly desired — the knowledge of how people lived, day by day, in big houses—was gained by reading in the evenings —not books on etiquette and the like, but women's journals of the finer sort. It was in the stories, rather than the

D

articles, that she found what she wanted. Incidentally, she suspected falseness in much that she had previously gathered from tales written for "the people"; she scrapped many of her notions gained in picture houses. This involved discouragement, for in general, as she perceived, it would be easier to behave like the persons in those tawdry novelette and gorgeous screen drawing-rooms than like the persons in these perfectly-printed, elegantly-illustrated pages. It was the tiny touches of refinement, the little graces of polite society, that troubled while they intrigued her, and at times made her feel well-nigh hopeless about the future.

According to his promise to Maggie, Colin took to consulting his daughter—sometimes humorously, some-times desperately—on questions of deportment. He did not start to do so an hour too soon, for Peggy, though unwilling to hurt her Daddy's feelings, had been on the point of exploding. It must be allowed that she was fairly kind and patient, but of the many seeds of instruc-tion sown by her, the best that could be said then was, that a few actually sprouted, while others might yet germinate in the darkness of that reluctant soil.

On an evening, in the second month of the big house, parents and daughter were in the drawing-room, Ronnie being, as usual, in the garage, adoring the new Daimler, and acquiring additional motor lore from the chauffeur, an old soldier, who was glad of the boy's company, and who, on half-holidays and Sundays, gave him lessons in driving.

A few hours earlier, the Daimler had brought Maggie home from town, where she had been shopping. She would have preferred the bus, but the Daimler was part of the " sticking it." So was the fashionable dressmaker,

for there her native dignity was tried to its limit.
To-night she was tired, with nerves on edge.

Colin, too, was not at his best; he was, in fact, in
one of his exasperating humours. He had been complaining of several things, including once more, the
late dinner. He had tried five of the chairs, and now,
with a curse, removed himself to another.

" Colin, Colin ! " murmured his wife, in weary appeal.

There was an unhappy silence till Peggy from the
couch, her legs tucked under her, laid down her journal
and spoke—

" Daddy, you've said ' Damn that chair ! ' exactly
five times."

He was taken aback; then, a frown between his
brows, he demanded grimly—

" Well, and what about it, my girl ? "

Neither look nor tone was familiar to Peggy, but she
held her ground.

" It wasn't playing the game," she said.

" What ? "

" Listen, Daddy ! If a stranger had been here and
heard your five ' damns,' he would have been shocked,
but—wait a minute !—Mother and I would have
pretended to think you were quite right to say them.
We would have backed you up—wouldn't we, Mother ? "

" Sure ! " answered Maggie, her blue eyes wondering.
" We would always back up your Daddy."

' Well, that's loyalty." Peggy tapped the paper on
her lap. " I noticed the word in a story just now; it set
me thinking about things."

Colin's thumb went up to the back of his neck and
scratched softly. " What are you after, Peggy ? " he
asked, irritably.

Her white throat moved as though she were swallowing something. "But I don't see why we should keep all our loyalty for a show off to strangers," she resumed. "Surely we can use some of it in the family. Your 'damns' were nothing, or next to nothing, Daddy, but they gave me an excuse to butt in. It's this whole evening I'm thinking of—and other evenings, too. You don't back us up, Daddy, and Mother and I are doing our level best. You keep on grousing at things that are necessary—you know they are ! You kick at things and you—you kick us ! You take the heart out of us ! You —oh, well, whatever it is, it's not loyalty—and without loyalty all round, there's just no hope for any of us ! "

Abruptly she slipped from the couch and left the room.

"Well," cried Colin, blankly, " I'm damned ! "

"Never heed, man," said Maggie, after a moment, "she didn't mean it."

"But—" He got up and came slowly to the hearth. "But maybe she was right ! " Softly—"By God, I believe she was ! Loyalty !—that's a word to keep in mind ! Maggie woman, I'm sorry. The next time I forget myself, just you name that word to me."

It was equivalent to so big a promise that we may believe he kept some of it.

VI

TIME passes, whether we progress or no.

Came the day—oh, sorry day!—when Colin Maclaggan finished his service with the L.N.E.R. Company. He was not the Colin of three months ago, the Colin we saw waiting in that dingy courtyard, on the chance of a last-minute passenger ; but the changes were hardly apparent to his comrades at Queen Street.

"Come into a bit o' money," he had told them, vaguely, in the beginning, for such things soon get abroad ; since when his daily takings in tips had literally gone to the dogs, being handed, with sage counsel, to that constant follower of the greyhounds, Hugh Jordan, without doing him a button of good.

He was, if anything, less vague at the two farewell suppers given to a goodly number of his comrades— the second supper being for those on night duty the previous week. In response to the toast of his health, he made a somewhat rambling speech on the benefits of railway locomotion and the variety in a porter's daily existence, and finished up with the following personal statement :—

"Well, chaps, the wife and I are going to settle down at a wee place called Glen Laggan. Maybe some of you have had the pleasure o' labelling luggage for it, though I can't mind ever having had the pleasure myself. But, though wee, it's on our own railway—God bless it !— and so you'll be able to travel on a pass when you've

47

a notion to come and see us—and, by Heavens, you'll all be welcome! (Applause.) Just one word more, chaps and friends :—The waitresses will now hand each of you an envelope which, on your honours, is not to be opened till you get home. God bless you all! I—I'm damned sorry to be leaving you all—and the Railway."

The envelopes contained five-pound notes, the only souvenirs Colin could think of ; but, as he said to Maggie, "It's not so long since I would have been dashed glad o' one, myself ! '

.   .   .   .   .   .

On the 14th of May, the Maclaggan family set out for the new home.

Cousin Bob, who was accompanying them, and who had recently paid several visits to Glen Laggan, would have had them make the journey by road, but on hearing that suggestion Colin had rebelled.

"What ? Bilk the Railway out o' the fares it's badly needing ? " he cried. "Anything but that, Bob. Anything but that ! "

" As you will," the obliging Bob replied. " The car can start early and meet us at Glen Laggan Station."

" The cars ! " corrected Ronnie, proud owner, at last, of a two seater. He, of course, was going by road !

To Colin it was an odd and embarrassing experience — seemed to savour of " swank "—to arrive at the Station, that afternoon, as a fare-paying passenger, and to have old comrades carrying the family belongings. To travel " first " was, of course, unthinkable.

" Bob," he whispered to his cousin, who was looking after such matters, " for the love o' Heaven don't be skimpy wi' the tips ! " Which advice to a less-understanding person than Bob might have seemed offensive.

Charlie Fortune came, almost at the last moment, to see them off—or, rather, to have a final glimpse of Peggy. They had met now and then, in a friendly way, during the past three months, sometimes with the company of Cousin Bob, and on each succeeding occasion it had seemed to Charlie that she had risen still a little farther above him. Well, it had just got to be !

Now they exchanged but a word or two—the sort of words so often exchanged at a railway carriage door—words which convey little and may conceal much.

" Charlie," said Mrs. Maclaggan, " you'll come and see us soon. We'll be wanting our old friends."

" Ay, lad," Colin added, heartily, " come for your summer holidays."

The train began to move. Charlie thanked them, and smiled gravely at the girl.

" So long, Peggy ! See and enjoy yourself."

" So long, Charlie ! Best of luck," replied Peggy, and, with an inward sigh, drew back from the window.

" I like that young man," remarked Cousin Bob. " I offered him a place in my business out there, but he won't leave Glasgow."

The sun was low when the train drew up at the little tree-sheltered platform which was their destination.

Ronnie and the chauffeur were standing there, also a soldierly man of middle-age, accompanied by a tall, very slim woman.

" Two of your neighbours," Bob remarked. " Colonel Silver and his lady—seem to be expecting somebody by the train."

As he spoke, the couple was joined by a young man, who might have been thirty, dark-eyed and pale, decidedly good looking—evidently their son.

The stationmaster opened the door, removed his cap, bowed to Maggie, and looked inquiringly at Bob.

" This, Mr. Stationmaster," said Bob, indicating his cousin " is the new Laird, Mr. Colin Maclaggan."

Colin held out his hand. "How's things," he said, pleasantly. " This is bonnier than the tunnel at Queen Street. Maggie—Peggy—shake hands wi' him ! Good old L.N.E. ! "

They descended.

The only porter was seeking the luggage of the pale young man, who was chatting with his parents.

" That," said Colonel Silver, " must surely be the new Laird. There was a rumour to the effect that he was connected with railway affairs—"

" The new Laird ! " softly exclaimed the son. " That's funny ! I bought an evening paper at Glasgow, and there was a par in it about Glen Laggan. It seems that, until the other day, he was a railway porter. Well, he looks rather like one, doesn't he ? " He checked a laugh, his glance caught by the fair face of Peggy.

" Good Heaven," murmured his mother, with superb disgust, " a railway porter ! "

Peggy's eyes moved in the direction of the group, perhaps in search of kindliness in the countenances of three people who probably loved one another, but found only admiration in one of them. She turned swiftly. " Come on, Mother," she said ; " let's get to the car."

Presently they were driving down the road to the Loch, gleaming placidly under the range of steep barren mountains ; then along the lochside, looking up the Great Glen that, splitting Scotland in two, provides her farthest and one of her fairest vistas. Soon appeared in sight, among the trees, the ancient ruinous stronghold of the Maclaggans, and then the white tower and turrets of Glen Laggan House. A minute later, the whole building, with its lawns and gardens, became visible.

Cousin Bob had been doing all the talking, addressing no one in particular. Now he held his peace. It was his great moment. No doubt, he understood when Peggy drew in her breath as though something had hurt her; when Colin slid his big ugly hand over Maggie's, and hers turned to clasp it.

And so the Maclaggans came home—feeling farther from home than ever in their lives.

As the car turned into the avenue, a man of middle age, big, brawny, black bearded, and a small, thin, mousey woman, standing by the gates, saluted; the man by solemnly lifting his cap, the woman by dropping her gaze and smiling shyly.

Colin, seeming to wake up, waved his hand cheerily.

"That was your lodge-keeper, Murdo McMurrich," said Bob. "A good sort, though a bit long-winded, if I may judge from the chats I've had with him. He has worked on the Estate from his boyhood. He will be your ghillie at the salmon fishing and, later on, at the shooting and deer-stalking."

"Is it me you're speaking to?" cried Colin. "Great—! Deer-stalking!"

"Whisht, man!" whispered Maggie, but not sharply. She had found some comfort in the fact that the woman had not stared at her.

"I'm no sportsman," Bob continued, "but I'm told that it only needs a beginning. Have you ever fired off a gun, Colin?"

"Often—but only at folk," Colin answered, with a twist of the mouth.

"Sorry! I had forgot about that. Well, I expect you'll get keen on the fishing, anyway."

Bob had planned—mercifully—that there should be nothing in the way of a formal reception. When the doorway came in sight, only two figures were to be seen on the broad steps—a stocky, ruddy man, with a heavy, drooping moustache, clad in bluish Harris tweeds, and a tall, straight one, of forty or so, clean shaven, in a dark suit, with glimpses of white linen and a black bow tie.

"Mr. Gregg, the factor, and Rosman, the butler," he explained.

"Well, that's a nice, wee homely touch, anyway," observed Colin—"a butler in plus fours!"

Bob's exclamation was, for once, impatient. "It is Mr. Gregg, the factor, who is wearing plus fours—"

"Well, well, you never know your luck. I would have thought—"

"Listen! We shall all shake hands with Mr. Gregg—"

"I see what you mean! We'll never let on we see the butler. I mind Maggie saying I oughtn't to be friendly-like with the servants."

"Colin," Maggie put in, "for pity's sake, let Bob tell us what we've got to do."

"There is no reason," said Bob, "why you should not recognise Rosman with a nod and a ' good evening.' He happens to be a superior sort of fellow for his position." Had there been time, Bob might have added that he had chosen Rosman from thirty-nine applicants, and that Rosman, holder of several University degrees, had given a satisfying reason for his desiring the situation of butler.

"Mr. Gregg," he proceeded, "may seem a bit dour to begin with, but he's all right, and you'll have to depend on him all the time, especially after I leave you, next month. As I've already told you, Gregg managed the Estate for the two previous proprietors. Well, here we are ! "

The car drew up at the entrance. The butler bowed gravely and opened the door ; Mr. Gregg, with a smile of welcome that seemed grudging, extended a large freckled hand to assist Maggie to alight. Presently Bob performed the necessary introduction. There was no awkwardness worth mentioning, if we except the little hitch caused by Colin's attempt to secure two suit-cases, which had been brought on the train, with a view to carrying them up the steps. Even railway porters have their habits.

They passed under an arch, with a heavy nail-studded door, a short vestibule, then under another arch, with glazed swing doors, and found themselves in the spacious hall, on warmly-tinted Eastern rugs spread upon oak planks. It would seem that the man who built the house had lacked respect for the lofty apartments of his period, for the ceiling, oak-panelled, as were the walls, was no more than twelve feet from the floor. In any light the effect was restful, without being dull. The place, furnished in lounge fashion, would be cool to enter in summer, snug in winter. Bob had made many alterations in the house, but none in the hall.

There, in the great fireplace, with its Victorian richness of burnished steel and inlaid brass, a fire of logs and peat offered its golden glow and aroma of hospitality. The walls were adorned with antlered heads and ancient Highland weapons, including some fine examples of those impressively fearsome instruments of death, Lochaber axes. Above the fireplace hung a magnificent painting, by a renowned Scottish artist, of a stretch of the Strath, a glimpse of the Loch and river, with Ben Nevis, under snow and sunshine, in the distance.

While Bob consulted the butler on some small matter, Peggy's gaze was caught and held by the picture, as her mother's was fascinated by the steel and brass below.

Ronnie burst in, crying, " Peggy, how's this for champion —eh ? " His glance was captured by the Lochaber axes. " Oh, Daddy, look at the choppers ! " He evidently expected a guffaw from his father, but Colin just then seemed lost in his thoughts.

" Ronnie," Bob said, quietly, " have you put away your car ? It'll soon be time for supper."

" Righto ! " The boy took the hint, without quite understanding it.

At a sign from the butler, a girl in uniform, who had been standing near the staircase, at the rear of the hall, came forward. She had reddish hair, a plump figure, a plain freckled countenance, and a beautiful smile.

The butler addressed Maggie with a deference that was, happily, not overdone.

" Ma'am, this is your maid, Jeanie. If it suits you now, she will show you and Miss Maclaggan your rooms. Will it please you, ma'am, to take supper in half-an-hour ? "

Maggie, who seemed to have lost her speech, turned helplessly to Cousin Bob.

" Yes, in half-an-hour, Rosman," said that useful person, and the butler retired. " Maggie, there's something I want to show to Colin, but he'll be up very shortly. Ask the maid for anything you want." He nodded to the girl.

" Ma'am—Miss—will you be pleased to come upstairs ? " she said, in the softest voice they had ever heard.

Bob turned to the factor, who had been standing solemnly aloof. "Mr. Gregg, will you come over to-morrow morning, at ten, and have a chat with us?"

With an assent as curt as his nod, Mr. Gregg departed. "Wake up, Colin!"

Colin drew his hand across his brow. "Bob, it's going to beat me," he sighed. "Are there many rooms in the house like this?"

"There's one, anyway, that isn't a bit like this," answered his cousin; "and I'm going to let you see it now. Come along!"

They moved into the corridor on the right and advanced to a door almost at the end of it.

"This is intended to be your own particular corner—your refuge, when you need one—and I hope to goodness you'll like it," said Bob. "It took me a bit of thinking out." He opened the door and led his cousin into the room.

Colin stopped short, wide-mouthed, staring about him. Presently a smile dawned and developed.

The room was simply and comfortably furnished, its principal appointments being a broad writing-table near the window, a handy round table, with smoking materials, a couple of luxurious easy-chairs at the hearth, a book-shelf on either side filled with volumes, each of which bore a title including the word "Railway," or "Railroad."

"Well?" said Bob, after a while.

But Colin was still eyeing the adornments of the primrose walls—engravings and coloured plates of locomotives, from the first "Puffing Billy" to the latest giant of the "Flying Scotsman," and of old and modern

railway trains and scenes ; also prints of the " Forties,
satirising railway travel in its early stages.

At last—" Bob, this beats all ! I'm simply da—"

" Don't say it." The little man pushed him into an
easy-chair. " How do you like the ceiling—my own
original notion ? "

Covering the ceiling, admirably drawn and painted,
was a great map of Scotland, the ramifications of the
L.N.E.R. being clearly shown in green.

" When the burden of being a Laird gets too heavy,"
said Bob, faintly smiling, "come in here and forget about
it. And maybe," he added, " not that I think you'll ever
need it, this room will keep you from getting over
proud."

Colin, hand out, would have risen, but just then the
butler came in. He set on the table a tray with decanter,
syphon, glasses, and retired.

" Sit still ! " said Bob. He mixed a drink in one of
the glasses, handed it to his cousin, and squirted a little
soda into the other glass.

" Bob ! " cried Colin. " After all this that you've done
for me, if ever I let you down, may God Almighty —"

Bob put up his hand. There was, perhaps, a trace of
emotion in his voice as he said : " No thanks required,
and no rash promises, Colin, old man. It's a simple
case of fair exchange. I've brought you here, and I want
you to be content here—you and Maggie, and your girl
and boy. I don't want you to feel like prisoners, or bound
in any way. But I do want you to give my idea an honest
trial. I believe in my idea of the old name in the old
place. I believe in you. That's all ! " He raised his
glass. " Maclaggan, of Glen Laggan, your very good
health ! "

Ten minutes later, he went upstairs with Colin, showed him the right door, and departed.

Colin strode into the bedroom. He was excited, but the sight of the interior subdued him for the time being. He had never dreamed of a white bedroom like it; compared with it the one in the Dumbartonshire mansion had been ugly.

Maggie, beginning to feel a thrill in the beauty and luxury of her new surroundings, was about to put on a new frock.

" Maggie woman," he said, huskily, taking her by the naked shoulders, " Bob's the greatest ever! I do believe it's all going to be quite easy—I'm saying, quite easy ! "

He completed her amazement by kissing her.

" Dearie," she murmured, " I dare say you were needing it, but you've had a dram."

" And so I have !—but that's not the point. The point is that I'm Maclaggan, of Glen Laggan—and so, by Heaven, are you ! "

Women are wonderful. " That's fine," she said, quietly, " and there's a nice clean collar for you yonder, on the dressing-table."

VII

ON that night, a peace unknown for weeks fell softly upon the Maclaggans. With the discoveries of never suspected simplicities, the complications and formalities of their new environment became less urgent, less oppressive. Strange as was everything within these unfamiliar walls, there was yet in the atmosphere a hint of homeliness, never for a moment felt in the " half-way house."

When Jeanie, the ruddy-haired maid, was inducting mother and daughter to their quarters, she said, without preface, what only a Highland girl could have said : " And it is a very fine thing, ma'am, to be coming back once more to the place of the forefathers, and I am wishing you all great happiness."

Maggie was going to have her domestic difficulties at Glen Laggan, but the remembrance of that little speech would help her to forgive many a fault. As for Peggy, at her bedroom window, a little later, gazing out at the loch and the mountains in the after-glow, she said to herself : " Loyalty—it'll all come right, if there's loyalty—the Highland sort."

Just before supper, the family joined Cousin Bob in the hall. All were rather subdued, excepting Ronnie, who having already made friends with Murdo, the lodge-keeper, announced his expectation of catching " some salmons " on the morrow.

Colin, by this time, was fairly inured to the formalities
of the table and the unwelcome attentions of servants
generally, yet he had dreaded an increase of such afflic-
tions at Glen Laggan. He had, in fact, imagined himself
banqueting in a place something like a cathedral, in an
atmosphere of awful solemnity, on dozens of strange,
uncanny dishes, the centre of many curious, not too
kindly glances.

His relief was, therefore, great when, presently, he
found himself in a room of not extravagant dimensions,
its furnishings and decorations quietly cheerful, and at
a table which shone invitingly, but neither groaned nor
dazzled. And the few dishes were the very things he
liked best, and the ministrations of the butler so unobtru-
sive, that his heart warmed to the man and those under
him. If this was being a laird, he thought, after the glass
of port recommended by Bob—he had not fallen in love
with the Burgundy at first taste—then being a laird wasn't
half bad! To Maggie and Peggy the repast was happier
than any they had known since leaving Glasgow, while
Ronnie, as usual, enjoyed himself to the full.

The butler having left the room, Bob said : " Now I
think it ought to be bed for everybody. Plenty to do in
the morning. You, Maggie, will be wanting to get your
bearings then, and you'll find Rosman helpful. Your
maid, Jeanie, too, will do her bit, if there's anything in
the Highland clan idea. Long, long ago, she told me,
when I interviewed her, one of her forebears and an
ancestor of yours, Colin, stood back to back in a great
fight till they were the only two left standing."

" That's great ! " cried Colin. " I must give her—"

" No, you must not ! " Bob became very grave. " I
can't tell you much about the other young servants, but

E

the cook, who admits to forty-nine, gets tight, as she very frankly informed me, once a year, on the 13th of April. However, that's a long way off—"

"Mercy!" exclaimed Maggie. "But why on the 13th of April?"

"On the 13th of April," Bob replied, graver still, "about thirty years ago, her young man—"

"Died—poor soul!"

"—jilted her, and, of course, she must celebrate the anniversary. So just remember, Maggie, never to plan a dinner party for her date."

So the first evening at Glen Laggan ended merrily enough, and up the broad staircase, at last, Hope went softly with the Maclaggans.

At the hour appointed, next morning, Mr. Gregg came over from his house, on the edge of the grounds, and awaited the pleasure of the new Laird in the office, across the corridor from the Railway Room, as Colin was already calling it.

Mr. Gregg was a widower, with two sons abroad and a daughter not long at home, after finishing her education in the South and on the Continent. Normally, a quiet, cautious, kindly man, he was now dour as well—dour, because he resented "this Maclaggan business," of which Cousin Bob had frankly told him the circumstances, and out of which he could see no issue, save ridicule and disaster for all concerned, including himself. Only because he and his daughter loved the place that had been their home for so many years, had he consented to continue as factor—it may have been with a secret hope that disaster would come quickly and render the estate lairdless once more. Incidentally, he was not dependent upon the salary attached to the factorship.

It should be remarked that he had not greatly admired the previous proprietor, the commercial millionaire, who spent only a couple of months of the year on his estate—a sporting visitor, rather than a laird in the true sense. But the millionaire had been a gentleman, and now these people from the slums of Glasgow, financed by their well-meaning, misguided relative, were going to make Glen Laggan their home. So Heaven help Glen Laggan, under its new Laird!

Still, as Mr. Gregg told himself bitterly, on that lovely May morning, duty was duty, even when it involved the hopeless task of trying to explain the affairs and workings of a Highland estate to an ignorant railway porter.

He stood to attention, as the well-meaning relative and the person from the slums came into the office. His acknowledgment of their greetings was no more than barely courteous.

"Be seated, Mr. Gregg; take the other chair at the table, Colin," said Bob. "As I can't be of any assistance, I'm going to leave you for an hour or so. Mr. Gregg, you might kindly give my cousin a general idea of things, and afterwards we'll all go out and have a look round."

"Very well, Mr. Maclaggan," was the polite reply. "I'll do what I can."

With a nod of encouragement to Colin, Bob went out. There was silence till the factor cleared his throat.

"Well, sir," he began, unfolding a plan of the estate, "I propose to put before you—"

Colin's hand went up.

"Wait a bit, if you please." In the brown eyes was distress, but they looked straight into the shrewd, greenish-grey ones. "Mr. Gregg, there's only one thing I want to say to you now. Nobody kens my ignorance better than myself, and I'm just going to trust myself in your hands."

It was hardly what Mr. Gregg would have expected. On his sunburnt countenance the red glowed for a moment. Essentially a believer in fair play, he realised that he had been in danger of denying it to this man who, whatever his deficiencies, appeared to have honesty and some courage, too. The position might be false—surely it was false !—but the man, he felt, was genuine. . . . After all, might there not be hope for such a man, despite all drawbacks, given time ? And it would be a big thing, a tremendous thing, if, in the end, one could bring, or help to bring, the man out on top !—Oh, but that was impossible !

Nevertheless, the man having appealed to him, resentment was no longer in Mr. Gregg.

" If I may say so," he said slowly, at last, " I appreciate your confidence."

" You'll help me—if it can be done—to win through ?"

" I am here to serve you, sir. I am anxious to help you in any way I can."

" Mr. Gregg, will you give me your hand on that ? "

Formality has its uses, but it makes a poor display in the face of sincerity.

" Surely I will, Mr. Maclaggan."

Bob, on his return, found the talk going briskly.

" But I'm afraid," the actor remarked a little drily, " we have not got very far into the estate business. We have, as a matter of fact, been discussing our daughters. I have mentioned that my Rona would be pleased to show Miss Maclaggan round the countryside, and the Laird " —the word came almost naturally, though Colin gave a small start—" seems to think it might suit Miss Maclaggan quite well. But now, perhaps, we had better be going into more serious matters—"

"You have both done a very good morning's work," said the little man, without a smile. The thing he had most hoped for had come to pass. Colin had, somehow, got on the right side of the man who could help him more than anybody.

Bluff has its victories ; so, too, has humility. Not that there was anything particularly humble about Colin when he set out with the others for a first glance at his estate. Head up, chest out, eye bright, a jauntiness in handling his cigarette, he was not just then an altogether impossible Laird.

VIII

PEGGY had already gone out. With a wish to be friendly, she had promised to let Charlie know of the arrival at Glen Laggan, and give him her first impressions of the new home; but morning had found her too happily unsettled for letter-writing; and, besides, the day's one post did not go out till the afternoon.

For a time she drifted among the shrubberies and gardens. There were plots bright with early flowers, but, just then, flowers, which could be seen in the city, hardly appealed to her. Desire was towards the grander things around her, the mountains, the greater bens still snow-capped, the wide, brown, tumbling moors, the glassy loch, the gleaming river, the waterfall sounding among the trees, and over all the vast blue, cloud-flecked, ever changing sky. To think that all these wonders were hers—not merely for a Saturday afternoon, or a Sunday, or a fleeting fortnight, but for as long as she chose to enjoy them!

Like so many of her working sisters in the City, Peggy had, as far as her circumstances allowed, been an open-air girl. With other girls, or one of her " boys," till Charlie came into her life, she had been wont to spend her free daylight hours, whenever possible, in rambling the countryside around Glasgow. Only in Charlie's company had she been content, or almost content, on a fine afternoon, to stroll the pavements. She wondered now if Charlie would be as keen on Glen Laggan as she was. Perhaps not, though she remembered his saying once that he was as fond of scenery as anybody, only it didn't seem to matter when he had her beside him. Poor old Charlie! Still, he wouldn't have given her back her freedom, had he been really desperately in love. All was for the best!

Nature did not, however, provide her only joy on that fine morning. It was lovely to be idle, delicious to be wearing nice clothes and fine stockings and smart shoes, though there was only herself to admire them. She was glad she had a pretty head, fine complexion, trim figure and neat legs, if only for the birds to see and chatter about. In that clean, sweet, soft air, which encouraged one to dream rather than to do, amid that spacious wild beauty, it seemed to her that she lacked nothing at all.

She arrived at a footpath that opened and strayed, carpeted deep with pine needles, into a fragrant wood. She entered and followed it for a furlong, then came to a sudden halt, thrilling. Through the trees appeared a towering wall, its grimness softened by ivy—the ancient castle of the Maclaggans. With shining eyes, she moved onward, and presently emerged into a clearing. Now she was looking at the front of the castle, which stood on a rock among trees, overhanging the loch. A great, uncompromising square it was, its roofless top ragged against the sky, long past restoration, a mere shell, though the stout walls, showing signs of recent preservation, might stand for centuries to come. The windows were few, and Peggy was thinking how absurdly small was the doorway, when she became sensible of another's presence.

She turned to see a man in grey tweeds rising—stiffly, she noticed—from a flat boulder near the opposite limit of the clearing. Dropping his cigarette, he came slowly forward, through the rough grass and patches of heather, using a stick. In his pale face, his eyes appeared black, and she recognised him as the young man she had seen on the station platform, the previous evening.

At a little distance, he halted and bowed, being hatless. In a pleasant voice he said—

"It has just, this moment, struck me that I am trespassing, and I want to explain that, for longer than I can tell, my people have enjoyed the liberty of walking through this part of these grounds. But I'm afraid we have omitted to ask the permission of the new proprietor, and so I offer you my apology."

Peggy, while not seriously embarrassed, was wondering what she ought to say, when he spoke again.

"My name is Silver—Wilfred Silver—and my people live at White House, beyond the wood"—he made a gesture rearwards—"about half a mile down the lochside." He took a step forward. "You, I think, are Miss Maclaggan"—another step—"and seeing we are neighbours"—a third step—"may I hope that you will shake hands?"

"Oh, yes," she said, softly, thinking of the news she would have to take home shortly. "I'm sure," she added, "my father will want your people to go on using this part of the grounds."

"Thank you so much." After a pause—"I suppose it is too early to ask if you like Glen Laggan."

"No, it isn't too early," she frankly answered. "You

see, I saw its photograph three months ago, and —and loved it."

" And the real thing does not disappoint ? " He was watching her face. A railway porter's daughter—but how pretty she was, how lovely were her eyes ! " I needn't have asked that," he went on. " Two minutes ago, you came out of that wood, a picture of happiness ! "

" Did I ? " She smiled, with a slight rise of colour. " I don't know why I didn't notice you then."

" You were too intent on that ruin to notice this wreck," he said, lightly.

For a moment she regarded him in puzzled fashion ; then—" You mean, you're a—an invalid ? I'm sorry."

" That is kind of you, but I'm on the mend, I hope. Had rather a nasty motor smash down in Surrey, two months ago, and got out of hospital only the other day. I came up on the same train as you, last night."

Peggy did not deem it necessary to mention that she had noticed him on the platform. " Your accident must have been an upset to your people here," she remarked politely.

" It was, worse luck ! They came South immediately they got the news, and returned only a few days before I did. Ruined my poor father's fishing—his chief pleasure here. He had taken, as he always does, one of the beats on your river for the two months."

" My river ? . . . Oh, I see ! " Peggy smiled, but she was annoyed with herself not seeing sooner. Of course, everything was hers, or, rather, Daddy's !

He made a gesture in the direction of the castle— " And what do you think of the home of your ancestors, Miss Maclaggan ? "

" It's grand—only I wish I knew something about it."

" Yes, it must have its stories—things must have happened in that old place—but I'm ashamed to say I know nothing, except that it was burned, by order of the Duke of Cumberland, soon after Culloden."

" The beast ! "

" He was, rather ! But he has his reward. He is remembered only as ' the Butcher.' Culloden was the gallant soldier's solitary victory, and he made the most of it Are you thinking of becoming a Jacobite ? "

She had read about Jacobites at school ; but at school one reads so much, without learning anything. He had taken her out of her depth again, but not, she was sure, with unkindly intent.

" Mr. Silver," she said, with a little air of dignity that touched and charmed him, " I know very well I have an awful lot to learn."

" Have you ? Well, whatever the awful lot may be," he said gently, " I don't imagine you will find it difficult. Wouldn't you like to see the inside of your castle ? It's a bit rough underfoot, and there's not much trace left of its former glories, except the huge fire-place of the kitchen, which is quite recognisable. Let me show you the way."

" Ought you to go into rough places when you're not fit ? " she objected.

" Oh, I'm fit enough for that. Please bend your head at the doorway, and keep it down till we're right inside."

She following him through the passage in the thick wall, past a dusky little chamber on either side, and stood upright in the desolation of the interior. A cloud had come over the sun ; the place was grey and chilly. They stood among fragments of masonry, fallen long ago, weeds and thorns. The walls seemed very high.

There was grass on their broken crests, and at one corner a little mountain ash flaunted itself bravely. Somewhere birds twittered, as though uneasy in their small hearts.

Peggy gave a shudder. " What an awful place to get into at night ! "

" I doubt whether any person has spent a night here since the burning," he said. " There are plenty of people around who would not come to the outside of this castle, an hour after sunset."

" Is it—haunted ? "

" Not that I've heard ; but in spite of motor 'buses and wireless, and so forth, the old superstitions do survive in these parts. Perhaps, you, Miss Maclaggan, are above that sort of thing. If not, it must be your Highland blood—"

" Are you chaffing, Mr. Silver ? "

" Indeed, no ! You see, I rather envy people who can experience ghostly sensations. Although we have been here for quite a long time—my great-grandfather built ' White House '—we are not really Highland. We are East Coast."

" So is Mother ! "

" Is that so ? Well, she will probably be amused by some of her maids' dread of the dark. I must try," he went on, " to find out the history of your castle for you—"

" Oh, please don't bother ! "

" But I'm curious on my own account, too. It seems rather absurd to live, as my people do, almost under its shadow and know nothing about it. But, you see, my grandfather was devoted to sport, and my father, since I can remember, has read nothing but military works, books on economics and detective stories—chiefly detective stories. Still, there may be something on his bookshelves —"

" Oh—be careful ! "

He had been standing almost facing her, his feet on a flat stone, leaning on his stick, its point on another stone—when the point slipped. But for her swiftness he would have been down. For a space her strong young arms held him ; he clung to her, his face almost at her lips. Recovering his balance, he stood upright, breathing quickly, yet not so quickly as she.

But she was first to speak.

" Have you hurt yourself ? You shouldn't have risked it."

" Forgive me," he said, after a moment. " I must have given you a fright. And thank you ever so much. You saved me from coming down on that old knee of mine, which would have put me back for Lord knows how long. Please don't look so scared. I'm not a penny the worse."

" Oh, you did terrify me, Mr. Silver," she said, " and I'm glad you're not hurt. But let's get out of this. Lean on me, if you want to. I've good strong shoulders."

She was charming, and he was still thrilling from the contact and feel of her ; his whole being was eager to touch her again. He wavered—and drew back.

" Thanks, Miss Maclaggan, but I'll manage. Would you mind going first ? " It was not often that Wilfred Silver denied himself.

They came out upon the clearing as the cloud passed from the face of the sun.

" Don't you want to sit down for a bit ? " she asked, thinking he looked paler than ever.

" Yes, I think I do," he answered, with a glance at

the boulder whence he had first seen her. He took out his cigarette-case and proffered it. If she took one, he would ask her to stay a little longer; if she refused—

She shook her head.

" You don't smoke ? "

" Gave it up ages ago "—meaning about three months ago, to oblige Charlie.

" You must have begun early ! "

She caught the quizzing look in the dark eyes, and laughed in spite of herself. It was all so different out in the sunshine.

He was serious once more. " Miss Maclaggan, I hope we shall meet again. My work is in London, but it will be a while before I can go back to it. I'm in for a pretty dull time."

" Dull ? You ? "

" Glen Laggan is not so new to me as it is to you, and, for the present, I'm like the local old woman of ninety-five, whose daughter complained that she could do nothing to amuse herself."

Peggy laughed again, but with sympathy. It was impossible to feel unfriendly towards this young man. Yet she could find nothing to say. She glanced at her watch, a gift from Cousin Bob.

" I must not keep you," he said. " Just tell me you will regard our meeting this morning as a full and proper introduction."

Etiquette is all very well in its way, but the girl who has held a young man, even a stranger, in her arms, for thirty seconds or so, cannot very well, the next time she encounters him, pretend she has never met him before !

" Why shouldn't I ? " said Peggy.

" Thank you for that and—everything." He held out his hand. " Goodbye, Miss Maclaggan."

She gave him hers. " Goodbye, Mr. Silver."

" You know your way home ? "

Was he chaffing her again ? With that dignified little air of hers, she pointed to the opening of the path.

" That's right," he said. " By the way, talking of superstition and darkness, would you dare to come along that path, through those trees, to the castle, say, in the late dusk ? "

At the time, she saw in it no more than a teasing question. Once more her head went up. " Because I'm a town girl, used to plenty of lights, you think I wouldn't dare," she said, " and maybe I wouldn't. . . . But maybe I would ! " She turned into the path.

" I believe you would ! " he called after her. " Goodbye, again ! "

Before she knew—" Cheerio ! " she said over her shoulder—and could have kicked herself.

Wilfred Silver watched till she had disappeared among the trees. " You little beauty ! " he said under his breath, and went over to the boulder. He lighted a cigarette and smoked moodily. So he had been smoking when she first appeared ; for he was a young man troubled about many things.

Now, however, it was the girl who provided the paramount problem. He did not regret having introduced himself to her. On the contrary, he truly and eagerly desired to see her again.

Railway porter's daughter ! Why, he knew no end of gentlemen's daughters who, looks apart, had not half her pride and dignity. The " cheerio " had, of course, been rather a lapse, but, somehow, he liked her all the better for it.

Still, a friendship with this girl would mean an awkward situation, since nothing, as he was perfectly certain, would ever induce his mother to call at Glen Laggan House.

IX

"A RAILWAY porter—good Heaven!" To Wilfred Silver his mother's words uttered on the station platform signified, definitely and finally, her attitude towards the newcomers. Socially, Mrs. Silver changed her attitude never; personally, she changed it extraordinarily seldom. She would sit for hours, with embroidery or a book, or at "patience," in a straight-backed chair, moving naught but her hands, and appear to be perfectly comfortable. Outwardly, at least, she had none of that modern restlessness which passes for activity.

Tall and fair, slender, thin-lipped, she had eyes that in strong lights were sea-green, and a clear, level voice that could say bitter things very sweetly. She came of an ancient family whose name is writ in British History, though not in letters of pure gold; there are people to whom it seems better, if the account be old enough, to have a name on the discredit side, rather than nowhere in the book.

She and Colonel Silver were at lunch when Wilfred, who had his Saxon name from her side, came in, after his meeting with Peggy Maclaggan. Like Time, Mrs. Silver waited for no man; like Time, too, she gave no regard to circumstances. Her son was an invalid, incapable of hurrying along the road, but that was no reason why a meal should be kept back a minute. She

received his apology graciously and expressed the hope
that he had not over-exerted himself.

"You are looking fagged, Wilfred," his father
remarked. "Where did you go?"

"Not far, Dad; through the wood and up to the
Castle. I sat there most of the time."

"I should avoid that walk if I were you, Wilfred,"
said his mother, "now that those dreadful people are
in residence. You don't want to offer them the opportunity of picking up an acquaintance."

Wilfred, on the way home, had not altogether made
up his mind, but now he decided to say nothing whatever
about his encounter with the girl. He said—

"They may not particularly wish to have our acquaintance, and, after all, Mother, we have no knowledge of
what they are like."

Mrs. Silver's straight mouth relaxed into one of its
chilly smiles. "My dear boy, use your common sense!
A railway porter! A person who carries luggage and
lives on tips!"

There was a pause, till the Colonel spoke. "As a
matter of fact," he said, using the introductory phrase
to which he was given when not very sure of himself,
"I met the new Laird, half an hour ago. He was walking
with Gregg and the person whose money, I believe,
purchased the property."

"They spoke to you!"

"On the contrary, they would have passed on had I
not stopped."

"Was that necessary, Andrew?"

"Well, really, I should have felt a churl had I acted
otherwise. As a neighbour, I offered my welcome.
That was all. But I may say that my impression of the

F

man was not unfavourable. While, undoubtedly, he lacks polish —"

" A rough diamond, with a heart of gold—spare me, please ! "

" I had no intention of inflicting so mixed a metaphor," he returned, with rather a weary smile. " I was going to say that, whatever his drawbacks, there is nothing in the least aggressive, or offensive, about him ; there is, indeed, something almost attractive. Then his cousin, if undistinguished looking, is quite presentable, though not so very long ago, I imagine, he was as unpolished as the new Laird. The world changes quickly nowadays, Elfrida, and we have got to take things as they are."

" Have we ? "

" At all events, the new Laird has come to stay, and I think he and his family ought to be given at least a chance. Certainly, I have no intention of ignoring the man when I meet him again."

" There is no reason why you should be rude," she said. " Also, there is no reason why you should go a step beyond ordinary out-of-doors courtesy. But you will have to be on your guard. People of that sort, on the slightest pretext, become horribly familiar."

" I should say he is much too diffident for that."

" At present the man is strange to it all, but the strangeness will wear off—and, then, he has a wife and daughter who, you may be sure, will egg him on to—"

" I shall leave you, Elfrida, to deal with the wife and daughter," he interrupted half-jestingly.

" I ? In what way should I deal with them."

" Gently, I hope. In the ordinary course of things, you will be calling at Glen Laggan House—"

"Really, Andrew, you are too absurd!" She turned to her son. "What do you say about it, Wilfred?"

"Well, Mother," the young man answered, with the briefest of glances, "those dreadful people, as you have called them, have not yet been here for twenty-four hours. I don't see why we should not keep open minds for a week or two, anyway."

"An excellent suggestion!" the Colonel observed.

"I fear I cannot follow it," his wife coolly returned. "I may tell you both, once and for all, that, so far as I am concerned, those people do not exist. We need not discuss them further."

Wilfred's shoulders gave an almost imperceptible shrug. The Colonel appeared to have accepted defeat. He seldom allowed himself to argue with his wife, for he seldom forgot the humiliation of his life. He was one of those most ill-starred men who, having married women with fortunes, have, with the best intention and worst results, directed their reinvestments. Elfrida, not a mean woman where money was concerned, had forgiven him; she had never directly reminded him of the disaster; but it is not possible to forget the thing that has altered the whole of one's material existence.

The Silvers had not been well off before the War; since the War they had been very badly off, indeed.

While they were still at table, the postman passed the window, and presently a maid brought in the mail.

For Wilfred there was one letter. He laid it down unopened, but, as though against his will, kept glancing at it.

"I guess I'll rest this afternoon," he said when his mother rose. "Not yet used to the Glen Laggan air."

"Quite right, my boy," said his father. "Take it easy and go slow."

There was concern in his mother's regard. "Yes; you are looking too tired, Wilfred. Go right to bed and don't get up before tea-time."

In his room upstairs, he read the letter—from a friend, a chartered accountant, in London. It was a fairly long letter, but the part that mattered to Wilfred Silver was this :—

"I have seen those moneylenders and explained the circumstances. They were pretty difficult, but in the end agreed to renew your Promissory Notes for four months, at the previous ghastly, but legal, rate of interest. I tried for the full six months, but they would not hear of it. So this means that on September 15th you have to provide £2,110, and I earnestly advise you to make every effort to do so, as there is not the slightest chance of a further renewal. I enclose the new Notes for signature. . . ."

Wilfred did not go to bed. He sat very still, in the shabby easy-chair—most of the furnishings of White House were shabby—and thought drearily. Four months ! A hundred and twenty days ! What miraculous thing could happen before the 15th of September to make his remaining asset, a bunch of share certificates of art silk and gramophone companies, worth to-day about £150—into the equivalent of £2,000 ?

Wilfred regarded himself as an honest gambler, an honest borrower ; but no man knows what he is till he finds himself in the morass of money difficulty.

At last, with a heavy sigh, he lay back in the chair. He was facing a window which looked out upon a wood. Over yonder, above the new green of the trees, the wall-tops of the Castle rose brown in the sunshine. He did not see them, but, shutting his eyes, he saw the opening of a path into another part of the wood, and a girl passing into it with a backward glance and a friendly " Cheerio ! "

X

"THAT seems a decent sort o' chap," Colin remarked, when the Colonel had gone on his way.

"He is," agreed Mr. Gregg; "and he happens to be your nearest neighbour."

"He is also one of your fishing—er—clients," Cousin Bob put in.

"That is so, Mr. Maclaggan. Since ever I can remember, the Colonel has taken No. 3 Beat for March and April. I daresay he has had to do without something else to manage it, for he's none too well off. The fishing, I should guess, is his one luxury. But his luck was badly out this year."

"How was that?" said Colin. "Fish not biting, eh?"

A heavy moustache is a useful thing for concealing small smiles, like Mr. Gregg's. "Not exactly," he replied. "Young Mr. Silver had a serious motor accident near London, and the Colonel and his lady went South, and were away for the two months. The Colonel never wet a fly."

Colin put back his cap and scratched his head. "Are you telling us," he said slowly, "that the man paid good money for fish he never got—and him hard up?"

"Yes, Mr. Maclaggan—but, of course, his being hard up is no business of ours, and, as a good sportsman, he accepts his ill-fortune without grousing."

"But, Mr. Gregg, you'll send him back his money! Is that not right, Bob?"

"No, no, Mr. Maclaggan," the factor answered quickly. "That would never do! In certain circumstances, you know, a kindness can be an offence. Maybe, later on, when you know him better, you might invite him to a day's fishing—"

They had to step to the side of the narrow road to let a big car pass. In the tonneau sat a large, clean-shaven, solemn-faced man, who gave Mr. Gregg a rather patronising wave, and whose appearance put the Colonel out of Colin's mind for the time being.

"Gosh! Fancy meeting him up here!"

"Do you know that gentleman?" the factor inquired.

"We ken him fine at Queen Street! 'Thrup'ny bit' we call him there. Mind you," Colin continued quickly, "there's nothing against a thrup'ny-bit, so long as the party doesna behave as if he had bought the Railway. Does that chap live about here?"

"He has a large place, twenty miles up the Glen, beyond Garry," Mr. Gregg replied. "Since you seem already to know him as a careful person, there can be no harm in telling you that, in his own district, he is called—in the Gaelic, of course—'The Man Who once Gave a Cigarette to a Ghillie.' And the ghillie could not smoke it, because there was a wee tear in the paper.'

"Man, that's the best yet!" cried Colin, with so resounding a guffaw, that the factor determined to be more discreet with his fun in future.

Later, in the blithest of humour, the new Laird sat down with his family to lunch.

"We've had a great morning, Maggie! Mr. Gregg is one o' the best—nothing stuck-up about him. He took us round, and I shook hands wi' some o' the—what d'you call them, Bob?"

" Tenants, Colin."

" Ay, tenants—that's it! Fancy me wi' tenants! Gosh, it beats all! And then, on the road home, a gentleman comes up to us—Colonel Silver—and he was as nice as nice, and said he hoped we would all be happy at Glen Laggan, and so forth."

" I met his son, this morning," Peggy put in, " when I was looking at the old Castle, and he was very nice, too."

" Well, if that's not splendid! It's fine when folk are friendly-like—eh, Maggie? And what age would he be, Peggy? About Ronnie's age?"

" A good bit older than Ronnie, Daddy. He's in business, I think, in London, but he had a bad accident — motor smash—do you hear that, Ronnie?"

" That's nothing against him," said her brother, pausing in life's most important pleasures. " It might happen to the best of us."

" Ay, we heard about the accident from Mr. Gregg," said Colin. " Well, well! You'll have to ask him up to his tea, Peggy—I mean, his dinner."

" I think we ought to wait till Mrs. Silver has called on Mother," said the girl. " Isn't that so, Cousin Bob?"

" Well, Maggie," said Colin, before his cousin could speak. " You can send Mrs. Silver a message by Ronnie, to say you'll be delighted to see her dropping in —"

" No, no, Colin," said Bob. " I'm afraid that wouldn't do. We must observe the established rules, one of which is, that the newcomer must never make the first approach."

" Is that a fact? Ah, well, I'm sure I'm not wanting to offend anybody, though I can't see how a kind word could do any harm."

" I can't say I'm looking forward to the ladies," Maggie remarked, with a rueful smile. " To tell the truth, I'm terrified."

" From what I have gathered from Gregg," Cousin Bob said, reassuringly, " you are not likely to be troubled too much by callers. This summer, as Gregg says, things are not what they used to be in these parts. Few of the people really belonging to the district live in it. Many of the big houses won't be open till August, and then some of them will be filled with strangers, out for sport only. Besides Mr. Silver, at the moment, there are only Lady MacVean, on the other side of the Loch, and Miss Carnachan —I forget where her place is, but she is the last of a very old family, and a bit peculiar—"

" Oh, mercy ! "

" Keep up your heart, Maggie—I'll stand by you ! " said Colin. " And here's another thing ! Mr. Gregg is bringing his daughter this afternoon to see Peggy. She's a great sport, I believe—rides a powny, and so forth. On a powny, I'm told, you can see places round about here that you can't get at any other way."

" Peggy," said Bob, " would you like to have a pony ? "

" Bob," Maggie exclaimed. " You've spoilt her enough already ! Don't—"

" Hoots, woman ! ' said Colin. " Let the man enjoy himself ! And what," he asked presently, " are you all for doing after dinner—I mean, lunch ? Mr. Gregg isn't coming till four."

" What about a drive ? " suggested Bob.

" Great idea ! But you'll excuse me. I'm going to step up to the railway, just to see what's doing. I—I've got a sort o' a home-sickness."

XI

IT was an unusually dry May—much too dry for the fishers in the neighbourhood. Six fine days went past, without Peggy revisiting the Castle. Not that she had forgotten it, or Wilfred Silver; but, as things happened, neither the time nor the opportunity had been hers. For this Mr. Gregg was more or less responsible.

At the outset, Rona was none too pleased at being appointed guide to this girl from nowhere, and she let her father know it; but, after her first hour at Glen Laggan House, she became more amenable.

"Goodness know how they're going to get away with it," she said, "but they're the sort of people one wouldn't hurt for worlds. I daresay I shall get to like them, and, of course, the girl's a peach to look at."

Rona, at nineteen, was a brown-haired, brown-eyed, brown-faced creature, of sturdy build, with the figure of a successful Channel swimmer. In pre-boyish-figure days an outspoken young man might have described her appearance as "cuddlesome." She had come home from a year on the Continent, starving for the freedom of her native glen. In passing, it may be mentioned that Ronnie found in her his first love. He had no use for "the skinny sort."

"I'm glad you feel that way about the Maclaggans," her father said, gratefully. "By helping them you'll be helping me. It's less than a forlorn hope, but I'd do a lot to see them come out on top."

Rona wagged her head. "The girl may do that, but I don't see it for the old ones. However, I'll do what I can for her, anyway."

Two days later she reported: "Peggy and I are going to get on. She's terribly in earnest about Glen Laggan, but she's a real sport, too. For a town girl, she can make pretty good use of her legs. We'll have some fun going around when she gets her pony."

Later, it was Colin Maclaggan who was the proud man when he saw his daughter setting out of a morning on horseback, with her new friend, to explore the mountainsides and corries and all the wildness that was still so strange to himself.

On the same day, Peggy received two letters. Charlie thanked her for hers, was pleased to hear she liked the place, and mentioned that things in Glasgow were as usual, the weather being rotten. Not a very satisfying letter! Mr. Wilfred Silver's was, at any rate, more interesting. It came along with a book, which did not look as if it had been on anybody's shelf for any length of time. Wilfred wrote—

"DEAR MISS MACLAGGAN,

I am sending you this little volume which contains something—though not much, I'm sorry—about your Castle. I have, however, got a story from an old man in the neighbourhood, which might interest you, though it is pretty gruesome. Severed heads and so forth! Since I saw you, I have been several times at the Castle, but I daresay you have already found many other interests in Glen Laggan. Yesterday, I saw you and Miss Gregg—through a field-glass—well up the mountainside, and wished—you cannot imagine how much—I had been fit to follow your example—and you. Please do not think of acknowledging the book. I do hope we may meet before long.

Yours sincerely,

WILFRED W. H. SILVER."

It was nice of him, Peggy thought, and she wanted to thank him, though, somehow, she did not want to write to him. While she did not mention his letter to her people, she did not conceal the book.

On the afternoon of the seventh day, Rona having an engagement, she decided, at the last moment, not to go driving with the others. Half hoping he might be there, she walked through the wood to the clearing.

At the opening of the path he was standing—waiting for her. His sombre eyes told as much, though hers may not have perceived it. He took her hand, but made no attempt to retain it.

"I saw your pale frock through the trees," he re-marked, lightly, "and said to myself that summer was coming."

"I think it has come," she replied. "I couldn't face a mountain climb to-day."

The weather had certainly become very warm, almost sultry. An hour ago, she had changed into the light frock of daffodil shade, white stockings and shoes. The week of Highland air had given her a lovely colour. If Peggy, in work-a-day garments, with the pallor of the City on her face, had been pretty, she was brilliantly so now.

Wilfred, who for seven days and, one might almost say, nights had been thinking of her , with two sorts of thoughts, forgot one sort and barely restrained himself. In the past, the fairness of other girls had moved him, but no fairness ever as hers.

" You are not yet finding Glen Laggan dull," he said, rousing himself.

" How could that be, Mr. Silver ? "

" Ah, well, perhaps you will never find it so—I hope not.   But you have had a week of the best weather, and have still to know the worst—days, when the Glen is filled with drifting wet mist—nothing to be seen, nothing to be done—when even the hardy Miss Rona prefers slippers and the fireside—"

" You know Miss Gregg ?   She's a wonder, isn't she ? "

" I know her—as a wonder.   I have not met her since she was quite a little girl—we have both been away so much.   But do you think you will be able to look out at nothing but mist, for days on end, and not weary ? "

" I think it will be ages before I have time to weary. I told you, I had a lot to learn."

" So you did, and I have been asking myself what you might be studying."

She gave him a shrewd glance.   " Sometimes, Mr. Silver," she said, carefully, " I wonder if you mean just what you say.   But "—briskly—" never mind that now ! I came here on the chance of telling you about the book. Thanks awfully !   I read it last night, when I ought to have been asleep.   It told me heaps of things I wanted to know about the Great Glen, and something about the Castle, too.   Fancy Maclaggans being here, nearly a thousand years ago ! "

" Does that matter to you, Miss Maclaggan ? "

" Yes, it does, though I can't tell why, exactly."

"You ought to have been a princess!" he said, his tone kindly. " Won't you sit down and have a little talk about it ? "

As if for inspiration, Peggy looked up at the Castle. She had her doubts about this young man, though she rather liked him, and he interested her very much. He was so different from the "boys" she had known in Glasgow.

" I've got a rug with me, so your frock won't suffer," he said presently. " Don't think I'm coddling myself. I brought along the rug on the chance of your honouring it. On that same chance I have brought it along every day, sometimes twice, for a week."

Her glance fell to meet his. " Oh, you don't mean that ! " she said ; yet she knew that this time, at any rate, he was sincere. And then she remembered. " Goodness, I'm sorry ! I meant to ask if you were keeping better. Are you ? "

" Much, thank you. Did nearly two miles this morning, without a rest. . . . Will you stay ? "

" Well "—a pause—" just for a wee whiley."

" A wee whiley ! " It was an echo, without mockery. His smile, though it brought a warmth to her tan, did not hurt.

" And what is wrong with ' a wee whiley ' ? " she bravely asked.

" Wrong, Miss Maclaggan ? It was charming—it fell out so naturally—just like ' cheerio.' "

" Oh ! And I called ' cheerio ' to you when I hadn't known you for ten minutes ! Mr. Silver ! "—abruptly— " do you think I don't speak naturally all the time ?

I'm not asking for nice fibs, but only for the nasty truth.
Tell me, please ! "

He regretted his " echo," but there was no way of
evading her demand.

" Then let me say," he replied, " that, sometimes, you
seem to speak rather—carefully."

She sighed.   " I was afraid of that."

" But what's the trouble ? "

" Oh, you know very well ! I'm not ashamed of
Daddy having been a railway porter, nor of having been a
shop-girl myself, nor anything of that sort—but I did
want to teach myself to speak nicely—and naturally, too.
You've been in Glasgow, I suppose ? "

" Fairly often. I'll not pretend that I don't know what
you mean. I seem to have read somewhere, once, that
the Glasgow people don't speak—only make sounds—"

" Oh ! " She smiled in spite of herself.

"—but, of course, it isn't quite so bad as that. As
for your speech, Miss Maclaggan, I wish you wouldn't
distress yourself. Glasgow comes into it only now and
then, and, if you'll allow me to say so, I like it. Still,
if you are aiming at eliminating Glasgow altogether, I
know you will succeed, as you will succeed in anything
you attempt."

She shook her head. " I wish you would be honest
with me, Mr. Silver. I'm no good at pretending,
myself."

" If you'll give me the chance, I'll prove my honesty.
Ask me, and I'll try to tell you when I think your speech
a little wrong. Now," he went on quickly, " let me fetch
the rug, and then we can sit down and talk quietly and
comfortably."

He brought the rug from the boulder and spread it

on a tuft of heather. When they were seated, she
asked—

"Did you really mean what you said about helping
me to speak better?"

"Do you really mean that you want me to—to pull
you up?"

"Of course, I do! I've always wanted somebody to
check me, and—there was nobody." Then, as an after-
thought—"But why should you, Mr. Silver?"

What a mixture of frankness, shrewdness and
simplicity she was! "Perhaps," he deliberately answered, "because I am hoping we are going to be
friends."

She gave a wise little nod. "I don't think I would
be sitting here, if we weren't going to be that," she
said. "But you'll have to be strict with me."

"Oh, rather!"

Their eyes met. They laughed.

The afternoon slipped away.

.   .   .   .   .   .

Rosman, the butler, was seeking for Miss Maclaggan,
to tell her that tea was served in the small drawing-room.
The motor party was taking tea at Foyers. He had
searched the gardens and been down to the lodge, where
he had learned that the young lady had not gone
out; so he now determined to try the grounds in the
direction of the Castle.

Rosman was looking the better of his life at Glen
Laggan. Maggie, who noticed such things in a motherly
way, had, within an hour of her arrival, thought him an
ill man, and had confided her fears to Cousin Bob, who
had partly reassured her by saying, "You should have
seen him a fortnight ago. He has come through a lot of

trouble, but he'll not give you any. Maybe I'll tell you and Colin more about him, later on."

Rosman, too, was feeling better—in mind, as well as body. It seemed to him that among those mountains, in this beautiful home, with those unsophisticated and not seldom amusing people, he might yet find peace. At all events, he had found privacy for his broken spirit. He was truly grateful to Mr. Robert Maclaggan, and, if only for that reason, would serve this odd Laird and his family with all his heart. As he walked through the grounds, he told himself that he would never want to go out of them. Nothing of the past, it seemed to him then, could enter there. . . .

He came to the path which, as he had learned during a recent evening stroll, led to the old Castle. She might be there. He had heard her talk of the Castle to her father. He liked this girl, though her fair beauty reminded him cruelly of a girl whom he would fain have forgotten ; he wished that nothing hateful and hideous would ever come her way.

He was near the end of the path, and in sight of the Castle, when he heard voices, recognising one of them ; but the presence of another person was no reason for turning back, his mission unperformed. Two paces more, and he was looking into the clearing.

He opened his mouth—and it remained open. A frown came between his brows. His hands clenched. A greyish shade came over his face. Horror stared from his eyes.

At last the strain relaxed. "God Almighty ! " he said under his breath, turned and, staggering a little, went the way he had come.

. . . . . .

G

Peggy looked at her watch.

" I must be going," she said, on her feet before he could rise to assist her. " Thanks awfully for the lesson, Mr. Silver."

" I don't know when I've enjoyed anything so much," he returned. " Do you think you need any more ? "

" Oh, don't make fun of me ! I feel as if it would take years."

" I should like that ! " he said, gaily. " Still, on the chance, I'm coming here to-morrow, and the next day, and—"

" Oh, please ! "

"—the day after, and so on and so on ! '

They went, laughing, to the opening of the path.

" Goodbye, Mr. Silver."

" Goodbye, Miss Maclaggan."

She took the path.

" Miss Maclaggan ! "

" Well ? "

" Please look over your shoulder and say it."

" Say what ? "

" You know."

" I don't ! "

" Your first fib ! "

" That's not fair ! But, anyway, I won't say it ! "

" What about my fee for tuition ? "

" Oh ! "

" Come, pay me ! "

" Oh, well, then—cheerio ! " she said—and ran.

His smile died. He put his palms to his face. If only, oh, God, if only . . .

Near to the house, she met the butler. Rosman had regained control ; also he had become possessed by a desire to see again the face, the glimpse of which had so shaken him, and was returning to the wood.

He stood aside, saying in his formal way : " I have put tea, ma'am, in the small drawing-room."

" Thanks—Rosman." Peggy was growing used to being waited upon, but she had still to watch that she did not " Mister " the butler. " Are you feeling quite well ? " she asked.

" Quite well, thank you, ma'am, though the sudden heat to-day—"

" You ought to take more fresh air," she said sagely. " Have you anything more to do now ? "

" Nothing—unless there is something you wish for—"

" There's nothing." She pointed towards the wood. " Have you seen the old Castle yet ? It isn't nearly so close there—a breeze comes up from the Loch. Try it, Rosman."

She went on to the house, reflecting that Rosman was far nicer than any of the butlers she had ever seen on the movies, though she had admired some of them quite a lot.

Rosman reached the clearing to find it deserted. He leaned against a tree and, with a hand that still shook, lighted a cigarette. Had memory played him a trick ? It was possible, of course ; but could there be two men with eyes like those he had lately seen—dark gloomy eyes, bold yet furtive—fastened on the face of the girl, who had seemed happily unaware of the gaze ? If only he had brought that snapshot with him to Glen Laggan— though, surely, of all places Glen Laggan was the last he should have imagined as holding any reminder of the tragic past ! Well, unless he were supported by certainty, he could do nothing.

That night, in his room—a fairly spacious apartment, which Robert Maclaggan had caused to be furnished as for a gentleman and a student—Rosman wrote to a friend in London, requesting a reply by return. Four days later it arrived, but it was from his friend's partner in business, who wrote thus : " Mr. Baildon, with Mrs. Baildon, has just sailed on a voyage to Australia, for his health's sake, and I do not expect him back till September. I regret I have no knowledge of the sealed packet to which you refer, or its whereabouts."

Rosman, having read, threw down the letter with a gesture expressive of defeat. Merely on the strength of one's memory, however vivid, of a photograph, one dare not say to a stranger, " Thou art the man ! "

XII

MAY came to an end, without a break in the weather.

"The fishing apart, it has been very fortunate," the factor remarked, one morning, in the office. "It has allowed you to see more of the place and people in two weeks than might have been possible in an ordinary month. You are beginning to feel at home, I hope?"

Colin smiled, dubiously. "In a way, I'm at home; in a way, I'm still a stranger. But you've been a great help—a mighty great help, Mr. Gregg," he added warmly.

"It has been no great task. But here is a small, though rather important point. You must drop calling me 'Mister.' I am your paid servant, as everybody knows, and when you give me the 'Mister,' especially before the crofters, they are—well, puzzled."

"I see what you mean," said Colin, after brief reflection. "Gosh, I've an awful heap to learn, Mr.— I mean, Gregg. And whiles I wonder what the folk are thinking about me."

"That's natural! But we'll just have to let them think till they make up their minds. In your case, I fancy, that may take a little time, though I gather from Rona that some of them have already made up their minds about Miss Maclaggan. Having the Gaelic, Rona can get at their thoughts."

" They like Peggy ? "

" They do. She has the right way with them. She is neither too stiff nor too easy."

" That's great ! They'll like Maggie, too, when she gets in among them. But I have my doubts about myself ! " Colin took out a packet of cigarettes, proffered it to the factor, and took one himself. " Man, I wish I could speak the language ! "

" That may come," said Mr. Gregg, more encouragingly than he felt. " Meanwhile, Miss Maclaggan is studying it—"

" I've seen her wi' the books."

"—and she and Rona are beginning to talk it on their excursions. If I may say so, you have a daughter who will make something of her life here."

" Ay, Peggy's clever. All the same, we're awful indebted to you and Miss Rona." Colin paused to light up.

Mr. Gregg's manner had become slightly awkward. " There's another thing I ought to say, if I'm going to do my duty. It is expected, even by those who don't do it themselves, that the Laird will attend Church." At Colin's glum look, he added : " Of course, if you are against the Church, as so many people are to-day—"

" No, no ; I'm not against it. I was brought up to go twice every Sunday, and I had an aunt married on a minister—quite a decent chap. But I doubt Maggie and me have sort o' col——relapsed. Still, I'm not against it—oh, no ! I ken there's a lot o' girning at the Kirk nowadays, but, as I said, not long since, to a signalman at Queen Street, that called himself a free-thinker, girning's easy and doesn't cost anything, either in siller or help. And as you seem to be anxious, Mr.—I mean, Gregg—for us to do the right thing—as we really are ourselves—I may tell you that my cousin was at us about it, only last night—and we're all going to yon wee Kirk up the hill, on Sunday first, though I doubt, sitting in a pew yonder, I'll feel like a monkey in a menagerie."

"Why not a lion?" said the factor, looking relieved. "At any rate, you'll please a number of decent people, who would be otherwise hurt."

"Well, well, we didn't come to Glen Laggan to hurt folk, anyway," sighed Colin, and opened another subject.

It was certainly an ordeal for the Maclaggans to sit in the small building, four miles from Glen Laggan, feeling painfully prominent, enduring the curious glances of not a few members of the congregation.

Colonel and Mrs. Silver were there, and, somehow, Peggy experienced a chill at the sight of the lady's eyes and mouth. As soon as the service was over, she hurried her parents out to the car, lest her Daddy should feel constrained to "pass the time of day" with the Colonel. She need not have worried, however, for Colin was only too thankful to get away, as may be gathered from his reply to Mr. Gregg's kindly inquiry, the following morning.

"Hellish—but, as Maggie says, we've got to carry on."

"It'll be easier next time, and you've made some old bodies very happy," said Mr. Gregg. "Now, there's some estate business for us to tackle. . . ."

On the afternoon of the same day, Colin, returning from a refreshing half-hour at the railway station—he had met a "goods" guard whom he had known long ago at Queen Street—was about to enter the gates of Glen Laggan House, when a small car drew up, and the occupant, whom he recognised as the Minister, jumped out, with a hearty greeting.

The Rev. A. Jarvie Fraser, recently appointed to the charge, was a young bachelor, good looking, smartly groomed, and likeable, though just a little too well pleased with himself, as one having authority. His manner was perhaps more affable than amiable. But Colin, as we know, was ever disposed to accept the ha'penny, giving credit for the shilling.

"I could not go past when there was a chance of shaking hands with the new Laird," said Mr. Fraser, showing beautiful teeth, under a trim black moustache. "I was not on my way to call, to-day, for I fancy that Mrs. Maclaggan is not yet welcoming visitors, but I hope to—"

"Come away in," said Colin, looking at the old silver watch he had set so often by the big clock at Queen Street. "We'll be having a cup o' tea now, and you'll be real welcome."

Thanks to his upbringing, Colin retained a certain respect for "the cloth"; but there was more than that and hospitality behind the invitation. Maggie had been dreading callers, and Colin felt that Mr. Fraser might make "an easy one," to begin with. In a way, he was right. Mr. Fraser stayed for an hour, and his talk was bright, kindly and amusing, especially when directed towards Peggy. Unfortunately, Peggy detected the hint of patronage in his manner towards her parents, and from that moment the Rev. Mr. A. Jarvie Fraser was doomed to the outer circle of her acquaintances for ever and a day.

"That wasn't so bad," cried Colin, when he had departed. "You got on fine, Maggie, wi' your first visitor!"

" Ah, but it's not men I'm feared for ! " said Maggie.

Perhaps that was why she was not utterly terrified by her next visitor, a week later—Miss Carnachan, of Garry, of whom a local crofter had long ago observed that she would have made a good enough man, had she been a foot and a half taller.

At half-past four, an aged car, with sounds suggesting a traction engine in distress, laboured up the avenue, took a crazy curve on the broad drive in front of the house, and with a cruel jar came to rest, not quite at the steps. From it, presently, descended its driver, a very small woman in a drab costume, which an expert in such matters would probably have dated five years back. In colouring and lines, or, rather, grooves, her countenance would have made you think of a walnut, and you would have put her age at seventy, or so, till a glimpse of her bright eyes and fine white teeth caused you to guess again. She carried a stout stick, for she was lame ; but she hobbled up the steps nimbly enough, and with a purposeful finger in a much-worn glove pressed the electric button.

Rosman opened the door—and his jaw dropped at the sight of her.

" Mrs. Maclaggan at home ? " she asked snappily of his legs, raised her glance, and gasped : " Michael Rosman ! What the devil are you doing here ? " Then she seized his hand and wrung it.

" Miss Carnachan," he said, " I had no idea that your home was in this neighbourhood. I thought—"

" Yes ; lots of people mix up the two Garrys. You were thinking of the one, thirty miles away. But that isn't answering my question."

" I'm earning a living and doing so, as far as possible,

out of the world." He looked over his shoulder, anxiously.

" Quite right !—We can't talk here. But I understand, and I just want to say that I was damned sorry to learn of your trouble, last year. I wrote to you, but the letter came back marked ' gone away.' When will you come to see me ? "

" Might that not be awkward—in the circumstances ? "

" Perhaps—yes. But if I can help, let me know." Her tone changed. " I take it that your—h'm—mistress is in. Is she receiving ? "

" I believe she will see you, Miss Carnachan."

" And the—h'm—Laird ? "

" He is in ; also Miss Maclaggan." Rosman lowered his voice. " You will be kind to them, won't you ? "

" That depends ! "

He hesitated.

" Lead on ! " she said, abruptly, and she was the sort of person who gets obedience.

Colin and Maggie were taking it easy in the Railway Room ; he with a railway book and cigarette, she with a seam and a paper bag of " black striped balls." From their expressions you would have judged that they were not unhappy.

Rosman entered.

" Miss Carnachan, of Garry, has called, ma'am. Shall I inform Miss Maclaggan ? "

As the door closed, Colin said : " God help us ! She's the peculiar one ! Have I got to show up, Maggie ? I wish Bob was here."

" You promised you would stand by me, Colin." Maggie rose, her fair face troubled, but determination in her blue eyes. At the door she said: "Run and brush your hair, man, and then come in with Peggy."

For about five minutes Miss Carnachan was terrible in her lofty politeness. They all hated her. Then, of a sudden, she became homely—at least, that was how they felt it. At the end of ten minutes, Rosman having brought in tea, she got up, with a thump of her stick, saying—

"You've had enough of me for a first visit, and, anyway, I do obey the social regulations—now and then."

"But, surely," said Maggie, who was just beginning to feel at ease, "you'll take a cup of tea before you go."

"Please excuse me. I seldom touch tea in the afternoon."

"Maybe," said Colin, kindly, "you would take a dram."

"Oh, Colin!" sighed Maggie, under her breath, while Peggy clenched her hands.

But no harm had been done.

"Thanks, Laird," she said, pleasantly; "perhaps when we are a little better acquainted. And to that end I hope you'll all come and see me soon. What about Monday, at four-thirty? Just ourselves, and no ceremony."

"That'll be grand!" said Colin, before Maggie could open her mouth, and thereupon Miss Carnachan declared it settled, and held out her hand to the hostess.

Peggy's finger was at the bell to ring for Rosman.

"No, my dear!" called the little woman. "Be friendly and come to the door with an old woman."

They all went to the door. There were one or two little courtesies that Colin had not needed to be taught, though the ungentle reader may suggest that the present

act was merely a relic of his railway portership. He ran
down the steps, opened the door, and handed the visitor
into her car.

With her hands on the wheel she turned to him, and
said—

" I'll tell you something, Mr. Maclaggan. In my lifetime, I have seen seven different proprietors of Glen
Laggan, but I have never seen one as like a Highland
laird as yourself. Now, for God's sake, don't pose as a
laird—*be* one ! Put that in your pipe and—bless you ! "

With these words, she unbraked and started her car
by letting it roll down the slope.

For a moment Colin stood, staring, then came slowly
up the steps.

" Maggie, do you think she was for being comical ? "

Maggie looked at her man, and suddenly felt rather
proud. " Peggy," she said, " doesn't your Daddy, wi'
his sunburnt face, in that smart rough suit, look finer
than anything you ever saw on the movies ? "

Peggy laughed and became serious. " That wee lady
says what she means, and means what she says. I would
trust her ! "

When Mr. Gregg heard of it, he rubbed his hands and
said to his daughter—

" There's a chance for them now ! What Miss
Carnachan says to-day, the Glen thinks to-morrow. It'll
be Mrs. Silver next, and she won't quarrel with Miss
Carnachan's verdict."

" I don't suppose she will," Rona agreed, " but I'm
wondering when we shall come to the snag. There's
sure to be one, somewhere, worse luck, and I'm getting
fond of Peggy."

" Maybe there will be no snag, after all. I was

afraid Miss Carnachan was going to be it, but now we can—"

"Hope for the best," concluded Rona. "You will have your hands full after Mr. Robert Maclaggan goes away," she added.

"Yes; I can't say I'm looking forward to that," said her father, becoming thoughtful.

Yet his optimism concerning Miss Carnachan was not unreasonable. There is no accounting for castes. This little old woman, wizened, lame, unfashionably attired, given to strong words, last of her line, living, almost in poverty, for nine months of the year in a decaying Highland mansion, the remaining three in a cheap London boarding-house—this little old woman, with little to show for her centuries of lineage, save some tattered parchments and antiques, was a personage apart in that wide district of ancestral domains and ancient families. She was an institution, a tradition— everyone accepted her as such, though none could have told why they did so. She was above peerages and wealth. The most elevated of her neighbours did not deem it stooping, to accept her invitation to a meal o scones and butter (margarine, for all they knew), bramble or apply jelly, home-made, and tea of the rankest; they were gratified when, once in a while, she deigned to appear at their dinner-tables. The gleam of approval in those bright brown eyes was a thing to win, the withering word from behind those white teeth a thing to be feared. Miss Carnachan, of Garry—only a name, yet *the* name in that countryside of great names ! Why ? Convention, says somebody. Very likely, since Convention makes cowards of most of us.

She had come to Glen Laggan House, with an open

mind, to judge for herself what those dreadful people, as she had heard them called, were really like. Ignorance she was prepared to overlook ; blunders she was ready to condone ; but anything savouring of affectation, pretence or aggressiveness would have found her without mercy. Within ten minutes she had learned what she wanted to know, and she had " accepted " the Maclaggans, not for what they were to-day, but for what, as she told herself, they might, if given a chance, be to-morrow. From more than one big house, in recent years, she had driven away, with a sneer at her lips for its new owners ; she left Glen Laggan House with a smile that was, at worst, whimsical.

" Poor wee body—she must be terrible hard up—but, gosh, she's plucky ! " was Colin's first thought on that first visit to Garry.

It was after tea, in the parlour, with its dingy crimson walls, its threadbare carpet, but with its old furniture and coloured prints worth a little fortune. Maggie and Peggy had lingered to look at the prints, and Colin, having followed his hostess through the French window, was standing with her in a small old-fashioned garden, the one cared-for spot in those wide, neglected, over-grown grounds.

" I attend to it myself," she had told him. " It is planted as it was in my grandfather's day."

Now she said abruptly : " What are you going to do with your boy, Laird ? '

Colin pointed towards an outhouse, where his son, having obtained permission, was examining with the keenest interest the " works " of the ancient car. " Well, ma'am, as you see, that seems to be Ronnie's line, and my cousin who's away in London for the week-end, thinks he should go in for it, after he's had a bit holiday here.'

"Quite good," said Miss Carnachan, " if the young man's mind is definitely made up. But, if not, why condemn him to the town ? Scotland has been bled nearly white by the cities." She swept her hand in the direction of the hillside. "You know what they are doing up there ? "

"Ay—planting a new forest."

"Yes—and there are many more to be planted. Why not put your boy, if he will go, into forestry—agriculture, too ? That will mean the town, to begin with, for theory; but afterwards the open. Less money in the open— maybe ; but better a fine life than a fat living ! And for all we know, Laird, Scotland may yet have to come back to the open for a bare one."

"Ma'am," murmured Colin, "you make a body think."

"Besides," she said, bluntly, "you are not going to live for ever. Do you want the next Maclaggan, of Glen Laggan, to be a motor millionaire, coming up for the shooting only, or, maybe, so busy, or so worried, a man that he lets it to a Sassenach ? Damned if I would like to think of that, if I had a son ! Don't let your boy grow up to regard Glen Laggan as merely a playground ! I believe it is going to be more than that to you, or I would not be speaking to you now. There are still a few lairds worthy of their lairdship—mind you, it is not a matter of money only—and I am looking to see one more of the right sort in yourself, before I quit Garry for good. And that's that ! "

She held out her brown hand.

"You're a wonder ! " said Colin, touched, though not

yet fully awake to the illumination and inspiration of her plain words.

"Meanwhile," she added, "I will give your boy an introduction to a friend on the afforestation work; and we'll see what happens." She raised her voice. "Mr. Ronald, come to the house and let me show you some of my antiques. I have some even older than that car!"

Altogether it was a pleasant afternoon for the Maclaggans, and there was plenty to talk about on the ten-miles' homeward run. Colin, however, remained out of the conversation. Miss Carnachan had given him, as the saying is, some nuts to crack.

A mile from Glen Laggan, he had the car stopped, saying, "I'll walk the rest o' the road, Maggie, and see you later."

The sun was still high, the air windless, and walking warm work, while Colin, stepping slowly, strove to concentrate on those words of his recent hostess— "There are still a few lairds worthy of their laird-ship, and I am looking to see one more of the right sort in yourself." . . . What exactly did they mean?

But the question would have to wait. At the first bend in the road, at the beginning of a steep brae, he encountered a distraction. By the wayside, stood a woman, grey-haired, sunken-eyed, her weather-seared face a network of wrinkles and furrows. She was about to resume carrying a sack which, to judge from its protuberances, contained peats.

Like a bird disturbed, the thought of Miss Carnachan flew out of Colin's mind.

"Here, mistress! This is in my line," he said, pushed

her gently aside, and swung the sack to his back. " Where do you want it carried ? "

Recovering from her surprise—or was it fright ?— she pointed up the road.

It was a silent journey. Self-consciousness returned to Colin, who was very shy of the Highland women ; and from this old body's expression you would have guessed that she did not know what to make of the business at all, at all.

Behind them came a car, an old one, though a youngster compared with Miss Carnachan's. It was driven by Colonel Silver, and Mrs. Silver was at his side.

" Who on earth is that ? " asked the lady.

" The new Laird."

" I ought to have known ! The ruling passion for carrying things ! But, surely, he does not expect a gratuity this time ! "

" Is not that a little too bad of you, Elfrida ? "

The car passed the couple. The Colonel was ready to salute, but Colin did not look aside.

" I told you," the Colonel remarked, presently, " that Miss Carnachan had called at Glen Laggan House."

" You did. It is just what one would expect Miss Carnachan to do. She has such a sardonic sense of humour."

" As a matter of fact, Gregg mentioned also that the Maclaggans were invited to Garry for this afternoon."

A thin smile appeared on the straight lips of Mrs. Silver. " The rise before the fall," she remarked. " Those whom the gods would destroy, they first make mad—sometimes with conceit."

" Don't you think you may be assuming too much ?

H

Would it not be wise, Elfrida, to reconsider your
decision with regard to—? "

"Enough, Andrew! As long as those people are
there, I will not enter the gates of Glen Laggan
House."

At the top of the brae, the woman turned to a thatched
cot, which seemed to Colin the poorest-looking he had
seen on the estate. By the side of the door he set down
his burden, took out his handkerchief, lifted his cap, and
mopped his brow.

"Gosh, it's warm!" he said, smiling.

With a sign she invited him to enter.

Inside, after the bright sunlight of the open, it seemed
almost dark. An orange glimmer of peats guided him
to the hearth. She wiped a low wooden chair and pointed
to it.

Colin, wondering if she might be a mute, sat down.
She left him for a minute or so, and returned with a
tumbler of very thick glass, filled with milk. With a
silent movement of her lips, she offered it.

Colin was not fond of milk, but he took it, thanked
her, and drank some. It was rich and sweet and not
quite cold.

"You've got a cow," he said, for the sake of saying
something.

She was standing a little way apart, fingers linked in
front of her, downcast. He decided that she was a mute,
though not a deaf one.

He emptied the glass, rose, handed it to her, thanked
her once more, and moved to the door. She followed
him.

Colin would have liked to give her a pound-note,
but he had promised solemnly, both his cousin and Mr.

Gregg, not to begin his lairdship with indiscriminate tipping.

He held out his hand. " Maybe you don't ken me," he said. " Maybe I should be telling you—I'm Maclaggan, the—the Laird."

She took his hand and lifted her sunken eyes to his face.

" You are more than that," she said, quietly. " You are a man."

XIII

COUSIN BOB had booked his passage to the Argentine for the 23rd of June. As the day drew near, you would have detected signs of depression and apprehension in the Maclaggan family. The little man, unlike most little men, had never been obtrusive in his counsel and guidance, but—with the exception of those few days of absence in London—he had always been at hand in a difficulty, to keep, as it were, the ship steady on her course through those strange waters. In the prospect of his departure the older Maclaggans, at least, felt that they were about to be left very much at sea.

On his last night at Glen Laggan, he sat with Colin and Maggie in the Railway Room, having a final talk. Peggy and Ronnie, with Rona Gregg, were out on the Loch, in the motor-boat. The air was warm and heavy; away to the Southward thunder rumbled almost constantly. It seemed that, at last, the fine weather had reached its breaking point.

" I don't see why you should worry," Bob was saying. " You have made a brave start, and everything is going smoothly. Tell me, is it more difficult than you expected ? "

" Far, far easier," Colin replied, " but—"

" You would not wish to give it up ? "

" No fears ! But, all the same, I feel that it has maybe been too easy, Bob ; that we're bound, one o' these days, to come up hard against it."

" In what way ? "

" Oh, dear knows ! There's such an awful lot o' things to be learned ! "

" But you're learning every day, and there's no desperate hurry. You have the years before you. Do you imagine I'll be bitterly disappointed when I come back in a couple of years, as I hope to do, if you have not learned everything ? If you do, then you've got the wrong idea of me. Go slow ; keep calm ; think less of what you are than of what you are going to be ; and never stop being yourself—and I'll be satisfied, because I'll be getting all I want of you. The same to you, Maggie ! "

" Ah, Bob, you're a great comforter," she said, " and Colin and I will never let you down, if we can help it. But we'll miss you terrible ! "

" Well, I want to be missed, Maggie. I've really nobody but you two and Peggy and Ronnie. But I'm going away, thankful that you have two stand-bys, like Gregg and Rosman."

" I can't think what I would do wanting Rosman," said Maggie. " He's a wonder ! The servants are a wee bit afraid o' him, but they like him. Though he never needs to lift his voice, he gets the thing done every time, and done well. At first I was afraid to keek into that beautiful kitchen, and now I don't think twice of stepping in and giving orders. I feel it's my own place, and that's thanks to Rosman."

" Ay, Rosman's the right chap for us both," said Colin. " But what's his trouble ? There's whiles something about the man's look that makes me heart-sorry for him."

"I'm going to tell you something about Rosman," Bob replied ; "but don't let it go any further. No need for the young people to know. I'm telling you, lest anything should happen while I'm away—not that I expect anything to happen—and he might need some friendly help. When Rosman, with a crowd of others, applied for the situation, I fancied him at once ; but he was so different, I had to ask him questions I should never have dreamed of asking the others. In the end he told me his story."

"Has he been in jail, poor soul ? " Colin asked in a whisper.

"He has been in hell. Rosman was born and brought up in a house something like this. He was the only child. His mother died while he was still at school. His father doted on him, and he wanted for nothing. At the University he went in for Physical Science and had a distinguished career. As there seemed to be no need for him to earn money, he remained at the University long after he had taken his degrees, engaged in research work. He was over thirty when the thing happened. His father, till then a careful man, had allowed himself to be drawn into some big financial business, the promoter of which was a scoundrel. When the crash came, and the promoter bolted, it cost the elder Rosman his entire fortune to get out of the affair with clean hands ; and soon afterwards he died. The son, with all his qualifications, had been a bit of a dreamer, and the best he could do for himself now was to get the post of Science Master in a school on the outskirts of London. He stuck to that, however, and after some years discovered that there was money to be made by writing popular articles and books on scientific subjects—"

" And now," exclaimed Colin, " he's a servant ! "

Bob smiled. " There is nothing on earth finer than a good servant, whatever the job," he said. " Well, when Rosman was getting on for forty, he married a girl much younger than himself, and, as I gathered, a beauty. They were happy enough, to begin with, but he soon discovered that his wife required a great deal of money and entertainment to keep her cheerful. He could not directly provide both, for his whole time was used up in earning the one to make the other possible. So she took to finding her amusements for herself, or with the help of new acquaintances. Rosman blames himself now for not having looked after her, but the man was living in a sort of fever of work. The more he earned, the more she wanted—"

" The hussy ! " muttered Maggie.

" —and his appeals went for nothing. Then, one night, she came home from a cocktail party, quite—drunk."

" Gosh—and her a lady ! " said Colin.

" In the morning, on the floor of her room, Rosman found a photo—a snap-shot—of a man, younger than himself, and extremely good-looking. She refused to give the man's name, but let slip the fact that he was the person who had introduced her to cocktails, cards, and so forth. Probably he was no worse than the other men she was meeting—possibly not so rotten as some of them; but Rosman still regards him as the man responsible for his wife's downfall."

" Well, I would think that, myself," Colin remarked. " And did Rosman find him out and give him a hammering ? "

"I hope Rosman may never find him," said Bob. "After that night, things moved from bad to worse. She went in for all the crazy things your so-called bright people go in for, and maybe some more, pledging her husband's credit all the time. And so, at last, Rosman found himself in the Bankruptcy Court—"

"Well, I'm—"

"Whisht, Colin," said his wife. "And what next, Bob?"

"She left him."

Maggie threw up her hands.

"A month later," Bob continued, "in a night club, she stabbed a man and killed him. She was not sober at the time, and she had provocation, but, all the same, she had brought the knife—a strong, steel, paper knife, the imitation of an old dagger—to the night club in her garter, and she had been heard to—"

"Maggie!" Colin exclaimed, "did we not read something like that in the papers—would it be in the winter?"

"I daresay," sighed Maggie; "but the papers are never wanting that sort o' story."

"Well, I'm not going into details, anyway," Bob went on. "Rosman, bankrupt as he was, managed to find money for her defence, but she got a heavy sentence —years—I forget how many. Rosman told me he was half-mad for a time—bought a revolver and went hunting for the man of the photo. But he had no clue, except the photo, and the man might have gone abroad; and at last, worn out, he came to his senses. He thought of using the revolver on himself, but got over that, too. His main idea now was to get as far as possible away from the world he knew, and the people who knew him. He had lost all notion for his old work—"

" But what," asked Colin, " made him think of being a butler ? "

" Reading the ' wanted ' advertisements put it into his head. There were houses in out-of-the way places that required men servants. He understood the workings of a big house ; he knew about wines, though he's been an abstainer since his marriage. But he had had no real experience, and therefore no references, and a score of people turned him down before he came to me."

" And you gave him his chance," said Maggie. " Just like you ! "

" It seemed a fair risk, in all the circumstances, and I think we've been lucky. I'm hoping he'll look happier, as time goes on. I'd like if he would go back to his writing, in his spare time."

" So that's why you gave him that nice room for himself ! But what's going to happen," she asked, " when that wife o' his gets out o' prison ? "

" Ah, then, I'm afraid, you'll lose Rosman ! "

" He'll take her back ! "

" And try to take better care of her. That, I believe, is his intention, though I could not tell you whether he still loves her. But that's looking ahead, Maggie."

" And the poor soul's a bankrupt ! " cried Colin.

Cousin Bob's undistinguished countenance had an unusually healthy look. " Well, as a matter of fact, he isn't now," he said. " I got matters arranged when I was in London, a fortnight ago—"

" You paid his debts ! "

" Pure business ! I wanted to make sure of the man doing his duty by Glen Laggan. So that's Rosman's story, as far as I know it."

" Bob," said Maggie softly, " you're a dear ! "—and if

Bob had been waiting for any sort of reward, he got it then, for the poor long-dead wife in the Argentine had been, after all, only a second best.

Colin lighted a cigarette and inquired : " Has he still got that photo ? "

" I believe so—and, for all I know, the revolver, too," answered Bob. " But I don't think you need worry—"

" I'm not worrying ; I'm just wondering what Rosman would do, if ever he came up against the man o' the photo."

" What would you do, if you were Rosman, Colin ? "

" Shoot, by—"

Rosman entered—hurriedly.

" Your pardon, ma'am, but there has been a little accident in the kitchen. One of the girls—your maid, Jeanie—has scalded herself. I have done what I could, but it might be well to have the doctor."

Maggie was on her feet. " I'll come. Colin, 'phone to Doctor Matheson. Ask what's best to be done till he can get here."

Afterwards there were those who hinted that Mrs. Maclaggan's solicitude for the girl, who was not seriously injured, was on a par with the Laird's carrying the peats for old Martha Macdonald—a little exhibition given for effect. Happily for Humanity, it is the minority that sneers. Those small incidents were to be remembered by the many when their remembrance was to mean much to Colin and Maggie, who had forgotten them.

XIV

ON the following afternoon, Colin went with his cousin to the station. There he dismissed the chauffeur, saying he would walk home.

The solitary porter was not at hand, and Bob, smiling inwardly, said briskly—

"Fetch along my suit-cases, will you?"

"Right, sir!" Colin picked up the cases and carried them up the platform, just as he used to do at Queen Street. But having set them down, he said quietly: "The Laird's charge for porterage is half-a-crown."

A laugh at parting is a good thing, when it comes at the last moment; it can hardly, however, be kept going for five minutes.

"Supposing," said Colin, presently, "something happened that made it impossible for Maggie and me to carry on at Glen Laggan—what about our bargain, Bob?"

"You're not a prisoner at Glen Laggan—I've assured you of that before," the patient little man replied. "There's no bargain on your side, except that you have promised to do your utmost to re-establish the old name. Let us leave it at that."

"You're mighty generous!"

"If you feel the strain too great, there's nothing to prevent you and Maggie from going away for a change.

117

In any case, you must go away for two or three months
of the year, if only to get ideas. Try London in the
coming winter—Maggie is willing—and see all you can.
It will be a chance for Peggy, too. Next year, go farther
afield."

" You think of everything, man ! And, then, about
the money ? I've always forgot to ask if I was to let you
know how I was spending it."

" You are not to mention money to me, unless you
can't make ends meet with what you have—which, as
I've told you more than once, is your own. Spend it
as you please. In the meantime, Gregg will keep you
right for the estate ; Peggy will help with your private
accounts and pull you up if you seem to be overdoing it ;
but before long, I'm sure, you will be handling these
matters for yourself. Don't let your heart get the better
of your head—and *vice-versa*."

A whistle broke the silence of the hills, and Bob turned
to take a last look at the scene he had always loved, if only
in his dreams.

" Yonder's my ambition of many years," he said.
" Make it come true, Colin ! Maclaggans in Glen Laggan
once more—and for good ! That's what I ask of you."

The stationmaster came along to bid farewell to the
man to whom he had been useful, and from whom a
handsome acknowledgment had come by that day's
post ; and, by the time he had finished his awkward
speech, the train was there.

Bob, the only departing passenger, got on board ; the
stationmaster put in his suit-cases, and retired. The
guard gave his green flag a casual wag.

Without further words, the cousins gripped hands—
and let go.

And so Bob Maclaggan—in person, at least—goes, as the old sagas have it, out of the story.

Colin watched the train crawl into the deep cutting, waited till the van, swinging round the curve, disappeared—till the heavy panting of the engine on the steep incline came but faintly and fitfully to his ears. For once he was in no humour for a " crack " with the stationmaster ; on the way to the gate, however, he remembered to hand the porter Bob's half-a-crown, with that gentleman's good wishes.

At the gate he met Colonel Silver, who had come up to collect a small parcel. During the past month they had met fairly often on the road, and had usually paused to exchange a few words. Now the Colonel said—

" I'm going back immediately. Perhaps we might walk down together."

" Sure ! " said Colin readily. While he waited he wondered whether their acquaintance was not now sufficient to justify his inviting the Colonel to a day on the river.

The Colonel, on his return, certainly gave him something like an opening.

" I don't think we shall have the thunder here," he remarked, with a critical look at the clouds, " but the rain is coming to-night. Badly needed, too ! "

" Ay," said Colin, cautiously, " the fishers have been having a thin time of it. Not a nibble for days, I'm told."

" Have you not been trying it, Laird ? "

" On the lawn," Colin replied, with a laugh. " I'm afraid I'm going to be no fisher. Murdo does his best to teach me the casting, but it's like throwing a steamer

rope, and I can see in his eye that he has very little hope.
I suppose," he added frankly, " my muscles have all
been de—developed, as you might say, in the wrong
direction. I think I'll have to leave the sport to my son,
Ronnie. He's keen, though he hasna nailed a salmon
yet."

" I have seen your son handling a rod, and he is going
to be a true fisherman—no doubt about it ! "

" That's fine news ! " said Colin, his heart warming.
He cleared his throat. " Well, Colonel Silver, now that
the rain's coming, the salmon'll be plentiful, I'm told,
and I needna say that I would be happy to see you pull
out a dozen or two—just any day that suits you."

It was like offering a drink to a thirsty man, who had
as good as vowed not to take one.

" That is extremely kind of you, Laird," the Colonel
replied, hoping he was speaking naturally, and wishing
to goodness Elfrida were less hopelessly unreasonable.
" At the moment, I am sorry I cannot definitely accept.
As a matter of fact—" He paused.

" Any time, any time ! " said Colin. " And if I'm not
about when the fancy strikes you, you'll find that Murdo
McMurrich has instructions to attend to you."

" Many thanks—I'll remember," said the Colonel, well
aware that while the river ran before his eyes he could not
forget. He put away temptation for the time being,
changing the subject. " The stationmaster mentioned
that Mr. Maclaggan had started on rather a long
journey."

" Ay, Bob's away back to the Argentine. A wee man
to look at, Colonel, but—" Colin halted and turned
round. Far away, among the hills, a wisp of white
vapour moved above the rock. " So long, Bob," he

said, under his breath, and resumed the walk, leaving the conversation to his companion.

The Colonel arrived at White House, having taken five minutes more than usual on his trip to the station and back, to find his wife at tea. Though he had intended to refer in off-hand fashion to his meeting with the Laird and, possibly, the Laird's invitation, he did not do so.

" Wilfred not in ? " he inquired.

" Not yet." After a pause she said : " Andrew, does it strike you that Wilfred is getting fit too slowly ? "

For the moment he forgot about the river. " It would have done so, if the doctor had not assured us, last week, that the boy was going on all right," he replied. " Don't you think he's looking better ? "

" He's brown, but the weather lately would have tanned a marble statue. It's not his look, but his want of spirit, that troubles me most. Of course, the accident may have something to do with that."

" Indeed, yes ! The wonder is that after such a smash he has any spirit at all. Besides, Elfrida, he must be finding the enforced idleness pretty irksome ; also, I daresay, he is worrying about being absent so long from duty. Though the Nicolsons have expressed a willingness to keep his place for him as long as possible, in these difficult times, one can never be quite certain, and I can well understand Wilfred's anxiety."

" Well, we all have our anxieties," said Mrs. Silver, "and if Wilfred is really getting back his health, that, in the meantime, is much to be thankful for. I told him," she went on, " of Ella's asking me to join her at Scarborough for July and August, and he declared he would get really ill if I refused ! "

"I don't promise quite so much as that, my dear," the Colonel returned, with an attempt at lightness, "but, after all you have come through lately, such a change as your sister offers is a godsend. Write to-night and accept!"

He turned to the window and presently remarked that the rain was coming. But his gaze was not on the clouds that promised, but on the earth that would receive— particularly on yonder tree-bordered reach of the river winding down the Strath. . . . The Devil, too, moves in a mysterious way, when he would have an upright man stoop to deception. The river. . . . The Colonel's ruddy neck became a little ruddier.

At the Castle, Peggy was saying she would really, really have to go. The past two hours had passed swiftly, sweetly, yet Wilfred had detected a constraint in her manner. He thought he knew the cause. This darling girl had, indeed, a lot of things still to learn, but ere now he had realised that she had learned a good many. So, since the end seemed to justify the means, and to be worth the risks, he told the first deliberate untruth in their acquaintance.

Keeping her hand, he said : "I'm always forgetting things, Peggy "—it had come to Christian names— "and I ought to have mentioned, a week or two ago, how sorry my mother is that she has not yet been able to call on Mrs. Maclaggan. My mother has not been too well—I'm afraid my accident was indirectly responsible— and may have to go away for a month or so. Will you tell Mrs. Maclaggan that she hopes to call, soon after her return?"

"Thanks—I will," said Peggy, frankly pleased. "You

see, Wilfred, I was beginning to think it was maybe not very nice, our being friends like this and meeting so often, if your mother did not want to meet mine. But now it's all right, and I—I hope Mrs. Silver will soon be better."

Peggy, the shrewd, kept him on his guard, but Peggy, the simple, always came near to breaking it down. In that moment he hated himself as much as he loved her, which was, in spite of all, not a little.

" And when," he asked, after a pause, " am I going to see you again ? "

She shook her head. " Dear knows ! I've a lot of things to do this week, and Daddy may want me. I'm afraid he'll be down on his luck for a while." She had already spoken of Cousin Bob's departure, and explained how he had said his goodbye to her immediately after lunch, desiring a quiet talk with her parents and no " send off " at the end.

Now she became suddenly aware that Wilfred still had her hand, and, with one of her little tilts of dignity, quietly withdrew it.

" Don't make it too long," he pleaded. " Don't stop your kindness to this poor crock."

" But you said you were feeling better every day, Wilfred."

" Yes—but it's infernally slow, and you—you are such a help, Peggy."

She did not like him quite so well when he spoke like that. Still, it must be awful to be unfit for so long. An idea occurred to her. Now that she knew about his mother, surely it would be all right to ask him to the house. Besides, it might be a sort of distraction for Daddy, just back from the station.

I

" Tea-time," she said, with an unnecessary glance at her watch. " Will you come along and see my people ? "

This was more than he had expected, and he had to think quickly. Difficult to refuse ; on the other hand, dangerous to accept. A week later, his mother safely away to Scarborough, it would be different.

" I wish I could," he said warmly, and truthfully enough ; " but I'm expected home, and if I didn't turn up, they would worry. You'll give me another chance— won't you ? "

" Righto ! Of course you must go home when you are expected. I'll tell them you are coming along— some day."

She turned into the path, took a few paces, and looked back, her expression a mingling of sweetness and mischief.

" Cheerio ! "

She was feeling awfully happy about Mrs. Silver. Somehow she had been dreading—she could not have told exactly what ; but now everything was all right and—correct !

Arrived at the house, she found that Providence had sent a distraction in the person of Lady MacVean, from the other side of the Loch. Perhaps Miss Carnachan had inspired the visit, for Lady MacVean did few things for the first time, without some outside inspiration. She was a large, middle-aged lady, with a tender heart in her ample bosom, as a novelist of the 'Eighties would have termed it, incapable of hurting a fellow creature, unless by some appalling inadvertence. She was so nervously afraid of hurting the Maclaggans, that they were " heart-sorry " for her, and did all they could to make her feel at home. To every second remark or so she answered

pantingly, " Charming, charming ! ' Colin sincerely
regretted his being debarred from offering her the dram
which seemed to be so clearly indicated in her case, and
shortly after her going, he exclaimed, " Maggie ! Was
she real ? "—a not altogether inexcusable question, since
Lady MacVean, though so solid in person, was so vague
in personality that any impressions she left behind faded
out almost immediately.

Of her impressions of the Maclaggans only two seem
to be now available. She confided to Miss Carnachan
that the Laird made her think of a converted cave-man,
while his lady was the living image of Julia Neilson, as
Nell Gwynne—the latter being, in the spinster's opinion,
not so far off the mark. Her departure to London, on the
day after her call, spared Maggie and Peggy, for the time
being, the trial of returning it, though, to be sure, Lady
MacVean had been a real tonic to their self-confidence—
which is the main reason for her name appearing in these
pages.

Colin, having repeated to his wife Bob's last words,
as it were, retired to the Railway Room and was about to
settle down to melancholy and a cigarette, when he
spied on the mantel a letter directed to himself in his
cousin's writing.

" What's Bob after now ? " he muttered, opening it.
The first thing he saw was a cheque for £200.

" More money ! What the blazes—? "

Sitting down, he read—

" DEAR COLIN,

It is time you were giving your wife some jewels.
She does not lack moral courage, but, all the same,
jewels are a support to a woman. Don't be too canny

in your spending, and get Peggy to choose for you.
I have not the pluck to mention this before I leave
you.

Bob."

" P.S.—With enclosed, ask Peggy to choose a little
necklet for her mother, with my kind regards."

" Bob, you're the limit! And you're right about
Peggy! " thought Colin, and went to find his daughter.

Jewels were not, as he had observed some months ago,
his job. He had proved that to his own sorry satisfaction
when he made the first biggish hole in the Thousand
Pounds, in order to buy an adornment for his wife. It
was a brooch, a monumental thing of richly-ornamental
gold, carrying a massive cairngorm, surely the largest
piece of amethyst in all broad Scotland.

Proudly—luckily privately—he had displayed it first
to Peggy, who, with tears in her eyes and a lump in her
throat, faltered—

" It—it's gorgeous, but, oh, Daddy dear, it would
never, never do! "

Now, having brought Peggy to the Railway Room, he
said—

" Did I hear you and your mother speaking about a
day in Glasgow, soon? "

" Yes—next Tuesday. There are simply dozens of
things we need."

" Well, then, my girl, when you're in Glasgow, get
this! " He handed her Bob's note and waited till she
read it. " And I'll give you four hundred pounds to
spend—"

" Daddy! "

" Not a word! I can beat Bob at his own game!

Listen ! What sort o' jewels do you think your mother might fancy, forbye the neck-thing ? "

" I know she would love a ring, or two——"

" Right ! Get her some rings, wi' my kind re—ye ken what I mean, Peggy ! " He refused to discuss the subject further.

" I'll have to watch your cheque book ! " said Peggy, who, however, had been given a commission very much to her taste. Money was so lovely when one hadn't to try to make it work wonders !

On the Monday afternoon, she rang up Charlie Fortune. She had as good as promised Charlie to let him know in advance of any visit to Glasgow. It would be horrid not to let him know, and then, by chance, meet him on the street ! Besides, it would be rather nice to see Charlie again.

" Peggy ! " came his voice in glad surprise.

" You knew it was me ! "

" Of course ! Are you in Glasgow ? "

" Glen Laggan ; but Mother and I are coming to Glasgow to-morrow—by road—leaving here at 6 a.m., to get a good long day at the shops. Mother wants you to meet us at lunch-time—"

" Your mother wants me ? "

" Well, both of us. . . . Will you come ? "

" Sure ! Where ? When ? "

" At one o'clock, at the North British Hotel—"

" Oh, not really, Peggy ! "

" Yes, really, Charlie ! It's not show off. Mother and I have just got to learn things. Don't you see ? "

" I see ! Well, I'll be there, on the stroke. Thank your mother kindly for the invitation. I suppose there's nothing I can do for you, to be going on with, to save your time ? If there are any odd, plain things for the house—"

" I'm afraid there's nothing plain wanted "—a giggle— " but, thank you, all the same, Charlie. It's things to wear we're out for this time."

" Just that ! And are you all very happy up there ? "

" Oh, rather !—except that we're missing Cousin Bob ! "

" I daresay ! One of the very best ! He came to see me on Friday."

" Did he ? Nice of him ! Did he say anything about me ? "

" Not a word."

" Oh ! "

" Not after the first hour of our talk, anyway. Well, then—I'm wanted in the office now—one o'clock on Tuesday, at the North British Hotel. So long, Peggy."

" So long, Charlie ! "

She put up the receiver, and remained gazing at it.

" Just the same old Charlie ! " . . . But was he ? Was there not a little difference, somewhere ? She wondered. . . . Anyway, it would be nice, maybe a wee bit exciting, to see him again.

XV

A S the Daimler sped through the mud and drizzle of the outskirts of Glasgow, Maggie gave one of her sighs.

" I'll never get used to all this soft living, Peggy ! "

" Seems to me you are getting used to it pretty quickly," returned her daughter, amused. " Wouldn't it give you just a wee bit of a jar if you woke up, one of these mornings, to find yourself back in the Parli'men-t'ry Road ? "

" True enough, dearie ; but there's mornings when I wake up and see my hands that haven't done a proper turn for months, and then I feel that it's far, far too soft to be—"

" And then Jeanie brings in the tea, and everything's all real and right ! "

" No ; I can't get over that, either. Every morning the tea at the bedside is like a miracle to me, though your Daddy takes it, as if Jeanie had been fetching it to him for twenty years. I suppose that's because his ancestors were used to it in the days of the old Castle."

" Anyway," said Peggy, not smiling, " Daddy's settling down nicely to everything. So is Ronnie."

" Ronnie ! Your Daddy was saying, the other night, he didn't know what to make of Ronnie—he's getting that pernicketty about his clothes, and that polite-like at the table."

" That's Rona ! "

" Rona ! Has she been speaking to him about his dress and behaviour ? "

" No, no ; but Ronnie fell for Rona the first time he saw her ; and that's the way it has affected him. Some boys take it that way," said Peggy, sagaciously.

" But Ronnie's far too young to be thinking o'—"

" He's not thinking—only dreaming ; and it's doing him a lot of good all round. A month ago, he wouldn't listen to me when I tried to teach him things ; but now he's getting to be a rare nuisance with his questions. However, I daresay he'll forget all about Rona, once he settles down to study, in Glasgow. I'm glad he's taking Miss Carnachan's advice. The motor business is all right in its way, but—"

" So am I glad, and your Daddy, too, though we don't fancy the notion of him, all by himself, in Glasgow."

" He could live in one of the hostels, and he'll be home for the week-ends." Peggy spoke of " home " as though the family had been at Glen Laggan for many years.

" I would sooner he was in lodgings, where I could depend on a decent woman to look after him, and see that his socks was always dry," said Maggie. " I think I'll ask your Charlie if he kens of a house where—"

" He's not my Charlie, but it would do no harm to ask him."

" I thought you and Charlie were—"

" Good friends—so we are, Mother," said Peggy, and changed the subject.

They had a busy morning in the City, and were not sorry, about one o'clock, to come to rest in the Hotel lounge.

" Oh, I'll never get used to this, either ! " whispered

Maggie, who, if looks counted for anything, was easily
the most attractive woman in the place.

"Yes, you will!" her daughter replied. "And just
wait till you see what I'm going to buy you, after lunch!"

"What? Tell me, Peggy—quick!"

"Something from Daddy, with his—h'm—regards!"

Maggie's brief excitement went out. "Well, well,"
she said mildly, "your Daddy must have his fun. I
expect it'll be something comical, if it isn't sweeties."

Charlie came in, looking less embarrassed by his
surroundings than Peggy could have expected.

Greetings over, she said: "This is Mother's funeral,
of course, but it would be an awful help if you would
pretend it was yours, Charlie—you know what I
mean?"

"Sure!" he answered, and presently escorted them
to the dining-room, requested a table, and ordered lunch,
as if he were used to it all. His manner was too quiet
to suggest stark assurance; rather was it the manner of a
young man modestly confident in himself.

But Peggy was puzzled, as she had been puzzled during
their telephone talk of the previous day.

In the course of the repast, Maggie brought up the
question of Ronnie's residence in Glasgow.

"That's easy!" at once said Charlie. "My young
brother is going abroad next month, and my mother will
be mighty glad to have your Ronnie in his place, to keep
the house cheery. He'll be well looked after, I can
promise you. Ronnie would be welcome at nothing a
week, but I don't suppose you'd stand for that, Mrs.
Maclaggan."

"Certainly not!" said Peggy. "But it's good of you,
Charlie, to offer, whether it can be done or no."

"Now, Mother, you've got to keep cool and leave everything to me. Both Daddy and Cousin Bob have ordered me to buy you presents, and it won't be of the slightest use to say you don't want them. Try to look as if you were in the habit of getting diamonds and rubies and pearls, and so on. No, not a word! Come on in!"

To herself she said, in effect: "Now be careful! No gorgeousness, mind!"

The hour that followed was filled with joyous excitement, not too well concealed, yet Peggy managed to keep her head. If the jeweller had never attended a customer more ignorant of gems, he had probably encountered many a one with less delicacy and discrimination.

For Cousin Bob's gift, she chose a small circle of diamonds on a platinum chain; for Colin's, a three-stone diamond ring, another of a fine little ruby between two diamonds, a pair of single-brilliant ear-drops, and, with what remained of the £400, a small diamond bar brooch.

"Oh, Peggy," Maggie said, as soon as they were out of the shop, "I hope there won't be a judgment on us for this! What extravagance!"

"What you need now," answered Peggy, who may have been feeling the reaction, too, "is a cup of tea."

The remainder of the shopping involved less excitement, but they were a weary pair when, at last, they got into the Daimler for the homeward journey. As they drove through the drabness of the City, Maggie remarked—

"Oh dear, it's terrible to think o' the folk that haven't got cars!"

"Well," returned her daughter, quite crossly, "don't think of them!"

Having been awake since 4 a.m., they slept, or drowsed most of the way, though Maggie started up at intervals to clutch the little package containing her new treasures.

In the late lingering twilight the Loch came in sight, calm, shadowy, mysterious, under the loom of the sombre mountains. All day it had been raining until an hour ago. Now the sky had the look of having been washed clean ; the mists were drifting from the bens. The sweet cool air of the moors poured in through the open windows. As the car slipped down the hillside, beyond the Loch, the house, dimly white, like a dream castle, pale lights in some of the windows, appeared among the dusky trees.

Peggy rubbed her eyes and roused her companion.

" We're nearly home." Next moment she gulped, caught at her mother's arm, and wept softly.

" Mercy on us, duckie ! " said the startled Maggie. " What's the matter ? "

" I don't know—I don't know—but it would just about kill me to give it all up ! "

" But we'll never do that—never ! " The woman's tone was almost fierce.

Colin was waiting for them on the steps. His welcome was warm, but not boisterous. Rosman, grave as ever, was in attendance at the door. They entered the cheerfully-lighted hall.

A woman, in nurse's uniform, carrying a tray, was going up the staircase.

Maggie caught her man's arm. " Ronnie ! " she gasped.

" No, no, Ronnie's all right. I'll tell you all about it in a minute. Come ben to the Railway Room."

There had been an accident, that afternoon, not far

from the gates. A number of small children were wandering homewards from the side-school, two miles away, when a charabanc laden with tourists came along. A genial old gentleman in the back seat dropped over a handful of pennies. While the children were scrambling a car came round the bend.

"Old 'Thrup'ny-bit' was driving," Colin continued. "I'll not say he was going too fast, or tooted his horn too late; but before he could pull up, he was into the wee crowd—"

"Oh, Colin!"

"I never saw a man so upset—and no wonder! None o' the bairns was killed, but five was sore hurt. There was a wee girl wi' a broken leg, and a wee boy wi' an arm broken in two places, and all were cut and bruised, more or less. When it happened, I was having a word wi' Murdo, at the lodge, and we soon got help and had the wee things carried up to the house—a sore job for them. Rosman kens something about first aid, and so does the cook, who was a V.A.D.; and I hadn't been a railway porter for nothing at all; so we all did what we could. 'Thrup'ny-bit,' poor soul, was for rushing them off to the hospital at Fort William, but that seemed a cruel journey, and luckily I got on to the doctor at once, and offered him anything in reason to rope in a couple o' nurses and smash the road record. Decent man, he did both things, and Rosman and the girls buckled to and had the rooms in the east wing ready in no time. And there are the bairns now, and their parents have been to see them, and they're all doing as well as can be expected. And I hope you're not put out, Maggie; but it seemed a dashed stupid-like thing to have all these pretty rooms, and not use some o' them in a real good cause. So, after you've had your supper, you and Peggy can step up and have a word wi' the night-nurse and, maybe, a keek at the bairns. And that's my story ended ! "

" Daddy," said Peggy, " You're a genius ! "

Colin laughed, saying, " Your mother still has her doubts about that."

" Colin," said his wife, as one waking up, " you ken fine I think you did the right thing. But the supper can wait. Come away, Peggy ! "

Left to himself, Colin picked a small, daintily made-up package from the many ordinary-looking parcels on the table, weighed it in his hand, shook it at his ear, and regarded it thoughtfully.

" Her jewels ! " he said to himself. " But Peggy doesn't seem to have got a great deal for the money."

However, it would seem that he was to think somewhat differently later on.

When he entered the bedroom, after midnight, Maggie was standing in front of the pier-glass. She turned swiftly. Her cheeks were flushed ; her eyes shone ; the jewels sparkled.

" Colin dear," she said, " I never could have dreamed of anything like this—oh, never, never—never ! "

Perhaps he did not hear her. " God save us ! " he said weakly, and sat down on the bed, staring. " Maggie woman, you're awful like a lady ! "

XVI

IN these days, Colin was a happy man. Everything was going " just fine." So he reflected, standing on the steps of Glen Laggan House, this fine morning, in the first week of July. The weather was looking more settled—not that the recent wet spell had depressed him. With so many things to do, think about and learn, dullness was out of the question. Still, it was grand to see the sunshine shimmering on the Loch, the gleam on the river running out of it and away down the Strath, and Ben Nevis over yonder, without a tatter of mist between its summit and the blue sky.

He had just come down from " passing the time of day" with the three young invalids—last night the two whose injuries were light, had gone reluctantly to their homes—and was now about to walk to the river and join Colonel Silver for an hour.

Alas for the Colonel ! Mrs. Silver had been gone but five days, and already he was beginning his third day's fishing, the gift of those " dreadful people." Yesterday Colin had watched him play and land a 24-pounder, and had gone home to practise casting on the lawn till his arms ached. " If it takes me ten years," he told himself, " I'll nail a salmon yet ! "

He took out his cigarette-case. Peggy had insisted on a big silver one. Shilling packets were not the thing at all for a Laird ! Peggy had also admonished him that he must never again say to the minister, or any other person, " Are you for a fag, sir ? " And " cig " wasn't much better. The correct way was to offer the case in perfect silence. To all of which advice Colin, half amused, half exasperated, had humbly promised his best attention.

The case was empty and, congratulating himself on having discovered the fact in time, he went back to the Railway Room to refill it. This he did from sixpenny packets—sixpenny, because he had discovered that the children round about were keen on cigarette pictures. At the same time, it seemed wise to replenish with petrol his silver lighter, also prescribed by his daughter— " a dashed fikey whigmaleerie o' a thing "—which, many a time, he would gladly have exchanged for a box of common " spunks."

He was thus occupied when the butler appeared to say that a man wanted to speak to him at the front-door.

" I asked him to go to the side-door," Rosman continued, " and told him the office was there, but he did not seem to understand. I should say he is a stranger here ; he is tall and thin and respectable looking ; but, I'm afraid, rather under the—h'm—influence, sir."

" Tight ?—at ten o'clock in the morning ! "

" Not so completely under as that, sir. If you wish, I shall endeavour to get him to go away, but though he would not give his name, he seemed to have your acquaintance."

" I'll see him," said Colin, and with misgivings went to the door.

Sure enough, it was Hugh Jordan, railway porter at Queen Street Station, inveterate sportsman and borrower of half-crowns.

K

Seven weeks at Glen Laggan had not made a snob of Colin, but it may be forgiven him that he was not glad to see Hugh Jordan. To several of his old comrades he had already sent hearty invitations, which had been awkwardly refused on the score of the " busy season " ; but Hugh was the last man he would willingly have made known to Maggie and Peggy. Nevertheless he held out his hand.

Mr. Jordan was wearing his Sunday clothes, but looked as if he had slept in them, and quite obviously, he was, as Rosman had put it, under the influence. Colin diagnosed it as " breakfast out o' a bottle."

" Hullo, Colin," said the visitor, with a sulky smile. " This is a swell boarding-house you've got into ! "

" Come in," Colin replied, desperately anxious to get him out of sight, lest Maggie, or Peggy, should come into the hall.

" This way."

Rosman was at the rear of the hall, aloof, yet attentive, and Colin, having put the guest into the Railway Room, called him over.

" An old railway acquaintance," he said, blushing. " I want you to fetch a good breakfast—ham and eggs, and so on—as soon as you can. And—and, Rosman, tell Mrs. Maclaggan and Miss Peggy, that—" He looked helpless.

" That you wish not to be disturbed—very good, sir," said Rosman, and went about his business.

Colin entered to find the visitor closing the window and muttering, " Bloody cold up here ! "

" Sit down, Hugh," he said. " Would you like me to put a match to the fire ? "

" I suppose you can stand the sixpence extra, or whatever it is," growled the visitor. "Who was yon snotty chap that came to the door? The boarding-house keeper?"

"The butler," said Colin, shortly, taking matches from the mantelpiece.

"Butler! Then this is a licensed house—eh?" Mr. Jordan's grin had become less sulky.

Stooping, Colin struck a light—"This is a private house," he said, quietly—and put the match to the paper.

"Private house—whose private house?"

Colin stood erect. "Mine."

The other scratched his head. "So the stories was true! Well, I never believed them! For "—with sudden viciousness born, no doubt, of the whisky and beer— "what hell's right have you to a place like this, and me and the rest o' us, yonder, working for a rotten wage?"

Colin's face was hot, but he answered steadily: "I'll tell you this much :—My right'll depend on what I make o' my job here, and it's a bit early to say anything about that."

"You call this a job!"

"That's what I call it, and that's what it is."

"Well, it's a soft job—the softest job I ever—"

"In some ways it is; but though I still ken very little about it, you ken nothing at all, and I'm not going to waste breath on talking to a man that can't understand."

"Well, I'm going to talk about it! I say it's a blasted shame that you should have all—"

"Hugh Jordan, you're in my house! If you don't like it, leave it! If you can't behave yourself, I'll put you out of it."

"Put me out? You!"

" Wi' one hand."

The watery pale eyes encountered the steady brown
ones, fell from the tanned, firm countenance to the
sturdy figure in Harris tweeds—and Mr. Jordan wilted
and came to his senses.

He had not intended to behave as he had done. His
object in " wangling " a day off in the beginning of the
busy season, with a pass for the journey, and in just
catching the 5.45 train that morning, had certainly not
been the offending of Colin Maclaggan. On the contrary,
his object had been, to put it baldly, Ten Pounds. But
those " halfs " and beers on an empty stomach—he had
not risen in time to take food—had played the very
mischief.

" Come on, Colin," he said with a dismal attempt at
heartiness. " It was only in fun. Maybe I was a wee
thing jealous, just for a minute ; but I'm really delighted
to find you so flourishing, and all that. And now, what
about giving the bell a push and bidding that butler o'
yours to fetch something to drink my best wishes—"

" He'll be bringing you your breakfast immediately. I
may as well tell you," Colin said mildly, " that we have
some rules in this house, and one o' them is—No drinks
before 7 p.m."

" Huh ! It wasna yourself made that one ! "

" I agreed to it, anyway. But it doesn't affect you,
seeing your train leaves at 4.10."

Rosman came in with a large tray, set it on the table
drawn in front of the guest, and retired.

" Does he do everything you tell him ? " Mr. Jordan
inquired, with a sneer of which his host refused to take
notice.

" Everything."

" I would be pretty low down before I would take on a job like that ! "

" Oh, you'll never sink to that height," said Colin pleasantly. " Well, take your breakfast. I'll be back shortly."

He left the guest glowering at the fine china and gleaming silver, yet with a hungry gleam in his watery eyes, and went to find Maggie.

" An old acquaintance from Queen Street," he informed her, " but terrible bashful. I'll just look after him myself, and Rosman can bring us lunch to the Railway Room. I doubt I'll not be able to come wi' you and Peggy to Miss Carnachan's in the afternoon, so you'll have to ask her to excuse me."

He went back to find Mr. Jordan tucking in, and somewhat more genial of aspect and manner. It had occurred to Mr. Jordan that £10 was very little—an almost insulting sum, indeed—to ask of a man who owned such a house and kept a butler. £20 seemed moderate ; £40 not excessive ; even £100—

So when Colin sat down, he said almost playfully—

" And when am I going to see the missus—eh ? "

" Never," coolly answered Colin, and gave no reason.

The visitor reddened, but deemed it expedient to hold his peace, and decided to ask for not more than £40— or, rather, £30. Colin chatted on railway matters, without rousing any apparent interest in his guest, who appeared to regard the map on the ceiling as merely comical, if not idiotic.

" You would think less o' the railway, Colin, if you was still on the platform," he remarked at last, setting down the empty cup, and yawning.

Colin, having rung for Rosman, offered cigarettes.

" I thought you would have smoked nothing but cigars, wi' gold bands on them," said Mr. Jordan.

" I can give you a cigar wi' a gold band on it—sorry I've none wi' two gold bands," said Colin, and produced a box. " Take another for the train," he added kindly.

" Thanks ! " This was better, thought Mr. Jordan, much better ! Colin was getting back his old good humour and softness. £35 did not seem at all absurd. He lit up and lay back in the luxurious chair, in front of the fire, now become radiant. He yawned again. He was extremely comfortable. The difficult part of his visit could wait awhile.

Colin got up. " I'll not be long ; but just ring if you want anything," he said, and went out.

Five minutes later, he peeped in. The guest was asleep.

" Hurray ! " murmured Colin, and having picked the banded cigar from the carpet, he transferred the key to the outside, quietly shut the door, and locked it. He was taking no chances of his Maggie being affronted.

Mr. Jordan slumbered till ten minutes after three, and was awakened then by his host, who said with a faint chuckle : " You've had a nice nap."

A meal, with coffee, was ready on the table. Mr. Jordan was feeling too fuggy to be hungry, but he was glad of the coffee. It was, he realised, high time he broached the subject of finance ; but to do so seemed to have become more difficult than ever. Still £25 was reasonable. He cleared his throat.

" And how," asked Colin, lighting a cigarette, " are the greyhounds ? "

Whereupon the poor needy one fell to pieces, so to speak, and incontinently confessed that the greyhounds,

blast them !—had sent him to Glen Laggan. He was in
debt ; there was no money in the house ; there was going
to be another baby ; and it was sheer worry that had
made him spend the last of his cash on whiskies followed
by beers. Would Colin lend him just ten pounds, which
would be repaid, as sure as God was in Heaven, within
three months ?

" Ay, I'll lend you ten pounds." Colin went over to
his desk, leaving the other furious with himself for not
having asked for more.

Colin took out his pen, bent over the cheque-book,
hesitated, and sat up.

" See here, Hugh ! I'll make you an offer. Give me
your word, in writing, to drop your damned greyhounds
—and the other thing—and I'll guarantee you a pound
a week for twelve months. Think, man ! Isn't it a
fair offer ? "

His mind was less muddy than it had been a few hours
ago, and Mr. Jordan did think. But he thought in the
wrong direction. He did not think that a pound a
week would make all the difference to his home ; he
simply thought that a pound a week would be a hell of a
long time in amounting to ten pounds. And, like most
gamblers, even when in the gutter, he had no sense of
proportion, but only an abiding conceit in his own
ability to make good in the end. So, without much delay,
he answered—

" Ay, it's a fair offer—a very fair offer—Colin ; but,
if it's all the same to you, I'll take the ten pounds now.
You needna imagine I'll be always like this. Though
I've been unlucky so far, I ken what I'm doing, and it's
only a matter o' time till I get all my money back, and
a braw lump for profit, into the bargain."

" Very well." Colin drew the cheque and handed it over.

The payee regarded it with some disappointment. " Thanks—but could you not have given me the cash ? I havena the price o' a beer on me for the road home."

" That's nice," said Colin heartlessly. " And now we'll be getting over to the station." For old association's sake, perhaps, he felt it his duty to see the visitor into the train, but he made no effort to carry on a conversation by the way, or on the platform.

When Mr. Jordan had taken his seat, however, he said—

" Listen, Hugh ! Yon offer is still open, and if ever you give me your word, I'll keep mine. But you must put it all in a letter. If ever you come to my door again, I'll—I'll take and put you in the Loch—by God, I will ! "

The guard fluttered his flag, and Mr. Jordan departed with his mouth open.

The stationmaster came up, smiling : " You will not be wanting that queer one back again, Laird ! " His manner was, perhaps, a trifle too familiar.

" No," said Colin, slowly, though pleasantly enough. " I am not taking any liberties from anybody." With that he walked out.

" Did he mean me ? " wondered the stationmaster, looking after him. Yet, being Highland, he did not think any the less of the new Laird.

A little way down the road, Colin halted to light a cigarette. Then it occurred to him that in dealing with Hugh Jordan he had done something he could not possibly have done, even a month ago. Presently he went down the hill, with a smile in his eyes, and his chest well out.

Near the gates of Glen Laggan House, he came face to face with Wilfred Silver. Thus far, they had more than once saluted on the road, but had never exchanged words. Now they both hesitated, and next moment the young man came forward.

" I should like to thank you, sir," he said, " for your kindness to my father. I don't suppose that anyone understands, as I do, what the salmon-fishing means to him. I thank you very much."

Whereupon that foolish heart of Colin Maclaggan warmed to the frank, handsome, dark-eyed young man.

" I'm sure the Colonel's right welcome, and it's a real pleasure to see him enjoying himself, Mr. Silver," he said. " Are you a fisher, too ? "

" Only in a small way, and at present I'm not up to anything in the nature of sport."

" Ay, ay ; Peggy—my daughter—has told us about your hard luck. But you're not looking so bad, either."

" I'm getting on, thank you. But now I'm detaining you."

" Not at all, not at all ! I'm alone this afternoon, and was just going home for a cup o' tea." Colin took courage. " Would you care to come up and take a cup, Mr. Silver."

" That is very good of you, sir," answered Wilfred, feeling that, at last, the gods were coming over to his side. " I'll be delighted."

" That's fine ! "

Colin, as has been remarked, was a happy man in these days ; and now, as he walked with Peggy's friend up the avenue, he was also rather a proud one.

XVII

ROSMAN, of course, had foreseen the possibility of Wilfred Silver's coming to the house. His manner, when he brought tea to the Railway Room, was that of the good servant, blandly aloof. He took no second glance in the visitor's direction.

None the less, the hateful suspicion was, if anything, encouraged by that one glimpse at close quarters; and, that night, Rosman came near to writing to Miss Carnachan, old friend of his people, on the chance of obtaining information as to young Silver's character and way of living. Yet, as before, he was balked by the question : How, after all, could he make certain, much less act, without the sealed package now in London, probably in the safe of his friend gone on a voyage to Australia.

As a visitor, Wilfred was the sort of man who can be charming alike in castle and cot. He was not, in spite of his mother, a snob, and he would have been highly astonished, as well as deeply hurt, had it been suggested to him now that he was a hypocrite.

Whatever his motives in making himself agreeable, he did not despise his present host. One need not be honest in order to recognise and respect honesty in another. Wilfred was not slow to discern that the ex-railway porter, however lacking in *savoire faire*, was no clown in an unfamiliar environment. More than ever he regretted his mother's prejudiced attitude.

There was plenty to talk about, and Colin frankly enjoyed his guest.

" But you'll have been in this house many a time," he remarked, after Wilfred had admired the scheme of the room.

" Only once or twice. My people have dined here occasionally. But Sir Henry did not spend much time here ; he came merely for the sport in the Autumn. Have you made many other changes ? "

" It was my cousin that did everything. Ay, he made some changes. He thought the place was too like a hotel, and tried to make it more home-like. Of course, you'll understand, Mr. Silver "—Colin smiled—" it's all like a palace to me ! Maybe, if you won't have another cup, you would like to see some o' the changes ? "

The little tour of inspection ended in the billiard room.

" I'm still a bit o' a stranger in here," Colin said, " but I expect the table will come in handy when the long nights arrive. I haven't played since I was a young man— I needn't mention that it wasn't on a table like that one ! —but Peggy is keen to learn, and Ronnie won't be much here in the winter ; so I'll have to try to get my hand in again. I suppose you're a champion, Mr. Silver ? "

" I'm a very ordinary player, but I know a fine table when I see it. You've got a beauty."

" I've still a lot to learn about fine things," said Colin, with an easy laugh. " I'm sorry I'm not fit to play you a game—"

" Why not, if you have nothing better to do "— Wilfred glanced at his watch—" and if I'm not staying too long ? "

The door flew open. Ronnie burst in, carrying a salmon by the gills.

"Daddy, I caught it myself! Murdo weighed it—it's fourteen and a quarter pounds!" He saw the visitor and became awkward.

"This is Ronnie," said Colin, looking proud. "You'll excuse him breaking in like this, but it's his first salmon."

"Then I know just how he feels. Let me congratulate you, Mr. Ronnie. A splendid fish!" Wilfred held out his hand.

Ronnie, ruddy and beaming, gave him a fishy clasp.

"Gosh, Ronnie, you should have washed your hands first!" Colin pointed to a door at the end of the room. "Mr. Silver, you'll get a wash in yonder."

"I'm sorry," said Ronnie to the visitor.

"No need," Wilfred returned kindly. "I asked for it, you know! Besides, I did the same thing to my mother when I took home my first fish. But mine was only an eight-pounder."

"I just had the luck," Ronnie allowed generously. "Colonel Silver," he added, "has got three, down yonder, and one of them is twenty-seven pounds."

"My father will be the happy man to-night, and blessing you, Mr. Maclaggan."

"He's surely welcome," said Colin, pleased.

Ronnie looked from one to the other. "Were you going to play billiards?"

"Not me!" his father answered. "But—Mr. Silver, if you could be bothered, maybe you would show Ronnie a stroke or two. He's just beginning to learn to strike the balls properly and—"

"Will you have a game with me?" said Wilfred.

"There now, Ronnie, there's your chance!" cried the delighted Colin. "Haste ye and get quit o' the salmon, and clean yourself."

"I'll not be a minute. Thanks awfully, Mr. Silver!"

Presently Wilfred was doing magical things with the balls, and explaining in brotherly fashion how he did them. Because of his motor smash, he was already something of a hero to the boy; now his *camaraderie* completed the conquest.

They were still playing when Maggie and Peggy came back from Garry, rather "set up," as they usually were, by the tonic quality of Miss Carnachan's company and converse. Rosman informed his mistress of the visitor, but it may have been that while doing so he watched the girl; in which case he must have learned that she was pleased, as well as surprised.

Maggie was hesitant about going to the billiard-room, but her sense of hospitality prevailed. Her welcoming of the visitor was an odd mixture of diffidence and dignity. Peggy's was an echo of it. Peggy had thought to say, "Hullo, Wilfred!" but she was abruptly made aware that this was quite different from a meeting at the old Castle. It seemed that he had, in one stride, as it were, come very near to her, and she was almost afraid.

"I met Mr. Silver on the road," Colin told them, "and got him to keep me company at tea; and now he's been giving Ronnie the treat of his life."

"This is a great day, Mrs. Maclaggan," said Wilfred. "Your son has landed his first salmon!"

"Fourteen and a quarter pounds, Mother!"

"Well, well!" Maggie would have looked just as pleased had it been a couple of ounces.

" Really, Ronnie ? " Peggy remarked teasingly. " Are you sure Murdo did not catch it for you ? "

" Murdo did nothing but gaff it—and you owe me fourteen-and-threepence ! " Ronnie proceeded to enlighten the visitor as to how his sister had laid him a shilling a pound that he would not get a fish that season.

" You have certainly earned your money," Wilfred said pleasantly, and looked again at his watch.

" Oh, don't be going yet ! " the boy exclaimed. " Please let me see that funny long shot again."

" Now, Ronnie, you're not to be a bother to Mr. Silver," his mother warned him.

" He's anything but that," Wilfred assured her. " But I've been here for a very long time, Mrs. Maclaggan."

" You're welcome ! " Colin put in. " If it's not asking too much, carry on wi' the lesson, and afterwards Ronnie can pass on what he learns to Peggy. I'm learning something, myself ! "

So Wilfred went back to the table, and Maggie sat down and tried her best to appear interested in billiards.

Before long Colin succeeded in edging his daughter to the farthest distance possible from the others, and whispered : " Should I ask him to bide for his dinner ? "

Peggy thought for a moment, then gave her head a little shake, murmuring, " That's Mother's business."

" It's you for the useful knowledge," he sighed, gratefully.

Twenty minutes later, Wilfred declared he must really go.

" How are the small invalids ? " he asked Maggie. " Like everyone else, I've been hearing about your hospital. Sir William was speaking about it yesterday."

" The children are going on nicely," she replied, " but

I'm afraid they'll be wearying before long. Sir William has sent them no end o' picture-books and toys and things, but—" She hesitated.

" They can't do much wi' the toys," said Colin, " and they get wearied wi' stories. All the same, old Thrup— I mean, Sir William—has turned out a white man. He has done his duty by the parents, as well as the bairns."

" Colin wanted to make a room into a wee picture house," Maggie remarked, " but I was terrified, though he promised to get films that couldn't take fire."

" And Maggie wanted a Punch and Judy show ; only I thought the bairns would soon get fed up with the same performance. . . . Well, well, we'll just have to do what we can to amuse them till they're fit to go home."

Wilfred hesitated and said : " I wonder if I could be of a little service, Mrs. Maclaggan. In a small way, I can do some juggling and conjuring tricks. This sort of thing."

He went back to the table and started manipulating the balls in miraculous fashion. Then one of them disappeared, only to reappear mysteriously from the top of Ronnie's head. . . .

" Gosh ! " cried Colin. " Half an hour o' that, now and then, Mr. Silver, would be the very thing ! Will you really do it ? "

" Delighted—any time you want me."

Wilfred soon afterwards went away, leaving as favourable an impression as any young man could wish to leave in the home of the girl desired.

Peggy and Ronnie, having gone with him to the door, Colin said—

" Maggie, did you not think o' asking him to bide for his dinner ? "

" I did—but I stopped myself."

" Stopped yourself ? Did you not think he was a real nice young chap ? "

" He did enough in half-an-hour to make me think all that ! "

" Then what made you stop yourself ? "

" Well, I thought it might look as if we was keen on him for Peggy."

" Oh ! " said Colin. " I see what you mean, but I hadn't thought o' it that way."

" We've got to think of it that way."

" Are you vexed wi' me for asking him in ? "

" Ask him again, whenever you like, but don't seem to run after him."

Colin nodded. " You're right, Maggie ! Still, would you be sorry if he and Peggy fancied each other ? "

" Ask me that next year. We'll both be wiser then about lots of things, and so will Peggy."

" I've my doubts about myself," said Colin, with a sigh. " And Peggy'll please herself, anyway. Well, what was Miss Carnachan saying ? "

Wilfred went home, feeling that the gods were truly on his side. Without effort on his part, a barrier had been removed. Glen Laggan House had, in the most natural way, been opened to him by its owner—he was glad now that he had not jumped at Peggy's recent invitation—and he had sensed nothing in its atmosphere that was not friendly. But he was touched not a little by the friendliness. He did not congratulate himself, because those simple people—he did not think of them as simpletons—had taken him on trust. On the contrary, he wished to God he could have made his first entry into Peggy's home as an honest man !

Was it too late to turn from the hidden path to the open one? What if he were to disclose his desperate situation to his father? As a boy, he had made his father his confidant; only since the beginning of his awful mess-making in London had he let reticence take hold, partly from shame of himself, partly from reluctance to add to his father's many worries. Even so, was it too late? After all, folly was not crime, and his father had never shewn himself as narrow-minded or hard.

Not for a moment did Wilfred imagine that his father could provide £2,000 by the middle of September—only ten weeks now; but the more he thought of it, the more possible it seemed that, with his father's support, he might be able to induce his creditors to postpone the day of reckoning for a considerable period; and, like most of us, he believed that, given time, he could work wonders.

He entered White House, determined to make confession before he slept, though tempted to delay, curiously enough, by the thought of dealing the blow to his father in the hour of elation after a successful day at the river. He might, however, have spared himself that little compunction.

Colonel Silver sat down to dinner in gloomy mood. He seemed to have forgotten about the twenty-seven pounder till the end of the meal, when his son referred to it.

" Who told you? " he demanded sharply.

Wilfred, somewhat dashed, accepted the opportunity and gave an account of his visit to Glen Laggan House.

The Colonel listened frowningly and said : " While I have no objections to your making friends with the

L

Maclaggans—quite worthy people, I'm sure—I think you must know, Wilfred, that your mother would strongly disapprove."

" Mother will change her ideas, once she knows them."

The Colonel wagged his head. " Do you intend to repeat the visit ? "

" Yes."

" Why ? "

" I happen to like the Maclaggans."

The Colonel shrugged, and there was a short silence. Then he looked like asking another question, but nothing came.

When the maid had served coffee and retired, he took from his pocket a letter and threw it across to his son, with the remark, " Things grow worse and worse. I found it when I came back from the river."

Wilfred read the printed announcement, which was to the effect that a certain industrial company would pay no dividend for the past year on its preference shares. He passed it back, murmuring, " That's awfully hard on you, Dad."

The Colonel softened. " I'm sorry, my boy, I was so ratty a minute ago ; but life grows more difficult as I grow older." He sighed. " And I ask only for peace in my old age."

So Wilfred, abandoning the idea of confession, continued on the hidden path. His engagement to Peggy was his one possible salvation. Once it was an accomplished fact, his mother, he felt sure, would at least countenance it ; but whether she did so or no, it would be announced in the papers, and he could not doubt that his creditors would then grant him the postponement that seemed everything to him now.

He must, however, hasten and intensify his wooing. He was growing fitter every day ; he could not much longer, he told himself, decently defer his return to London. There was bound to be a limit to the patience of his employers ; to try it too far would mean the loss of his position, with its very fair income.

He spent a restless, unhappy night.

In the morning a messenger brought a formal note from Peggy. Her mother would be greatly obliged if he could manage to give the children a little entertainment in the afternoon. That cheered him. The gods were certainly on his side. He almost persuaded himself that the crooked course before him would, in some miraculous way, straighten itself.

Yet by evening he was not so sure of the gods. He had delighted the small invalids, and earned the unaffected commendation of his host and hostess, not to mention the admiration of Ronnie ; but he had learned from Peggy that during the coming fortnight she was going to be very much occupied with two girl friends from Glasgow, whom she did not suggest his meeting.

While that fortnight was a miserable one for Wilfred, it was by no means filled with happiness for Peggy. It held, indeed, the first great disappointment and discouragement of her new existence. The two girls were employed in her old place of business, and she had planned, with much thought and enthusiasm, to give them the holiday of their lives. She presented them with their railway tickets and no end of things to wear, both pretty and serviceable, she arranged picnics, car and motor-boat excursions, so that they should see the countryside which she had come to love with a sort of passion ; she lay awake of nights, thinking of trifles for their gratification.

She made a list of other girls, whom she would invite later on.

It is not to be supposed that those two girls were altogether ungrateful, that they enjoyed themselves not at all. But they had their own fixed ideas of what a summer holiday should be ; they missed the throngs, the promenades, the fun of crowded bathing, the bands, the pierrots, the picture houses, the ice-cream saloons, and so forth ; they as good as told Peggy that she was buried alive. While they admired the beautiful home and accepted its luxuries, they were embarrassed by its formalities and—possibly to cover their embarrassment —indulged in contemptuous little remarks and asides about them. They went home, leaving a wounded, angry Peggy with the impression that they had wasted their precious holiday by spending it at Glen Laggan.

"Never again ! " she declared to her parents, who were hurt, too.

Colin, however, demurred. "Ah, but I wouldn't say that, my girl. You've been unlucky the first time, but I'll warrant you've got other friends that would think Glen Laggan the best ever. You'll try again, later on ! What do you say, Maggie ? "

"Your Daddy's right, Peggy. Still, I would advise you to ask some boys, too, just to make the scenery more exciting."

XVIII

ON an afternoon, when rain squalls were lashing up the Glen, Colin and Maggie were sitting by the fireside in the Railway Room, now to them the most familiar apartment of the house. Rosman had lately removed the tea-tray. Maggie was reading a story in a woman's journal recommended by Peggy, because it gave rather a vivid word-picture of a fashionable dinner party; Colin was frowning at a page of an *Elementary English Grammar*, which he had promised his daughter to study in his spare time.

"The man that wrote this book," he said suddenly, bitterly, "was a proper scoundrel! I would walk twenty miles to see him hung, so I would!"

"Come, come, dearie," said Maggie, looking up. "I'm sure the poor gentleman meant well when he wrote it. I've learnt a lot from it. If it wasn't for the *were's* and *was's*, and the *did's* and *done's*, and the *gone's* and *went's*, and the —"

She was interrupted by a sound suggesting a reaping machine gone wrong.

"Hurray!" cried Colin, jumping up and throwing the book on the shelf. "Fancy her coming on a day like this! Now you can ask her that question about—"

He was at the front door and down the steps before Miss Carnachan, of Garry, had bumped her car to a stop.

"What a day!" he said, assisting her to alight. "Gosh, you're wet!"

" Only Glen weather," she returned cheerfully, " but the damned old caravan broke down half way, and I got a bit damp and muddy, pulling it together. I'm afraid," she added, hobbling smartly up the steps, " it will not survive to attend my funeral, after all ! "

Maggie was at the door, with a sympathetic greeting.

" Don't worry about me. I'm tough," said the little woman, wriggling out of a raincoat which had seen better years. " But if you have a fireside, lead me to it ! "

She had not hitherto been in the Railway Room. She sat down in Colin's chair, placed a pair of stout shoes on the fender, and heaved a great sigh of satisfaction.

" There are summer days in the Glen when a fire is as welcome as at Christmas. I was so afraid you would put me into the drawing-room."

Maggie's hand moved to the bell.

" No tea, if you please ! " Miss Carnachan turned to Colin. " Laird, do you remember, the first time I called here, you offered me a dram ? "

" So I did," said Colin, looking unhappy ; " God forgimme ! "

" God will ! I'll take it now, and ask Him to bless you ! "

" Ring, Maggie, ring ! " cried Colin.

" Oh, it's not so urgent as all that," she said, laughing. " Still, I'm feeling my age to-day. Guess what it is, Laird."

One may suspect that she enjoyed embarrassing people. Colin looked uncomfortable, while Maggie regarded him with anxiety. Surely to goodness he would not say more than " fifty-nine ! "

" Out with it, Laird ! " said Miss Carnachan.

Colin cleared his throat and blurted, " Wi' your

liveliness, you can't be much more than fifty and a bittock."

"Thanks! I'm seventy-two! This is my birthday, and as nobody remembered, I thought I would come over and tell you two good people. Yes, that's why I'm here."

"Seventy-two!" said Colin, before he knew. "You're a warrior!"

The butler came in.

"Rosman," said Colin, with emotion, "fetch a—a big bottle o'—o' champagne."

"Very good, sir."

"No, no!" she exclaimed. "Just a drop of the Auld Kirk, please. I never sing before 9 p.m."

"Very good, ma'am," said Rosman, solemnly, without a glance at his employer, and retired.

"Have I put my foot in it again?" Colin ruefully asked. "We've only once had the wine—when my cousin Bob was here—and Maggie, there, said she would as soon have stone ginger; but seeing it was your birthday, Miss Carnachan, I thought—"

"You thought very kindly, Laird," she said, gently; "but when I asked for the dram, I asked for medicine—you understand?"

"Miss Carnachan," Maggie put in, "will you bide and take your dinner wi' us?"

"Mrs. Maclaggan," came the reply, "I'll tell you a secret. All the way from Garry—except when I was cursing the old caravan—I was putting up a prayer: 'O Lord, drop it into their kind hearts to ask me to dinner, for it's no fun being the last of your line, on your seventy-second birthday, and clean forgotten.'"

Then a smile added to the furrows of her weather-beaten

countenance. "I accept, with pleasure, your kind invitation."

"That's great!" said Colin. "And we'll have the wine then, to drink your health!"

"Delighted! On the whole, I prefer champagne to cocoa, in which I would have toasted myself—perhaps— had you not asked me to stay. Another secret, Mrs. Maclaggan! On chance—or, rather, in faith—I brought my dinner things in the caravan."

"Maggie," Colin exclaimed, "isn't that the best ever?"

"He means," said Maggie softly, her blue eyes misty, "that you've done us a great honour, Miss Carnachan."

For once Miss Carnachan seemed at a loss. Then she said—

"So a king and queen might say to the beggar who had confidence in their charity. Yes, I've done you the greatest honour in my power."

A little later, sipping her whisky and soda, smoking a cigarette, she surveyed the apartment.

"Laird," she said, abruptly, "doesn't this room keep reminding you of the past?"

"It does that, Miss Carnachan!"

"And you don't want to forget the past?"

Colin looked puzzled.

"If I were a man," she said, "I would take off my hat to you."

His puzzlement became bewilderment.

The spinster turned to her hostess.

"I think *you* know what I mean?"

Maggie nodded. "Colin's not ashamed that he was once a railway porter; no more am I; and I hope the children will never be," she said, quietly.

Colin laughed. "I see! What for would I be ashamed?" he said. "But, maybe, Miss Carnachan, this room makes me think o' the future, too. You see, one o' these days, I might go back to Queen Street."

"Colin!"

"He's only trying to make our flesh creep," Miss Carnachan remarked—and at that moment Ronnie came in.

"Daddy, come on to the billiard-room! Mr. Silver—" He stopped short at sight of the visitor, then came forward and shook hands cordially. "Are you keen on billiards?" he asked her.

"I was, about fifty years ago. Are you, Ronnie?"

"I'm learning. Mr. Silver's teaching Peggy and me. You should see him at it. He's a wonder!"

"Laird," she said, "don't let me keep you. Are you a pupil, too?"

"I am, but there's no hurry. I'll be along in a few minutes, Ronnie."

Ronnie having gone, Miss Carnachan said—"Is that young man never going back to his work in London?"

Quickly Maggie asked: "Do you not like Mr. Silver?"

"I didn't mean that. I hardly know him—or his parents, for that matter; but the last time I passed him on the road, he looked fit for more than loafing."

"He was to have gone back this week," said Colin, "but his employers have given him a bit longer—till the middle o' August—so he'll have a day or two at the shooting, with his father."

"On your moors, of course!"

"Well, and what for no, Miss Carnachan? Ronnie'll be trying his hand at the gun, but I'm giving it a miss—

this year, anyway. If you have any friends that would like a week or two at the sport, I'll get Mr. Gregg to arrange it for them, and welcome."

" You are very good. If the Lord loveth a cheerful receiver, He must think a lot of Susan Carnachan! Is your daughter going to shoot ? "

" There's not many things that Peggy doesn't have a try at! She and Rona Gregg and Ronnie have been practising on clay pigeons. Mr. Silver's teaching them."

" I have two not too well off young friends in the South, who would jump at your offer," said Miss Carnachan. " They would probably fall in love with Miss Peggy, but they are fine young men, although I say it, and she can't meet too many of that sort. In case you change your mind, Laird, I'll write to them to-night."

" Splendid! " said Colin—and seemed to remember. " But Maggie was wanting to ask you a question about Mr. Silver. Go on, Maggie! "

" Colin thinks I should ask him to dinner, one night, but I wasn't just sure if it would be the—the right thing."

" Why not, Mrs. Maclaggan ? "

Maggie evaded answering the question by saying, " You see, he has been very kind to Peggy and Ronnie, and such a help with the children upstairs. Every afternoon he does something to amuse them."

" H'm! " said Miss Carnachan. " Well, I can see no reason why you should not ask him to dinner."

" What about the Colonel, too ? " Colin inquired.

" That's rather different, Laird. Wait till your wife and his have met." She turned to Maggie. " Forgive my butting in with a suggestion, but, if quite convenient,

would not you ask Mr. Silver for to-night? I should
like to make his better acquaintance."

"Great idea! I'll go now and ask him," cried Colin,
and went out in high spirits.

He was a subdued man, however, when, half an hour
later, Peggy informed him that he would have to dress
for dinner.

"Dress!"

"White front, black tie and dinner jacket. Mr.
Silver has gone home to change. Cheer up, Daddy!
You've got to begin some time, and it's Mother's first
dinner party."

"Well, well, I wouldn't let your Mother down for
anything," he sighed. "All the same, I doubt I'll look
awful comical."

Yet, once he was into the garments, which Maggie
had been cherishing hopefully since May, he was inclined,
in furtive fashion, to "fancy himself," and was considerably uplifted when Peggy told him he looked "a treat."
Maggie was, of course, by this time used to wearing pretty
things, but it was the first occasion for donning her
jewels, otherwise than in secret, and between them and
the excitement of her first party she presented an example
of womanly radiance.

"I wonder, Laird, if it has occurred to you," Miss
Carnachan, discreetly remarked, "that you have a
very pretty wife."

"Ay, Maggie looks not so bad in her fine feathers,"
he admitted, and regarded his wife with some astonishment. "And Peggy's not so bad, either."

Of Peggy, her fairness set off by a sea-green frock, it is
enough to say that the first sight of her made Wilfred
Silver wish more than ever that he was an honest man.

At the outset, the dinner looked like being a stiff, uncomfortable affair, but before it was half-way through, Maggie had ceased to be a Martha, while Colin, having forgotten his shirt front, presented the figure of a happy host, rejoicing in the entertainment of his friends. Towards the close, he gave the toast of the lady guest.

" I ask you all to drink to Miss Carnachan. This is her birthday. She is seventy-two years of age, but still going strong. Let us hope she will go stronger, the older she grows. Miss Carnachan, your very good health ! "

" Thank you, Laird," muttered the spinster, " and God bless you all for your kindness to a lonesome old woman."

Altogether it was a cheerful evening, and no one could have guessed that Miss Carnachan, alert and apparently interested in everything, was keenly watching Wilfred Silver all the time.

Colin and Maggie accompanied her to Garry in the Daimler, Ronnie with Peggy—Wilfred having gone home —driving the " caravan."

Near the end of the journey, without preface, she asked—

" What's the matter with that young man ? "

" Mr. Silver ? " said Maggie anxiously.

" Yes. He talks brightly and plays the piano almost as well as he plays billiards—but he's just a bundle of nerves."

" I didna notice he was nervous," said Colin, " but I suppose it's the result of his accident."

Miss Carnachan did not pursue the subject. In a very different tone of voice she said—

" Now I want to thank you both for a happy evening,

and to make a confession. I was feeling sick of people who are afraid of me, and I wanted to know if you really liked me. My age is sixty-one, and my birthday is in November. Can you forgive me—you, Mrs. Maclaggan?"

For a moment Maggie was taken aback; then she understood. "Sure!" she said, and gave the skinny little arm at her side a squeeze.

"Maybe," said Colin, clearing his throat, "you wouldna mind telling us the exact date in November. I could do fine with another birthday dinner party—eh, Maggie?"

XIX

ONCE a fortnight, Colin and Cousin Bob exchanged greetings. Colin's was not the pen of a ready writer, but his letters were dutiful in detail, and he sometimes spent the better part of a day in composing one. Bob's were generally brief and businesslike.

The letter Colin held in his hand this afternoon was longer than usual, the typescript running on to a second page, which was the page that matters to us.

"I daresay"—wrote Bob—"you still see something of that capable young fellow, Charles Fortune? You may remember that I was favourably impressed by him. Indeed, I think I told you that I had made him an offer, which he turned down. But I am still looking for a man of his type to assist me in certain directions. To such a man I could promise a really good future out here. I do not wish to press the matter unduly, but when next you happen to see Fortune, you would oblige me, by mentioning casually to him that you understand my offer is still open, and that it might even be improved, if he cared to write to me on the subject. I take it that you will be seeing him within the next few weeks, and shall be glad to have your report in due course."

Colin read the passage to his wife and added : "I don't

suppose it would be worth while saying anything to Charlie, now that he's doing so well in Glasgow. He'll be a big man there before he's finished."

" Still," she returned, " Bob has asked you to speak to him. When Peggy and I saw Charlie in Glasgow, he said he would be coming to see us, one of these Sundays ; but if I was you, Colin, I would write to him at once. You could write, asking him when he was coming, and then mention—casually, as Bob says—about the offer still being open."

" Right you are ! I'll get Peggy to write. Where is she, this afternoon ? "

" She and Rona and Mr. Silver and Ronnie are away in the motor-boat. They're going to have tea at the head of the Loch."

" Well, well," said Colin, " these young folk have a proper rare time. I whiles think that Peggy and Ronnie get more out o' Glen Laggan than you and me."

" And so they do—and will, I hope," she said, " not but what we're getting a good deal—eh, my man ? I'm satisfied, anyway."

" Are you that ? "

" Sure ! At first I thought that all you and I could do would be to try and hold the fort till Ronnie grew up ; but there's a lot more in it than that."

He nodded thoughtfully. " So there is—a lot more ! And so you wouldn't like to go back to the old life, Maggie ? "

" I'm sure you've asked me that a thousand times ! Whiles I waken up in the dark and wonder if there was anything serious behind your question."

" Dear, no ! "

" Well, don't ask it again, Colin. I'll answer it now,

once and for all. It—it would just break my heart to go back! So now you know!"

"Ay, ay, woman, I know," he said, softly. "But, you see, I just like to feel sure, every now and then. I'm satisfied myself, though I can't help feeling, now and then, that there'll be something to pay for it all one o' these days."

"Then, if it's got to be, we'll pay the price between us, and say we've had good value," she said, with an uncertain laugh, "broken hearts and all! We'll have had a taste of Heaven, anyway!"

"That's true—though, if Bob hadna took thought for everything—everything, Maggie—it might have been an awful dose o' Heaven's opposite!"

He brought out his big silver case, admired it for a moment before taking out a cigarette, and got up.

"I'm away to see Gregg—and get another scolding."

"What have you been doing this time?"

"Promised an old man and his wife new windows. I was in their wee house—up Glen Doran—on Thursday —you mind what a wild day it was!—and I could guess what the draughts would be like in the winter. B-r-r-r! Gregg says, if I don't ca' canny, I'll spoil the folk and ruin the estate; but, of course, he's joking."

"Still, Colin, should you not be guided by Mr. Gregg?"

"I should—and I'm going to reform—but it's awful nice to be able to give folk new windows, and so forth!" He lit up. "What are you going to do till tea-time?"

"I'm going to read the Grammar book," Mrs. Maclaggan replied, with the sweet smile of a tortured martyr.

"Tits, woman! Read a novel!"

She shook her head. " With Mr. Silver coming about the house, it's not fair to Peggy. Whiles, when I make a mistake before him, I fancy it gives her a wee grue. I'm going to get my singulars and plurals right, if it kills me ! "

" Then may the Lord help you ! " said Colin, and went cheerfully to receive the scolding.

Maggie took up the *Elementary English Grammar*, but one may doubt whether she gained much instruction from its pages that afternoon. Her thoughts kept turning to her daughter and Mr. Silver—and Charlie Fortune. She was not exactly worried about Peggy, but she was puzzled. She would have liked very much to know what, if anything, had happened between Peggy and Charlie, five months ago. She had seen for herself, on that last visit to Glasgow, that the two were still friends, though Charlie had shewn an independence quite new to her. Yet that independence might have come from a hurt pride, and she was loth to think that her Peggy was the sort of girl to have changed her mind with the change in the family circumstances. As for Mr. Silver, Peggy appeared to accept his devotion pretty much as she had accepted Charlie's—as a matter of course, yet not un-kindly—not that that was to be taken as a reliable indication of the state of her heart !

Maggie would not have been the tender mother she was had she not indulged visions of her daughter, married to a gentleman, like Wilfred Silver. In some ways, it seemed the best thing that could possibly happen to Peggy, though, in other ways, it might not be the happiest that could befall Colin and herself. Maggie was wise enough to perceive the drawbacks to, as well as the advantages of, such a union ; but, first and last, it

M

was Peggy's future that mattered. Even in these days the younger generation owes something to the older, however loudly it may deny its indebtedness and protest its independence.

Though still shy of Mr. Silver, Maggie was attracted to him by reason of his lack of " side " and his fine courtesy towards Colin, no less than to herself. She liked the way he took nothing for granted, yet accepted favours without fuss ; she admired the beautiful manners that came so naturally to him ; without envy, she wondered if her Ronnie, with a like upbringing, would have acquired the same accomplishments. And, perhaps, she felt a certain tenderness for him because of his nervousness, first noted by Miss Carnachan, and now occasionally evident to herself.

At the same time, she never saw Wilfred in company with Peggy, without experiencing a little hankering for Charlie Fortune.

" Ah, well, what must be, must be," she said to herself, and strove to fasten her attention on the important statement, that an interjection was a word of exclamation expressing some strong emotion.

Peggy came home about seven o'clock, having invited Rona Gregg and Wilfred to dinner—much to her father's satisfaction. Colin was getting the host habit. He may have pretended differently to Maggie, but he liked getting into his dinner jacket and sitting at the head of the perfectly-appointed table, beaming alike on guests and family. It was grand to be able to give folk a proper, good dinner, and see them enjoy it ! Sometimes it may have been that he saw himself in imagination, presiding at a bigger table and a more elaborate feast, with many guests. If so, the conceit was surely pardonable. Good fortune may stimulate worse things than the instinct of hospitality.

To-night, to be sure, he had a moment of disappointment when Wilfred—the only person besides himself who took wine—refused a second glass of Burgundy. He might have pressed the matter, had not Maggie managed to catch his eye. It had seemed to her that Mr. Silver, though genial and amusing as ever, was more nervous than she had yet seen him.

After dinner, she found an opportunity to ask him— diffidently—if he were feeling not so well.

For an instant his dark eyes—tired, yet far too bright, she thought—looked into the serene soft blue of hers. "Thank you," he answered, with the ghost of a smile, "I'm quite all right—only I've been rather off my sleep lately."

"That's not good," she said, shaking her head. "Your mother wouldn't like to hear that, I'm sure. But it's a mercy you didn't have to go back to London, with all the traffic and noise."

"Perhaps," he said slowly, "it's worse to lie awake in the silence, Mrs. Maclaggan, if—"

Ronnie was at his side.

"Mr. Silver, are you ready for the foursome at billiards—you and Peggy against Rona and me?"

"Ronnie," his mother interposed, "Mr. Silver is maybe a wee bit wearied. Get your Daddy to—"

"Daddy prefers to mark, Mother."

"I'm ready, Ronnie," said Wilfred, getting up. "Thank you again," he added quietly to his hostess.

For a couple of hours he played patiently and cheerfully with the novices. After that, to oblige Ronnie, he performed what he called his parlour tricks with the balls and other things; and then, since Peggy had suggested it, played light music on the piano and sang foolish songs till midnight. Finally, rather than hurt his host, he took a whisky and soda.

The night was warm and dark. Half-way home, he stepped from the road and threw himself down on the heather. Not more for the sake of Peggy's grey eyes than her mother's blue ones, he felt like abandoning his schemes and submitting himself to the worst. But the mood passed.

The worst was too dreadful. It meant either extreme financial embarrassment for his father, or disgrace for his people, as well as himself. And now remained but two weeks till he must return to London. The past two weeks had been, in a sense, vain. He had been in Peggy's company nearly every day, but never once alone with her. He almost wished he had never entered Glen Laggan House. Had their meetings beside the old Castle continued, he would have won her—if she were to be won—before now. He must try to get those meetings resumed. . . .

In the dawn he went home, feeling dead beat. He slept till six, and then came back to it all again.

.   .   .   .   .   .

Peggy was about to go to bed when her mother said—
" Colin, tell Peggy what Bob wrote about Charlie."
" Righto," said Colin, got the letter from a drawer in the writing-table, and read the passage indicated.
" But I'm sure he doesn't want to go to the Argentine," said Peggy, and yawned.
" You never can tell," Maggie remarked. " Bob seems willing to do a lot to get him."
" Anyway," said Colin, " it's our duty to pass on Bob's

message. So you might write to Charlie in the morning, Peggy."

Peggy was well used to writing letters for her father, but she replied. " Wouldn't it be better if you wrote yourself ? I know Charlie would prefer it."

" Hoots ! You ken how I hate writing letters. Just write him a nice wee note, asking when he's coming to see us, and mention—"

" Casually," Maggie put in.

" Ay—mention casually what Bob was saying about him."

" Very well," said Peggy, without enthusiasm, and left the room, leaving her mother still puzzled.

Peggy went upstairs in something like a temper. She had never liked Wilfred so much as she had liked him to-night—and now they had gone and reminded her of Charlie, thereby making her feel once more unsure of herself in the horrid, uncomfortable way of five months ago. It was, of course, none of her business that Charlie should be tempted to throw up his splendid position in Glasgow and go abroad ; but neither was it her business to put the temptation before him. Not that it mattered to her whether he stayed in Glasgow or went to the Argentine ! So far as Glen Laggan was concerned, he might as well be in Buenos Aires, ten thousand—or whatever it was—miles away, instead of merely a hundred !

Like Wilfred, she was late in going to sleep, but, unlike that harassed young man, she evaded her problem till the sun was high, and then discovered a way out —for the time being, at any rate.

It was her mother who, at lunch, inquired whether she had remembered to write to Charlie.

"Yes; I wrote and asked him when he was coming. If he's coming soon, Daddy can tell him—casually— about Cousin Bob; if not, then we can write again. Cousin Bob didn't say we were to write, and he didn't say it was awfully urgent."

"Well, well, if he comes soon, it'll be all right, I daresay," said Maggie, feeling like a deep-sea angler who once more brings up the line, with the baits gone. "But it would be a pity if Charlie missed the biggest chance of his life for want of a wee letter."

"If Charlie doesn't turn up this Sunday, or the next," Colin said stoutly, "I'll write to him, myself—or tell Peggy what to say. I suppose it wouldn't be fair, when he's so busy, to ring him up on the 'phone."

"No, it wouldn't!" Peggy answered firmly.

It might, or it might not, have been enlightening to Maggie to have seen her daughter's letter, now in the post. On a picture card of the Loch, Peggy had written these words—

"Daddy is asking when you are coming up this way.—P.M."

Not too hearty, at all events!

XX

THE card reached Charlie's home on the following morning—Friday—but after Charlie had left for the City. At present his business day was a long one, and it was near to ten o'clock when he returned. His mother was away for the week-end. In the sitting-room, his father, at the fireside, with pipe and a motor journal, directed his attention to the card on the mantel-piece, at the same time giving him a keen glance.

Mr. Fortune, as it may be remembered, had spent the earlier part of his working life as a railway porter, and had then inherited a motor garage. In many respects he was a different sort of man from Colin Maclaggan. Certainly he would have been hopeless as a Highland laird. On the other hand, Colin would have been equally hopeless as owner of a number of big garages and an extensive trading business in cars. Colin, whatever the opportunities, could never have made himself a rich man. Robert Fortune, at the age of fifty, had made himself a wealthy one, and even in those difficult times was making himself wealthier. He was not, by the way, unacquainted with the Stock Exchange, though he was no blind gambler.

He noted his son's eager look at the card, and then the slight expression of disappointment.

" Charlie," he said, abruptly—he was usually abrupt—" I've got a word to say to you."

"Give me a minute or two," the young man replied.
"I've a note to write for the ten o'clock collection."

"Write your note!" Mr. Fortune went back to his
journal.

Now Charlie, on his way home that night, had made
up his mind to take a run to Glen Laggan on Sunday.
He had told himself he was a fool, but the craving for a
sight of Peggy was not thereby rendered more endurable.
He would 'phone in the morning, lest his coming should
be inconvenient. But, somehow, Peggy's curt message
suggested something more formal than a "ring up."

So, at the writing-table in the window, he wrote a
polite note to Mrs. Maclaggan, to the effect that he would
call on Sunday afternoon, in the hope of finding her and
the family at home, and said nothing at all about Peggy's
card.

Then he went out to post it, and on the road tormented
himself with wishing he had written to Peggy, after all.
But there was not time for that now, and, arrived at the
pillar-box, he thrust in his missive, assuring himself that
he had done the right thing.

He was nearly home again, when he reflected that he
had cut things pretty fine, and ought to have looked at the
indicator on the pillar-box, to make sure that his letter
had caught the collection—the last for the night; just then,
however, he heard a clock strike ten, and was satisfied.

Nevertheless, public clocks may go slow, or postmen's
watches may go fast, and, as a matter of fact, the pillar-
box had been cleared about a minute before it received
his letter, which would rest in that scarlet security till
after the mail-bags were safely on the morning train for
Glen Laggan.

Every day, thousands of people, from one cause or

another, "miss the post." Once in a while it does really matter to somebody.

Charlie rejoined his father, sat down and lighted a cigarette, though he was more than ready for bed.

"Things in town going all right?" said Mr. Fortune, laying aside the journal.

"All right, Father."

"That's good! Well, you've a real chance now to save money."

"Now—yes."

"But you saved a bit before you got the management o' Lawtons'—eh?"

"A wee bit."

"How much?"

"Four-fifty." Charlie smiled. "Do you want the loan of it?"

Mr. Fortune was amused, but sobered quickly. "And you've got a life policy for a thousand."

"Yes—but only one premium paid."

"Ay; you took it out when you thought you was going to get married."

It may have sounded brutal, but Charlie knew his father.

"That's so," he said quietly.

"Maclaggan's girl thought it wasna good enough?"

At that Charlie stiffened, saying, "You are mistaken!"

"If I'm mistaken, it's because I'm in the dark." Mr. Fortune sucked at his pipe. "See here, Charlie, in one way it's none o' my business, but in another way it is. Listen! A while back, you came home one night and told me you was engaged to be married; and, the very next night, you told me it was off. But you never told me why."

" I'll tell you now. I broke it off."

" You ? But why the blazes ? "

" Because I felt—to use your own words—it wasn't good enough."

" How ? "

" Surely it's plain. She had become the daughter of a man with at least ten thousand a year."

" Well ? "

" And I was still an assistant in Lawtons'."

" Well ? "

" That's all."

" Is it ? I think you've forgot something."

" What, Father ? "

" Me ! Why the hell did you not come to me ? "

Charlie stared. " You mean—for money ? I never thought of it ! "

" H'm ! Well, maybe you didna. I brought up you and your brothers to stand on your own legs. But this is an ex—exceptional case, as they say." Mr. Fortune reached up and placed his pipe on the mantelshelf. " Charlie," he said, " I'm not asking out o' curiosity. Are you going to Glen Laggan ?—I read your postcard."

" I've just written to Mrs. Maclaggan to say I'll call on Sunday."

" Good for you ! So you'll be seeing the girl again and—"

" That's all over."

" Not at all ! That postcard's all bunk. It's not her Daddy that wants you ; it's herself. Only she's a bit offended at something. Now—"

" I tell you, Father—"

" Hold your tongue, lad ! If you still want that girl, I want you to have her. I want you to have her to please yourself—and to please me. You can call it swank, if you like, but I want to be able to tell folk you're a son-in-law o' Glen Laggan. See?"

Charlie shook his head, smiling, sadly. "I know you mean it for the best, but—"

"Listen till I tell you a secret! At this moment I'm worth a bit over a hundred and fifty thousand pounds—"

"You're—what?"

"And when I say that, I mean that I could show you the bulk o' it in cash, on a fortnight's notice!"

"But that's wonderful!"

"It is—just about as wonderful as Maclaggan getting Glen Laggan, without doing a hand's turn for it! But that's not the point, Charlie. This is it!" Mr. Fortune took breath. "When you've got to Glen Laggan, on Sunday, and when you've made it up wi' the girl, you can tell Maclaggan that you have Thirty Thousand Pounds in the Bank—and, by Heavens, I'll see that it's true!"

On Saturday, the postman was late, and Peggy, who had been watching, went down the avenue to receive the household budget. Somewhat to her astonishment it included nothing from Charlie, but one from Wilfred. Why had not Charlie written at once? What had Wilfred, who had been at the house, the previous afternoon, entertaining the children, to write about. She answered the second question by reading the letter on the spot.

It was short. "Dear Peggy,—Can't we have a quiet talk, just by ourselves? I shall be at the Castle all Sunday afternoon, hoping to see you, if only for ten minutes. I'm feeling awfully down. Do pity me and come.—Wilfred."

She did pity him. Perhaps, without knowing, she had

pitied him from the day of their first meeting, when within the Castle she had clasped him, stumbling, to save him from falling, unwitting that because of her he would soon fall lower than ever she could imagine.

Yes ; she would get out of the motor run with her parents to-morrow afternoon and go to the Castle—and, anyway, Charlie, if only as the business-like person he pretended to be, ought to have replied to her card by return !

Thus woman, modern as ancient, uses her powers of reasoning to the confusion of man and the confounding of herself !

Towards four o'clock, on Sunday afternoon, Charlie drove up to Glen Laggan House, his heart sinking a little at the sight of its magnificence and the spacious beauty of its surroundings. His father's amazing offer had not gone to his head. He could not insult Peggy by imagining that she would be affected by it ; to himself it meant only a little courage, rather than much confidence. The money did not make him a better man—only a better match.

As he drew near the house, Rosman, who, it would seem, had been taking a stroll in the grounds, ran up the steps and took his place at the door. Charlie, having expected to find a butler, did not mistake him for a guest, and asked for Mrs. Maclaggan.

" Mr. and Mrs. Maclaggan have gone motoring for the afternoon, sir."

" They did not leave a message ? My name is Fortune."

" No, sir." The name was not new to Rosman's ears.

Charlie perceived that his letter had not arrived. After a slight hesitation he asked for Miss Maclaggan.

" Miss Maclaggan is expected home at four-thirty, for tea. Mr. Ronald may be in then, also. Will you come in and take a seat ? "

" Thanks—unless I might take a walk in the garden ? "

" As you please, sir." Rosman's glance was shrewd. " As far as I know," he said, " Miss Maclaggan has not left the grounds. You might care to take a walk round, on the chance of finding her."

" Is—is she by herself ? "

" She went out alone, sir, half-an-hour ago."

" Then I'll do as you say—thanks."

" If I may suggest it," said Rosman, " you might try the old Castle—a favourite spot of Miss Maclaggan's. I will point out the way."

Whether there was design behind his courtesy, only Rosman could have told ; but it may be remarked that his thoughts of Wilfred Silver were not grown kindlier since the young man had become a familiar figure at Glen Laggan House.

They went down the steps, and from the corner of the house Rosman supplied directions.

In a little while Charlie was walking slowly along the silent, shady, needle-strewn path towards the Castle. He was not now feeling so hopeless. While he admitted that he could not give Peggy anything like what he was going to ask her to give up, he was no longer a man who could give nothing at all, nor was he going to ask her to give up everything. Already, among other airy inventions, he had built a pretty cottage in Glen Laggan, a second home, to which Peggy should escape from the City whenever the Country called.

No, he was not feeling hopeless, and maybe his chief support was the thought that during those ten weeks

Peggy had been living in such an out-of-the-way place as this. So far as men were concerned, she might almost as well, he imagined, have been in a nunnery. As her beauty had been out of his sight, so, almost certainly, had it been hidden from the eyes of others.

And, to sum it all up, if Peggy had really cared a bit for him, five months ago—and he would never believe that she would otherwise have promised to marry him— there was still a chance of his winning her back.

Raising his gaze, he beheld the ancient ruin looming through the trees. He smiled softly. He used to despise such things ; yet perhaps, after all, there was something worth while in ancestry—if one lived up to it. He did not wonder at this being " a favourite spot " of Miss Maclaggan's !

He was almost at the end of the path, where it opened upon the clearing, when he heard a voice—a man's ; then a second voice—Peggy's.

He stopped short, but not before his eyes had seen that which caused the pretty cottage and all other airy inventions to collapse and vanish away.

XXI

IT need not be assumed that Peggy, had a letter come from Charlie, would not have gone, on that Sunday afternoon, to the Castle to meet Wilfred, but it may be supposed that she would have gone in a different frame of mind.

That she was still piqued by what she was pleased to consider Charlie's inexcusable carelessness, is suggested in the fact that, before leaving the house, and after telling Rosman she would be home for tea, she said to him—

"If there is a 'phone call from Glasgow, ask the caller to ring up again, after seven o'clock."

"Very good, ma'am," Rosman replied, opening the door for her; and presently he noticed that she did not take the direction which would have led her out of the grounds.

Still, there were two Peggys just then.

"If he rings up in the evening," thought the one, "he'll have to speak to Daddy or Mother."

"To begin with, anyway," thought the other Peggy.

After which she managed to dismiss Charlie from her thoughts, or, at any rate, to the back of her mind.

To meet Wilfred at the Castle had always been something in the way of an adventure, and though she knew him so much better now, she was conscious of a thrill as she approached the tryst. It was not a joyous thrill. Very soon he would be going away, and when would he come back ? She did not seek to deceive herself. Un-doubtedly she would miss him—miss him badly—the most charming and interesting man she had known ; the most sympathetic and understanding. If only she understood herself a little more ! It was all supposition of course, but she could not play lightly with certain persistent small questions. For instance, would she like Wilfred as well, if they were both far away from this lovely, romantic Glen Laggan, and all the easy existence within it ; and could she like him enough to give it all up for good ?

As she passed through the trees, she wondered whether he had something very particular to say to her ; if so, whether she really wanted to hear it. Thus far he had never ventured, openly and directly, to make love to her ; yet there had been times when she had been more aware of love-making than ever she had been with Charlie Fortune. Half curious, half fearful, she drew near to what she guessed might prove to be dangerous ground.

Remembering his note, she wondered also why he should be so " awfully down." It could hardly be because of his health, for she happened to know that only the other day he had got a " clean bill " from the doctor. There was nothing now to delay his return to London, and surely, after those months of compulsory idling, he ought to be glad in the prospect of getting back to work. But perhaps the " down " feeling had already passed off, and she would find him in one of his lighter humours. On the whole, she hoped so. Yes, while his love-making was sweet and thrilling, as an under-current, she did not desire that it should come in a storm on the surface— not yet, anyway.

Through the last screen of branches she caught sight of him. He was sitting on the flat boulder where she had first seen him, and she noted at once that he was not smoking. His attitude was lax ; he was gazing moodily at the ground.

So he was still " down " ! For a moment or two she experienced a rising disappointment ; then pity, as in a gust, came and overbore it. He was, at least, her friend. No one could have proved himself a better comrade. From the first hour of their acquaintance he had, some-how, made her feel proud and happy—and suddenly she asked herself whether, without his comradeship, Glen Laggan would ever have become so dear to her.

She stepped out from the trees. " Hullo, Wilfred ! " she said softly.

He sprang up and came to her. He caught both her hands, saying, " It's awfully good of you ! It must be nearly two hours since I saw your car driving down the Loch, and I had all but despaired of your coming. Will you come and sit down ? I brought along the old rug, on chance."

" Only for a few minutes, then," she answered, releas-ing her hands. " I've got to be back at tea-time. Ronnie's bringing Rona—she's teaching him the Gaelic, now ! You'll come, too—won't you ? "

" I'm never out of your house, Peggy," he said. " But we have half an hour till then. You can't imagine how I've been missing our talks in this quiet place."

There was a pause while he arranged the rug and she seated herself, with her usual pretty little display of demureness. Then, with an upward glance, she remarked, for the sake of saying something, that she had not seen him at Church, that morning.

N

" Father and I are inclined to go slack when Mother's away," he replied, with smiling lips and sombre eyes. " As a matter of fact, I spent the morning here."

" Here ? Reading ! "

" Thinking," he said heavily, " of my sins—and you."

" My memory doesn't seem to have been in very good company this morning," she returned, speaking lightly, feeling uneasy.

" That is true," he muttered, and now she detected bitterness in his tone—a new thing to her ears.

" Wilfred, what is the matter with you ? " she asked, breaking a silence. " Are you feeling not so well ? "

" I'm all right. Don't I look it ? "

" Your eyes don't. They look as if you—."

" It's want of sleep." he said quickly. " I've been quite off my sleep for a very long time."

" That's awfully bad," she said, with a sage wag of her head. " Didn't you ask the doctor, when you saw him the other day, about it ? "

" He asked me."

" Well ? "

" He thought it was probably owing to my having too little to do here."

" I daresay he was right."

" That's too bad of you, Peggy," he said, with something like his old humour. " Have I not been working hard all those weeks to amuse you ? "

" Evidently the wrong sort of work for you, Wilfred," she replied, relieved. " But, seriously, it will do you good to be back in London, at your proper business. I don't see how you, or any real man, could be happy, just passing the time, for months."

" Perhaps I haven't been so very happy all the time,"

he said, gloomy again. "Well, I've fixed to go on the 14th—ten days from now."

Her eyes on the dark wall of the Castle, she said : "That will let you get a couple of days at the shooting."

"Do you really think the shooting matters to me?" His voice told her he was hurt.

"Peggy, can't you say you will miss me?"

She turned to him slowly, yet almost frankly. "Of course, I'll miss you—so will all the others. But it's one of those things that can't be helped, and so there's no use making a song about it, as Daddy would say. On the 15th you'll be back in your office, in London, and then—"

"Not till the 16th. On the way, I'm spending a day with my mother, at Scarborough."

"I'm sure Mrs. Silver," said Peggy, who, for some reason unknown to herself, always became stiff when Wilfred mentioned his mother, "will be delighted to get all the news."

"There is only one piece of news I want to give her."

"Only one? Why, there must be hundreds of—"

"Only one—about you, Peggy."

"Me!" She stared—and through her bewilderment became aware of his pallor. "Wilfred, you are *not* well!"

"Let me speak." He cleared his throat and wet his dry lips. "I—I can't keep it back any longer. Day after day, I've broken my heart for you; night after night, I've lain awake, longing for you. You're the sweetest, dearest thing in the world, Peggy. I'm not worthy of you, but, before God, I'll try to be. I'm poor, but, if you'll trust yourself to me, I'll give all that's in me to making life happy for you. Peggy darling, I love you—have loved you since the first hour I saw you. Will you marry me ? ''

It was an avalanche of words, with a passion that overwhelmed her—yet only for a brief space. She emerged, breathless, terrified, half-fascinated. She got up and stood there, her breast heaving.

" You ought not to have said that," she whispered, weakly, reproachfully, at last.

He rose also ; he laid his hands on her shoulders. His dark, tragic, haunted eyes caught and held hers.

" Peggy, I believe in you," he said, and his voice was strange to her. " You wouldn't fool me deliberately. You've been so sweet to me all along, it isn't possible you could have cared nothing at all—is it ? ''

"Please, Wilfred," she said helplessly, "please, don't! ''

" Is it ? ''

She was dumb.

His hands slipped beyond her shoulder ; all at once his arms enclosed her. For a moment she was close to him ; for a moment his mouth was on hers. . . .

In that moment, Charlie Fortune looked from the wood.

Her strong young arms forced him away. She drooped before him, murmuring, " Why did you, oh, why did you ? ''

" But, Peggy, you do care —a little ? ''

" I don't know." She put her hands to her face. " Oh, I don't know—really, I don't."

Gently he took her by the arm. " Sit down, dear. Let's talk about it quietly. Forgive my being so rough, but I love you so—desperately."

She was glad to sit down. For a while he did not disturb her, and her emotion had subsided when he said—

"But, Peggy, you do care a little—don't you? Do answer me!"

"I like you—I like you very much, Wilfred," she faltered, "but—"

"I'm content! I know I can win your whole love." He paused, as if a thought had occurred. "Perhaps I ought to have asked sooner; is there anyone else?"

"No—oh, no—at least, I don't think so."

"Aren't you sure?"

"I'm not sure of anything just now. I'm sorry, but you've upset me terribly."

"Dearest, forgive me again. But you are sure that you like me very much—aren't you?"

"Yes, I'm sure of that. Only—"

"Then you're going to promise to marry me," he said boldly, but with a great, new fear at his heart. Someone else?—no, he must ignore the possibility. "Peggy, dear—do you hear me?—you're going to promise to—"

"Wilfred, I can't—I—I couldn't promise such a thing to any man, unless I was sure—quite sure—of myself."

"I'll take the risk. Promise, Peggy! It's life and death—"

"No!" she said, with unexpected firmness; "No!"

"My God!" He turned his face from her.

It was the merest whisper, yet she heard it, and again her heart filled with pity.

"Don't take it like that," she said tenderly. "We've been such good friends. It's awful to think of it ending like this. I—I do hate hurting you."

Quickly he turned to her. In her tenderness did he see a spark of hope?

"Peggy, don't make it end just yet. Give me the

last little chance. You haven't had time to think. Take time—take till the day before I go away. Then give me your answer. Till then I promise to be as I've been till now—your friend—nothing more."

" I'm afraid," she began—

" It's I who must be afraid. But don't end it just yet. Let me—live a little longer."

His pleading won.

" And on the thirteenth," he said, " we shall meet here and—"

" No ; I will write, Wilfred."

He accepted it with a bowing of his head. There was silence till she told him she must be going, adding kindly—

" You will come, won't you ? "

" Thanks, yes. I always enjoy tea at Glen Laggan House," he answered, smiling so bravely that had pity and admiration been enough, her doubts of herself would have been slain then and there.

XXII

AFTER the brief glimpse that signified downfall to his hopes, and when the stunning effect of the shock had passed, Charlie's first thought was to return to the car and drive off, without a word to the butler. Then, remembering that he had given the man his name, also that his letter would be delivered on the morrow, he became dubious over the idea. Finally by the time he reached the house, pride having revived, he determined to pay his visit as planned, or almost so. This morning, having hesitated till the last minute, thinking of Mrs. Maclaggan's suggestion that, when he did come to Glen Laggan, he should stay overnight, he had packed and placed a suit-case in the car.

"You did not find Miss Maclaggan at the Castle, sir?" said Rosman, appearing in answer to his ring.

"I have just been there. Where ought I to park my car?"

"If you will step in, I shall take it round to the garage presently. It looks like rain. Shall I fetch up your suit-case?" To Rosman it seemed that this was not quite the same young man whom he had directed to the Castle, twenty minutes ago.

It occurred to Charlie that he ought to explain. "I'm not staying the night," he said, "but I wrote to Mrs. Maclaggan, on Friday, from Glasgow, saying I would call this afternoon. My letter seems to have missed the post."

"I see, sir. Miss Maclaggan should be home in a few minutes. Meanwhile, after your long drive, you will want a wash and, perhaps, some refreshment—a whisky and soda, or—"

Charlie refused the refreshment. Ten minutes later, he was sitting in the drawing-room, wishing himself a hundred miles away. His thoughts were not bitter, only sad; he was vexed with himself alone. Peggy was not to blame. Five months ago, he had given her her freedom. There was no getting over that. He had fooled himself with his theory that in that period she would not make the acquaintance of other men. He ought to have taken her curt message on the card as an intimation to the effect that she was no longer interested in him, even in an ordinary, friendly way. Well, he hoped the man, in whose arms he had seen her, was of the right sort; he wished her nothing but—

Peggy came in, with Wilfred. A minute sooner, or a minute later, she would have received warning of the visitor's presence from Rosman; but Rosman, as chance would have it, had gone to the garage. Now she was completely taken aback—pale for an instant, then rosy; and the blush was—in part, at least—born of resentment. Why had he not let her know he was coming?

The awkwardness of the moment was not mitigated by Charlie, who, heartsick at the sight of her, was slow in coming forward. Wilfred, cursing inwardly, told himself that here was the "someone else."

Peggy, recovering, stiffly welcomed the unexpected guest, and made the two young men acquainted, naming Mr. Fortune as an old Glasgow friend.

It was Wilfred, however, who kept the talk going, by proceeding amiably to discuss, as a motorist, the road from Glasgow. And before long, happily, Ronnie brought in Rona Gregg, and that buxom and hearty young Diana, who, like John Knox, " feared the face of no man," but none the less loved a room full of boys, became the preventer of pauses for the next hour.

Peggy, presiding at the tea-table, spied Charlie looking rather " out of it," as she thought, and let her heart soften towards him. At her sign he removed to a seat beside her.

" Were you waiting long ? " she inquired.

" Not long, Peggy. You've got a lovely place here."

" You like it ? But, I expect, you would soon weary of this sort of life, away from everything."

" Maybe—but I want to tell you, Peggy, that I got your card on Friday night—I was away early in the morning, and late in getting home—and wrote at once to your mother—I was going to have 'phoned to her anyway—"

" Mother never got your letter."

" I've guessed that ! I suppose I must have just missed the last collection. I'm sorry." Having got it off his mind, Charlie looked as relieved as a heart-broken young man may look.

" I'm sorry, too," she said, sincerely enough. " We would have been at home, if we had known you were coming."

Charlie may be forgiven for wondering whether she really meant the " we " to include herself.

" Does Mr. Silver belong to this part of the country ? " he asked.

" His people are our nearest neighbours, but his business is in London. He had a bad motor accident a while ago, and has been home to recruit. He's going

back to London next week." Her speech may have
sounded slightly breathless.

"I see," said Charlie, who did nothing of the sort.

"His father, Colonel Silver, was the first person
here to welcome Daddy, and so—we've been rather
friendly."

"I see, Peggy." He hated to suspect her of concealing
things. Yet if she were engaged to the man, surely she
might have told him. If she were not engaged—well,
maybe he was a bit old-fashioned.

Next moment, with a twinge of shame, and another of
pain, he perceived the possibility of that embrace having
been the first.

Glancing across at Wilfred who, apparently, was
enjoying the chatter of Rona and Ronnie, he remarked :
"It must have been a very bad accident. Mr. Silver
doesn't look too fit now."

"Oh, he's all right now," she answered, "except that
he's a bit nervous at times."

"Yes, that's it ! I was wondering what it was. When
he's not speaking, his eyes look as if he were terrified of
something—"

Peggy raised her voice. "Will anyone have more
tea ?" Replies being in the negative, she turned again
to Charlie.

"Daddy will be glad you came to-day. He wants to
have a word with you about a letter he got from Cousin
Bob."

"Mr. Maclaggan, in Buenos Aires ?"

"Yes—but it's Daddy's affair, so I won't say anything
more."

"I can't think what it can be about, unless he's
thinking of adding ironmongery to his big business out

there," said Charlie. "He's a great wee man, your Cousin Bob!"

"He's all that! I often think of him, always in the background, while all we have here comes from him." Peggy sighed. "Sometimes it doesn't seem quite right."

"But it's perfectly right! He couldn't have done without you all. He told me, himself, that if you hadn't all been what you were, his dream of Glen Laggan could never have come true. But he didn't need to tell me that about you, Peggy. Anyone can see that you were made for this life."

She smiled and frowned. "Don't try to make me feel too—comfortable, Charlie. We haven't been at Glen Laggan three months."

"I was never any use at compliments, and I'm not trying to pay them now," he said slowly. "When you came into this lovely room, a wee while ago, you belonged to it—you belonged to it, just as surely as I didn't!"

"Charlie, you're not to talk like that!"

"Well, then, I won't. I'll talk about your Cousin Bob—the greatest man I've ever met—one of those men that do really big things, without anybody taking much notice. I could see that, not in his talk, but behind it. And I'd be very much surprised if Glen Laggan was the only splendid thing he has done, or will do. I tell you, Peggy, he made me change my mind about wealth. Wealth's neither bad nor good. It's the man that has it."

"I had no idea," she said gravely, "you thought so much of Cousin Bob."

"I'm telling you now. I met him only a few times, but a few times with a man like him is worth a thousand times with the ordinary sort of man that's just a working and feeding machine, and a talking one, too! Do you know, Peggy dear—oh, I beg your pardon—" He stopped short, like a runner at the verge of a precipice.

"Yes?" She pretended not to have noticed it, though the "Peggy dear" had brought a sudden mist to her eyes.

"Do you know, Peggy," he resumed, with the enthusiasm gone from his voice, " he very nearly got me away to the Argentine, last June. If the managership of Lawtons' hadn't come along—"

"Was that why you wouldn't go to the Argentine?"

"I suppose it was, though I must say I didn't consider going abroad very seriously then."

"Would you consider it more seriously now, if you got another chance for the Argentine?"

"I surely would!"

Rona called out—"Peggy, Mr. Silver seems to have his doubts about our going up Cleishabhal in four and a half hours. Come and make him believe! Are you a mountaineer, Mr. Fortune?"

"Not since my parents lived four stairs up, Miss Gregg," Charlie replied, with the humour that sometimes rises from despair.

The talk became general and remained so till the arrival of the Laird and Mrs. Maclaggan.

If Charlie desired comfort for his bruised spirit, he must surely have found some in the welcome of his hostess and her distress at her absence on his arrival. Only the Post Office was to blame! She was "terrible glad" to see him, and his room had been awaiting him for weeks. Had he been shown his room? What? He could not stay the night? Too bad!

"Never heed, Maggie! We'll have him back in no time, now that he's found the way," said Colin, his arm about the young man's shoulders. "Now we'll make the most of the time there is."

Colin had already scented a dinner-party. He would take no refusals. Miss Rona, if she didn't think she was bonnie enough in her present frock, could run home and dress, but Mr. Silver was going to stay where he was. It was going to be a great evening!

Of Wilfred it should be recorded that he looked to Peggy for his decision.

"Of course, you must stay," she said, quietly—but what else could she have answered? Now she was troubled about many things.

Charlie, his hurt soothed somewhat in that atmosphere of unaffected friendliness, may have felt a fleeting regret that he had not allowed the butler to take his suit-case from the car. Then Colin, clasping his arm, conducted him to the Railway Room.

They had just finished their chat there when Maggie came in, dressed for dinner, and still rather shy of her fine feathers, though they were modest enough, as such things go. But Charlie now beheld her so attired for the first time. He rose up, transfixed.

"What do you think o' her, Charlie?" said Colin, chaffingly. "Duchess o' Glen Laggan—eh?"

"Colin, behave yourself!"

"And she's put on her jewels in your honour! Come, my lad, what do you think o' her?"

Charlie reddened, but answered steadily, "Mr. Maclaggan, she's just beautiful!"

And, while she blushed, Colin cried delightedly—

" Gosh, Maggie woman, it's not the first time I've heard you called that ! I'll have to get specs ! "

" You would never think he was a laird, would you, Charlie ? " she said, recovering her dignity. " But maybe he takes after his savage ancestors. Come away to dinner ! "

Laughing, they went into the hall, where the sight of Peggy in her " pretties " brought it all back to Charlie. With a different heart, he would have enjoyed the ensuing hour very much, indeed. The host, after a passing regret for the absence of a shirt-front and dinner jacket, was at his heartiest. Wilfred was really amusing, and Rona, magnificent in scarlet, the adoration of poor Ronnie, bubbled over with fun.

But a cheerful countenance may take some supporting. Charlie, though never sinking to the level of the proverbial skeleton, was thankful when the feast, which concluded with an embarrassing toast to himself, was over.

As soon as decency permitted, he took his departure, in a downpour.

Wilfred left shortly after. At home he found his father poring over business documents.

Without a glance, the Colonel said : " Aren't you taking a little too much from Glen Laggan ? "

Wilfred, head aching, nerves twittering, replied : " Aren't *you* ? "—and in the next breath added ; " I'm sorry I said that."

The Colonel winced, sighed and sat up. " A very just retort ! " he said. " I have certainly taken too many favours from Maclaggan. But the fishing is my only distraction in these days, and, God knows, I need distraction." He sighed again. " I am wondering, to-night, how long we shall be able to afford to live here.

Not long, unless things improve beyond any hope of mine." His head went down again. "Wilfred, for the first time in my life, I have borrowed money."

Wilfred had an impulse to go to his father and cast himself on his knees; but it passed, and he remained there, downcast, dumb.

The Colonel raised his eyes. "My boy, you're looking done up. Get to bed at once. We must discuss these hateful things another time."

"I'm sorry," said Wilfred again, helplessly—and went.

In his room, the sweat on his face, he wrote once more to his accountant friend in London, the gist of the letter being "Is there no way out?"

.   .   .   .   .   .

At ten o'clock, Rona, escorted by Ronnie, went home.

"Peggy," Maggie remarked, in the hall, "you're looking wearied."

"I'm going to bed." With an effort—"I wonder if Daddy remembered to speak to Charlie about Cousin Bob."

"We'll go and ask him."

They went to the Railway Room.

"Of course, I remembered!" said Colin. "That was what I brought him in here for, before dinner, and I must say I got the surprise o' my life!"

"How?"—from Maggie.

"Well, as you ken, I was cock-sure he would never dream of throwing up his fine job in Glasgow; but he seemed to be greatly interested in Bob's offer."

"It wasn't really an offer!"—from Peggy.

"Well, it was next door to an offer. It would be really an offer as soon as Charlie said he was open for it. Anyway, Charlie's going to think it over, seriously, for a month—not longer—and then he'll write to Bob. But, between ourselves, I think Charlie's as good as booked for the Argentine."

" Well, well ! " Maggie murmured.

Peggy moved to the door.

" I've always thought of Charlie as a home-bird, but young folks must do what they think best for themselves," Maggie continued. " I'm vexed we were all out when he arrived. I was saying to Rosman I hoped he had looked after him—"

" Oh, Rosman," said Colin, " would do that all right ! "

" Charlie wouldn't come in at first ; preferred to look round the garden ; so Rosman, thinking Peggy might be at the Castle, showed him the way—"

" Good-night," said Peggy, and went out quickly.

XXIII

COLIN relinquished the heavy rod to Murdo, his ghillie, and stretched his arms.

"I doubt I'll never get the hang o' this fishing. I really thought I had nailed yon whale, but I suppose I was too quick in giving the chugg," he said, ruefully. "Murdo, do you think I'll ever catch a salmon?"

Murdo, a magnificently-framed Highlander, as ponderous of speech as of body, slowly replied—

"Well, now, that will be a very hard question to answer, sir, for no man is knowing what is coming to him in the future. You see, sir, as I was telling you nine or ten times before, the salmon fishing is taking a great deal of practice; and the younger the man, the easier will be the practice. That is why Mr. Ronald is a fisherman already. I am not meaning to say that you are too old— ho, no, not at all, sir! As the saying is, while there is life there is hopes, and very likely the oldest man in the Bible was still full of them when he was near a thousand years of age."

Colin, lighting a cigarette, smiled behind his hand. He rather enjoyed leading Murdo on. Murdo, whose verbosity and occasional bluntness irritated most people, only amused him. Also, while still apt to be shy with his other tenants, Colin felt at home with Murdo. From Murdo, who seemed to know the life history of every soul on the estate, he obtained an insight into their little worldly affairs, their joys and sorrows, which he could never have learned directly. Colin, at this time, it may be remarked, would fain have moved disguised among his people, after the manner of King James the Fifth, in order to learn how they lived and, incidentally, what they thought of himself.

"Murdo," he said, " I believe you are not expecting me to catch a salmon this season, anyway ! "

From under shaggy brows the ghillie eyed the river that had run through his fifty years.

"It is the God's truth, I am not ! " he answered frankly, at last. " And I will not be greatly expecting you to do it next season, either "—a pause—" but, maybe, perhaps and possibly, in the season after that, if we are all spared and enjoying good health, you will be getting a nice fish, sir, for you are a very meritorious gentleman ! "

He would, doubtless, have rambled on in the same strain, but for a sound that came suddenly to their ears from down the river—the cheery whir of a reel.

" The Colonel has struck another one ! " he announced. " Now, sir, if I was you, I would be going and watching him playing the fish, and be getting a good lesson to yourself." The Laird assenting, he continued, as they went along the bank : " Have you ever noticed, sir, that the Colonel is a different man when he has the rod in his hand ? He is no longer looking as if the cat had eaten his breakfast, and put it all up again on the good dining-room sofa. Ho, no, not at all ! He reminds me of my wife's brother, who learned to play music on the har-monium—and with both his two hands, mind you ! He was a poor miserable-looking sort of man at his work, or when you met him on the road, or saw him in the

Kirk—oh, my goodness, especially in the Kirk! But when he was sitting at the harmonium, with his feet trying which would get there first, he would be looking as joyful as a very bird of Paradise! Ay, ay, it is a grand thing to see a man looking always happy, like yourself, sir!"

With such converse they remained in the background till the Colonel's ghillie had gaffed the fish, and landed it safely, and then Colin went forward to congratulate the Colonel.

Without doubt, it would have been a bitter draught to Mrs. Silver, could she have been present then, to witness her husband's cordial manner towards the chief of "those dreadful people."

"Your kindness seems to carry good fortune with it, Laird," he said. "I cannot remember a month when I enjoyed such excellent sport. But now that it has become almost a daily privilege, I ought to be ashamed of myself for taking so much."

"Don't speak about it! Dear knows, you're welcome, and I'm glad the fish are so obliging."

Not for the first time, the oddity of the situation occurred to Colin. Here he was, until lately a man of no possessions, standing on his own land, receiving thanks for favours done to a gentleman, whose suit-case he might have—probably had—carried in the past, a service rewarded with a gratuity!

To a nature less ingenuous than Colin's such a situation might have induced a keen satisfaction of the meaner sort; but having no shame of the past, Colin had no conceit in the present, and therefore no unkindly thoughts of the boot being on the other foot, and so forth. It was "queer"—that was all. Besides, he was beginning to feel something like affection for this man, who seemed always to be lonely and never altogether cheerful. It would be fine when Mrs. Silver was home again, he thought, visualising a dinner party in Glen Laggan House, at which the Colonel and he would get on like a house on fire ! Meanwhile—

" What about to-morrow, Colonel ? I can't get up any excitement for the grouse, but, as I've said to you before, I've a lot to learn. The young people are as keen as mustard, anyway ! Your son was saying he fancied you preferred the fishing, but I thought I would ask you, myself. So, if you care to join the young people on the moors, they'll be proud, and I'll be the same."

" You are too kind." The Colonel was less embarrassed than touched. This ex-railway porter had an extraordinary way of being friendly without offence. " But Wilfred was right," he said. " I do prefer the river. Just at present "—with a wan smile—" I am not in the best of—h'm—form, and the solitude suits me best."

" As you please," Colin returned, wondering a little. " In that case, I'll tell Murdo to attend—if he doesn't haver too much for you. I'm afraid Peggy has trysted your present ghillie for the shooting."

" Thanks ! Murdo is known to me," the Colonel said, with something like a laugh. " I can always listen to his voice, without hearing his words. On the whole, I find him rather soothing."

" That's fine ! Well, I'll not interrupt your sport any more. Good luck ! "

Colonel Silver looked at his watch. " Four o'clock ! I'll stop. Don't want to be too greedy ! " he said.

They walked together along the mile of winding

moorland paths leading to the high road. The talk was
mainly of salmon-fishing. The Colonel was full of the
lore of the salmon, and had the statistics of the river for
forty years at his finger-ends. Colin was intrigued.

"It's a bigger thing than ever I thought it was," he
said, "and I'm beginning to understand what it means
to you, Colonel, after being acquaint wi' it all your life."

"I'm a very bad case, as you know," the other
remarked. "I once, indeed, thought of writing a book
on the subject."

"That would be great!"

"I have the material, but not the ability—no, not the
ability."

"You never can tell till you try. I've got a big book
yonder about the salmon-fishing. The chap that wrote
it has got his likeness on the front page. To look at him
there, you would never think he could have wrote an
invitation to a funeral!"

The Colonel laughed. "What is the title of the
book?"

Colin told him.

"Ah, I have not come across it."

"I'll send it along to you, Colonel."

This talk about a book may seem too trivial to record,
but, as things chanced, the book was fated to make all
the difference in the world to a number of people.

Soon afterwards they parted. Colin went up the
avenue, with the intention of at once dispatching a
messenger with the book to White House. The intention
was, however, put out of his mind, for the time being,
by the sight of Miss Carnachan's decrepit car at the
door.

Miss Carnachan's two young friends had arrived from

the South, that morning, and she had jerked them over, as she expressed it, to introduce them to the " damned decent soul," meaning Colin, who was going to provide them with a fortnight's shooting, and his family. Miss Carnachan, however—whether out of mischief or otherwise—had supplied no advance information regarding the Maclaggans.

They were well set up, attractive fellows, keen on the coming sport, ready to be pleased with everything else. Never having been north of Yorkshire, they accepted Colin as a typical Highland laird, and Maggie, who, by the way, was making progress in her grammar, as a consort worthy of her position. Never having caught a salmon, they gratified Ronnie—once he had assured himself that their English manner of speech did not really indicate " swank "—by treating him with considerable respect. Perhaps, on the whole, they were easier as guests than two young Scotsmen in the same grade of society would have been.

As for Peggy, who came in a little late, if they had anticipated a specimen of bouncing, brawny girlhood, they must have been disappointed—or relieved. Peggy, while she did her hospitable part, was subdued and at times distrait. The past nine days had not been happy ones.

Tea was hardly over when Colin decided—vain for Miss Carnachan to protest—that there must be a dinner party, that evening, in honour of the young Englishmen, and charged his daughter straightway to send a note of invitation to Wilfred and another to Miss Rona and her father. Six guests ! Great ! The biggest yet !

Impossible to rebel, though in that hour Peggy regarded her Daddy as an inconsiderate tyrant. With a sick heart, she wrote, in her Mother's name, to Wilfred. She had seen him on six days out of the past eight, and he had played his part well, but his suffering had been evident. She wished she had not made that promise. Already she knew what her final answer would have to be. She was terribly sorry for him, but she could never love him. On each of those six days she had—very gently— tried to make him understand ; but if he understood, he had given no sign.

Now, with the pen in her hand, came the thought of ending it there and then. It might be brutal to do so, but it seemed cowardly to refrain. Yet she refrained. After all, in the Maclaggan code, a bargain was a bargain. She had promised her answer for the 13th—she must keep to that. Yet a letter seemed cowardly, too, and now she told herself that, instead of writing when the time appointed arrived, she would face him and give her answer as kindly as she could.

So a messenger went to White House, and returned with a reply, directed to Mrs. Maclaggan. Wilfred thanked her very much, and was sorry he could not come to dinner, that evening. That was all. Peggy was relieved for the time being. Afterwards, when the guests were gone and the house was quiet, she wondered why he had refused the invitation.

About Charlie, too, she wondered. Probably she did not, and never would, realise that since her first meeting with Wilfred she had not once given him a thought, without giving another to Charlie. Since that afternoon, two Sundays ago, however, the connection in her mind between the two young men had become closer and clearer than ever before. Now, for the hundredth time, she asked herself the unanswerable questions :—Had

Charlie really gone to the Castle ; if so, at what particular
moment had he arrived at the opening to the clearing ?

While she lay awake the wind began to whimper and
whine about the windows of her room. Before long it
was coming in heavy squalls, with great blatters of rain.
Dismal prospect for the Twelfth of August, now within
a few hours of its dawn ! But the coming event, which
had mattered so much to her, ten days ago, mattered
nothing to-night. Glen Laggan itself and all it
represented, though still dear, were become less
precious.

Over yonder, at White House, Wilfred Silver, still
dressed and wide awake, was pacing the floor of his
room, or lying for a few minutes on his bed, or crouching
in a chair, palms to eyes—always on the verge of a mental
collapse. He had, that day, received a reply from his
accountant friend in London. It was no worse than he
ought, reasonably, to have expected, nevertheless, it had
crushed him.

"I am sorry, Wilfred, but I have got to be blunt.
There is absolutely nothing to be done here. If you
cannot settle with those people next month, you
will have to go through the mill and endure the
publicity. Once again, I strongly advise you to appeal
to your father."

Up to a point, the defeat of one hope, even if it seem
the last, may mean the uprising of another ; but, in the
case of Wilfred Silver, that point had been passed. He
no longer looked to Peggy for salvation. Already he
knew what her final answer would be. Perhaps he had
known since his hope in her culminated in that wild kiss

in the shadow of the Castle, yet had allowed the dying thing to go on deceiving him. Now it was dead.

When the dawn came to his window, wailing and weeping, he sat down at the table, all the youth gone from his face, to write to her. . . .

XXIV

AN inglorious Twelfth! The five young people had been early on the moors, but had received quite enough weather punishment by midday. Their early return to Glen Laggan House—with one grouse, shot by Miss Rona—was joyfully acclaimed by Colin. Happy thought! A lunch party!

"But, Peggy," he asked, next moment, "where is Mr. Silver? I thought he was going to be with you all."

"He didn't turn up, Daddy. I daresay he thought we wouldn't attempt the moors in such awful weather— we were almost blown off our feet! Of course," she added, "he may have found other things to do. He is going away, the morning after to-morrow."

"So he is—I had forgot. But surely he'll be coming along later on. If he doesn't, you must ask him to dinner, to-morrow night."

"He'll want to spend to-morrow night with his father," Maggie put in.

"So he will. Pity we can't ask the Colonel, too. However, Mr. Wilfred will most likely be dropping in in the afternoon."

They were all going to sup, that night, at Garry. A dinner party was beyond Miss Carnachan's resources, domestic, as well as financial; the supper she was providing would mean her doing without many little things for months to come. But she had her Highland pride, and while, as she frankly admitted, she received cheerfully, she could give gladly, without thought of the morrow. Her two young English guests imagined that, though Garry House was falling to pieces, their hostess was quite comfortably off.

After lunch the young people went to the billiard-room. Colin looked in to tell them of the magical things they would see on the table, once Mr. Silver arrived. But the afternoon passed, and Wilfred did not appear.

Peggy was dressing, rather listlessly, for the evening when Jeanie brought her a letter, saying, " There will be no answer wanted."

With misgivings, she opened it. Was it an appeal, timed to influence her just before she wrote the promised final answer ? If so, she felt it would weaken her resolve to send him a friendly line in the morning, and meet him, face to face, as an honest girl should, in the afternoon. She did not want to be a coward. He was her friend, and he was going away, and maybe she might be able to say some little thing to cheer him, which would not seem at all the same in cold ink.

Taking courage, she unfolded the sheet and began to read :—

" DEAR PEGGY,

I have been thinking about you all night. I know what you are going to write to me. I know how kindly you will write it, and how the writing of it will be painful to you. And so this is to tell you that I shall not expect to hear from you to-morrow. I love you enough to spare you this much. If you have been worrying about it, forgive me. I have decided that it will be much better for us both, if I go away without seeing you again. Thank you for all the sweetness you have put into my life during those weeks of our friendship. Try to be as gentle with my memory as you have been with myself. Goodbye, dear.

WILFRED."

Time passed.

Maggie came in to learn what was keeping her daughter. Not for a long time had Peggy wanted her mother so much. The splendid independence of youth breaks down, once in a while.

"Dearie, what's wrong? You're crying!" Quickly Maggie shut the door.

Next moment Peggy was on her breast, faltering a vague outline of the trouble.

"There's something about his letter that's too sad for anything," she ended.

"Poor lad! But you can't help not loving him, dearie. Be sorry for him, but don't break your heart. What's making you so terrible vexed?"

"I don't know, Mother, I don't know. I'm afraid— and I don't know why."

"Come, come, my Peggy. If time doesn't cure, it helps folk to endure. It's a mercy the poor lad has his work in London, to keep his mind busy. There now! Here's another hanky." Then Maggie said the practical thing. "They're all waiting, ready, for us, downstairs. Bathe your eyes, honey, and I'll go and tell them you won't be long. Haste ye!"

On the way to Garry, Peggy determined to write a few words to Wilfred, just to wish him well, and after that she began to feel less unhappy. The English boys were

amusing in a way that was new to her, the one as a
buffoon, the other as a cynic, and the distraction made
brooding impossible.

Arrived at Garry, they found Mr. Gregg and his
daughter already there. It was the first time the factor of
Glen Laggan had been honoured in this way by Miss
Carnachan, and while he had a sincere respect for the
little lady, he may have suspected something more than
hospitality behind the invitation. And Miss Carnachan
made no bones about it. Before he had been two
minutes in the house, she said—

" Mr. Gregg, I want you to help me—back me up. I
suppose the Laird is aware of the Garry Games, next
month ? "

" Oh, yes. He has sent in his subscription and is
providing a couple of prizes, as well."

" Good for him ! But tell me now—is he going to
be present at the Games ? "

Mr. Gregg shook his head. " I have assured him that
the kilt is not at all necessary, but—"

" Time enough for the kilt, a year or two hence ;
though, once he sees the kilts at the Games, he'll be
wanting to adopt it. He could carry it all right."

" Better than some who will be in it at the Games ! "
Mr. Gregg remarked, smiling grimly behind his
moustache.

" I believe you ! But, what's he afraid of ? "

" Oh, just the people—the grand folk, as he calls
them. And I gather that Mrs. Maclaggan feels the
same."

" Fudge ! Don't they realise that they have my
support ? "

" I am sure they realise, as I do," said Mr. Gregg,

with unwonted *empressement*, "how valuable that support is to them!"

Miss Carnachan permitted a smile. "Thanks for the pretty speech! But, seriously, don't you agree with me that they ought to attend the Games?"

The factor hesitated before he answered: "In a way, I do agree. The Laird's absence would hurt—might even offend—his own tenants, some of whom will be competing. On the other hand, I can understand his diffidence. He is not the sort of man who wants to be an object of interest—"

"Thank God, he isn't! I understand very well that it will mean taking a plunge, but he has got to be made to take it. You have mentioned his own tenants—is not Glen Laggan sending a team for the tug-of-war?—yes, I thought so!—and for that reason alone he ought to be present."

"That's so!"

"Very well! Now, Mr. Gregg, it is understood between us that the Laird does not leave this house to-night till we have his word that he will attend the Garry Games.—Ah, here comes the car!"

The company being gathered together, she inquired of Ronnie, who seemed to have won a corner of his own in her regard, concerning the day's sport.

"The weather was too awful," he began—

"Tut! Only Glen weather! You'll come to love it yet! What was the bag?"

Ronnie blushed. "Half a brace—and Rona got it."

"Well, well; half a brace is better than no grouse! Still, I did a little better, with nine brace."

"Save us!" cried Colin. "Miss Carnachan, are you telling us you went to the moors in yon wind and rain?"

"Not quite, Laird. The moors came to me. As Mr. Gregg may not have told you, I have many admirers in these parts, all fairly good shots."

"Miss Carnachan," said Ronnie, "if I get a grouse to-morrow, it's yours!"

"Proud to receive it, Ronnie, and to eat it, too," replied Miss Carnachan, who would be living almost exclusively on gifted grouse for weeks to come.

Supper was a hilarious affair. The shabbiness and threadbareness of the spacious old dining-room, which had not been used for years, were less evident in the soft illumination of oil lamps and candles; its chill, damp atmosphere had been mitigated by three days' firing. For the time being, poverty had shrunk into the shadows. The food was simple and homely, but on the shining mahogany were things of silver, of crystal, of china, that would have caused the eyes of a connoisseur to bulge. Save for the indifferent assistance of her sole retainer, an elderly woman, muttering gloomy prophecies in the Gaelic, all had been prepared, polished and laid out by her own hands, what time she rejoiced in her temporary ruin. The whisky in that exquisitely-cut decanter represented the second last quart of a spirit which her father had deemed precious, twenty-five years ago, and which she had never tasted. She had had to purchase the port, yet it was by no means "the worst possible."

A little mad, someone may say, but Miss Carnachan, of Garry, made no half-friendships, and when she gave to friends, she gave with both hands. She had grown weary of her outwardly free-and-easy, but inwardly formal, social existence in the Glen, and those Maclaggans had brought a new interest into her old life. They *must* succeed! She was not going to see them beaten!

Later in the evening, it was discovered that the wind had changed, the clouds were passing, and there was a moon. One of the English boys proposed a motor-run, and the hostess approved. She regretfully admitted that there was nothing in the house for the enlivenment of young people. No gramophone, no wireless. The ancient piano, standing six foot high against the wall, was musically defunct. And, Heaven forgive her, she did not possess a pack of cards! Yes, the motor-run was the very thing!

They went off in the Daimler, Ronnie driving, with Rona at his side, Peggy behind, in the company of the two young Englishmen who were, perhaps, affected by her fairness in the moonshine, for the buffoon became dull, and the cynic grew sentimental.

In the room she called the parlour Miss Carnachan approached the subject which she had taken so much to heart.

" Well, Laird, it's to be hoped they get a better day for the Games, next month. A wet and windy Twelfth is bad enough, but it is not sportsmen only who would be disappointed by a day like this, on the first Saturday in September."

" I'm sure I hope it'll be fine," said Colin, cordially. " The folk in Glen Laggan have been talking about the Games for weeks."

" It's the event of the year! Everybody will be there. You and Mrs. Maclaggan will see more of the real Highlands in that field than you would see on a hundred-mile motor tour!"

" But, Miss Carnachan, we're not going to the Games."

" What? Laird, what are you saying?"

"It seems best to give the Games a miss—this year, anyway."

"Mrs. Maclaggan—Mr. Gregg—do you hear what the Laird is saying? Not going to the Games! Preposterous!"

"Well, you see," said Maggie, "Colin and I talked it over, and we came to the conclusion that it would be wiser not to go."

"Did he talk *you* over?"

"No, no!"

"Did you not want to go?"

"It wasn't a case of wanting, or not wanting. I dare say I would go, if Colin was going; but I think he is right not to go."

"But why on earth? Laird, explain yourself!"

Colin, looking embarrassed, answered frankly enough: "I thought it would have been plain to you, Miss Carnachan. Maggie and I aren't—prepared. We've still too much to learn."

"Nonsense! Besides, you'll learn no end at the Games."

"I shouldn't wonder!" Colin dryly agreed. "Mr. Gregg, there, can tell you why we think it wise not to go. I asked Mr. Gregg—supposing we went to the Games—would we keep among the ordinary folk. When he answered that that would hardly do, I decided not to go."

"Are you afraid," she said, kindly, "of the—the extraordinary folk?"

Colin reflected before he spoke. "It's not exactly that. Wait a moment till I tell you something, Miss Carnachan. I never had any use for the man that butts in everywhere, crying, 'I'm as good as anybody, I am!' I've seen

plenty of that sort of man in my time, and I never thought
they were as good as even myself! I can't hope that all
the ladies and gentlemen up here are as kindly disposed
as you and Colonel Silver, and so, to make a long story
short, I don't feel like butting in amongst them. I'm
not ready—maybe I'll never be ready—but, if I can help
it, I'm not going to do anything now to make it more
difficult for Ronnie and Peggy later on."

"That's beautiful!" Miss Carnachan said quietly.
"But still, Laird, you are wrong! At any rate, you are
seeing only one side of the question. You are not the
sort of man, I know, who butts in, and I think I may tell
you that you will not find, among my friends up here,
many unkindly-disposed persons. But even were it
otherwise, you have your duty to perform. Your
position has its responsibilities, its penalties. You have
the makings of a modern laird, the opportunities of
becoming one. You have come fresh, as it were, to the
job, without traditions and prejudices, and with, I
sincerely hope, a good many illusions. It is the people
who do their duty, without looking round to see whether
their neighbours are doing theirs—it is such people who
keep their illusions—illusions that are worth more than
the Bank of England! Sounds like a damned good
sermon, doesn't it?"

"Gosh, you're a wonder!" said Colin, while Maggie
looked a little like crying, and Mr. Gregg grinned behind
his moustache.

"Now to the point!" she continued. "How will
your own people—I mean the people of Glen Laggan—
how will they feel, if, in the very first summer of your
lairdship, you avoid what to them is a very, very important gathering? You have not bought those people;

they have not been sold to you ; none the less they are
yours. If you don't feel that they are yours, then you're
not the laird I've taken you for ! " She turned to the
factor. " Mr. Gregg ! Apart from the tug-of-war team,
are there any other competitors in Glen Laggan ? "

" Oh yes, Miss Carnachan, several—especially Murdo
—your lodge-keeper, Laird—who is hoping to carry
off the prize you are giving in the local piping
competition."

" Murdo ! Is that so ? "

" Murdo," remarked Mr. Gregg, " is reputed to be
able to charm the salmon with his piping, but I am sure
he will never do his best at the Games, if you and Mrs.
Maclaggan are not there."

Colin looked over to his wife. " We didn't think of
anything like that—did we, Maggie ? "

" Not seriously, anyway," she replied. " Miss
Carnachan, do you really think it would make a difference, us going to the Games ? "

" All the difference in the little world of Glen Laggan !
What do you say, Mr. Gregg ? "

" I am hoping you have prevailed on the Laird to
change his mind."

Colin gave a short laugh. " It seems I've got to do
that ! " he said. " Whatever I've been put here for,
it's surely not to hurt folks' feelings, pipers' included !
Are you willing, Maggie ? "

" We'll just do it," said Maggie.

" I congratulate you on your wisdom ! " Miss
Carnachan said, never doubting her own.

" All the same," observed Colin, turning the big, soft
pillow, " I doubt it'll be the worst yet."

Maggie, who was thinking about her daughter and "that poor lad," pretended she slumbered.

In her room, Peggy was writing her note to Wilfred. . . . " I hope you are sleeping better. I wonder how you are to-night. . . ."

Well for her then that she did not know !

XXV

THE next day was fine—a perfect day for the moors. Peggy went out early, with Rona and the young men, but came home before lunch. For the afternoon it had been arranged that she and her mother should take the last of the small invalids, now almost fit, home to his parents, and then drive to the town to do some shopping.

Maggie was by no means glad to lose the youngster, a jolly little Highlander, who had become very much at home in the big house.

" Dear knows, I'm not praying for another accident," she said to Colin, while waiting for the car, in the Railway Room, " but I could do fine with another wee hospital— if the patients were enjoying themselves."

" I dare say I could get that sort of patients for you," Colin replied, from the writing-table. " I doubt my old friends at Queen Street'll never be unbashful enough to come to Glen Laggan, but I can't think they would mind their bairns getting the change o' air. I'll see about it, Maggie. In the meantime, you might kindly clear out, or sing dumb. I'm striving to finish my letter to Bob. There seems to be an extra lot to say to him, this fortnight."

Maggie moved to the door—and came back.

" Colin, there's something I ought to tell you—not that

223

you need be mentioning it to Bob. It's about Peggy.
She has refused Mr. Silver."

The pen dropped. Colin sat up. " Is that so ? " he
said, softly.

" Are you vexed ? "

" Are you, Maggie ? "

" No ! "

" Well, that's a mercy. Someway I thought you might
be. I've fancied lately you had got fond o' the lad. I'm
not just sure o' myself. I've liked to see him in the house,
and his father's a real nice chap—"

" I like him, and I've whiles been sort of sorry for
him, though I can't tell why. Just a feeling, you understand ? But when all's said, I'm not sorry our Peggy is
not going to marry him."

He nodded. " Well, well, it's Peggy's business, and
we're not in a big hurry to get quit o' her, are we ? "

Rosman appeared, announcing that the car was at the
door. When he had gone—

" It's queer how quick we've got used to things,"
Colin remarked. " The butler comes in and says ' The
car, ma'am,'—and we never turn a hair ! And we're
not in a stew because our girl turns down a Colonel's
son ! I'm sure I'm glad you're not disappointed."

Left to himself, he sighed.

Before going out, Peggy handed Rosman a letter,
asking him to have it sent to White House.

Soon after the car had gone, the postman arrived—
late again !

Nowadays Colin received a fairly large mail, not a few
of the items being " appeals." Mr. Gregg attended to
the estate letters, and till lately Peggy had been helping

with the others. Colin, however, was beginning to manage a good many things for himself. He was not of the stuff of which figureheads are made, and each succeeding day seemed to find him busier, in one direction or another.

In the bundle handed over by the postman was a bulky registered package. Rosman, about to sign for it, saw that it was for himself. . . . His signature was less clear than usual.

Setting the package aside, he took the letters to the Railway Room.

Colin glanced up, and stared.

" Rosman, are you not well ? "

" Quite well, sir, thank you."

" You look as if you had been seeing a ghost ! "

The butler's smile was certainly pale.

" Look here ! " Colin went on ; " Strikes me you're not getting enough exercise in the fresh air ! Have you ever been out o' the grounds yet ? "

" No, sir—not yet. I find the grounds very enjoyable."

" Then you're going out of them to-day—now ! Tell one o' the girls to look after things, and take the whole afternoon off. Same again to-morrow ! "

" Thank you very much, sir," Rosman answered from the door.

" Wait ! " Colin's manner became awkward. " Rosman, I happen to have a notion—from my cousin —o' what you've been through. If you ever think there's anything I can do, just come and tell me. I promised my cousin to look after you. That's all ! "

Rosman hesitated, as one who would speak and cannot find the words. Then abruptly he bowed and went out.

Colin wagged his head. " Something wrong there ! "

he thought, and some minutes passed before he returned to his letter-writing.

Recovering the package, Rosman went quickly to his own room. He locked the door. He was trembling; his gaze was wild. The ugly past had crashed into the quiet, almost peaceful present. The self-control of months was snapped.

"Now I shall know!" he muttered, tearing at the stout, sealed wrappings; "Now, by God, I shall know!"

He laid bare another sealed package, with his name on it, also a letter. As it were an unwelcome duty, he glanced impatiently through the letter.

"DEAR SIR,—

Referring to our correspondence of May, I thought it well to forward your letter to my partner, at present in Australia. This morning I have received his instructions for finding and delivering to you the packet left in his care, and now have pleasure in forwarding it herewith, by registered post. Kindly acknowledge receipt."

Tossing the letter aside, Rosman proceeded to break the seals and undo the wrapper. The contents consisted of written and typed documents, a bunch of news-cuttings, several loose photographs, and an oblong cardboard box. All, excepting the box, related to his young wife, now in prison, the blood of a fellow creature on her name and memory.

From one of the cards her weak, pretty face looked up at him. His expression softened, but only to grow harsh again, savagely so. Turning the photo on its face, he went through the papers till he came to an envelope, on a corner of which was a cross roughly scored in red ink.

Now he was going to know—know for certain! He

was trembling so violently that he rent the envelope in seeking to release its contents, a snapshot of the head and shoulders of a young man in tennis shirt and blazer. It was of post card size and exceedingly clear.

Rosman, now shaken by a frightful emotion, had to sit down. His pallid face shone with sweat, his teeth were clenched ; his eyes glared.

Now he knew—oh, now he knew ! The thing was beyond question ! It was a good likeness, but, features apart, the striped club tie and the badge on the blazer belonged to Wilfred Silver ! He had noted them often. And his wife, though she had refused to give the man's name, had admitted the photo to be that of the man who had introduced her into the cocktail, gambling, loose-living set—the beginning of her miserable end.

There had, of course, been other men to help her on her brief downward career, but Rosman's hate had become concentrated on the man of the photograph. He had been the first ! To Rosman it mattered nothing whether this man were worse, or less evil, than the others ; nothing that his crime might have ended with the introduction to the set ; nothing that it might, possibly, have been made in mere unpremeditated, thoughtless folly. For Rosman it was enough, more than enough, that this man had opened the door and shown the way ! Twelve months ago his hate had been molten ; now it was hard and cold, very cold, but all the deadlier for that.

Time passed. He became composed. His nerves steadied. He lighted a cigarette. Why brood and delay ? Let him act—now !

He got up and opened the lid of the cardboard box, disclosing—carefully packed with wads of paper—a sturdy, well-oiled revolver, and a small carton of cartridges. With hands that seemed familiar with fire-arms he tested the trigger, broke open the barrel, and presently inserted the cartridges. Placing the weapon in his jacket pocket, he glanced at the little alarum clock on the dressing-table.

Ten minutes to four—a likely enough time to find Wilfred Silver at home. Or he could wait—oh, yes, he could wait for his revenge just a little longer!

He recollected Miss Maclaggan's letter, not yet dispatched to White House. It would add to the simplicity of his extremely simple plan, if he took the letter with him. He could ask for Mr. Silver, saying he had instructions to deliver a message personally and obtain an answer; and then—and then, while Mr. Silver was reading the letter, he would shoot him in the breast—not in the head. Somehow he did not want to shoot him there—no, not in the head. . . .

Colin went on with his letter to Cousin Bob.

" . . . and so Maggie and I have just got to face up at the Games, and try not to disgrace you there. . . . Otherwise things are moving quite nicely. I am now able to look after the bank account myself. Peggy was a great help, though awful strict and particular. If I was sending £5 to a poor chap at Queen Street, she would put me through an examination to make sure I could afford it. Peggy is not mean—she would give the £5 herself—but she is terrible afraid of me spending so much that we will not be able to keep things up at Glen Laggan. But there is no fear of that. As far as I can make out, there will be lots left over—thousands —at the end of the year. Anyway, I am not worrying.

You told me not to. . . . I am liking the Burgundy very well now. . . . Last night I made a break of 14 at the billiards. I am still studying at the Grammar. It is H—! . . . We have been having some wee dinner parties. I am sorry to say there was some trouble in the kitchen, because I did not give longer notice, and Maggie got the wind up, but Rosman made it all right with the cook, and all is peace once more. Rosman is great, but I have just been telling him he must go out more. . . . Peggy shot a grouse this morning, but she was crying when she told me about it. I do not think she will make a good sportsman— not with the gun, anyway. Young Mr. Silver is for London in the morning. We will all miss him—one of the best, like his father. . . . We are all well— splendid—and always remembering your good self. Maggie wears your jewel at the wee dinner parties. She is getting keen on her fine feathers, and looks quite nice in them. . . . God bless you, Bob, and we are all trying and hoping to be credits to your great kindness. Now I will close, with kind love from all at Glen Laggan.

Your much obliged Cousin,

COLIN."

He was in the middle of a refreshing cigarette when his glance fell on a book he had laid on the table, two days ago—the volume on salmon-fishing promised to the Colonel.

" Dash ! " he thought. " If I don't attend to it now, I'll be forgetting again ! "

His finger was on the bell when it struck him that

Rosman would not be on duty. He was still a little diffident about making requests to the maids, and, after a moment's consideration, he determined to be his own messenger. It would not be a case of making a social call at White House—Colin was getting on with his etiquette—for he would simply hand in the book, with his kind regards—no, compliments—for Colonel Silver, who, almost certainly, would be down at the river. He would take the short cut by the Castle, and so be back by tea-time.

He left the house, walking leisurely, about ten minutes behind Rosman, who also had chosen the short cut, believing he would thus reach his destination without encountering anybody.

Rosman, familiar with the way to the Castle, walked quickly, in an oddly automatic fashion, servant of a solitary fixed idea, a man hypnotised by hate. Nothing mattered till he did the fell deed ; beyond that he could not see.

But he was not so familiar with the way beyond the Castle. Arrived there, he was compelled to halt, search-ing for a path through the wood on the farther side of the clearing, where the ground sloped downwards. He soon discovered the path, an ill-defined track, little used. He stepped forward, but only, after a few paces, to stop short, his eye having been caught by a movement down yonder among the trees. Yes—somebody was coming slowly, very slowly, up the path.

Rosman had no wish to be seen, much less to meet anyone, just then. The approaching figure might well be one of the gardeners, all friendly, garrulous fellows. He turned, ran to the Castle, and dodged into the low doorway. Inside, on either hand, was a small, almost dark chamber, with a slit in the front wall, through which in the long ago eyes had peered and, maybe, missiles had been discharged.

He stepped into the chamber on the left, took his stand by the slit, and waited.

He was beginning to think he had been mistaken, that the figure must have been proceeding in another direction, or have turned back, when silently it appeared among the nearer trees.

Wilfred Silver stepped into the clearing. He was attired for the moors and carried a sporting gun, yet he looked, not as a man returning from the mild adventure of bird-slaying, but as one who had been hunted almost to death. He stopped, and those dark eyes of his, all their lustre gone, gazed around, vaguely, piteously.

Rosman saw nothing piteous—nothing save the enemy whose life he desired. Taken aback by the unlooked-for appearance, he had quickly recovered to realise that fortune had delivered his enemy softly into his hands ; and now he brought forth the revolver and held it ready at the slit. At the moment, the enemy was too far away for a sure shot, but let him continue along the path, past the Castle, and he would come within easy range. It might, thought Rosman, with a shudder, have to be the head, after all ; but even so—

At last the enemy moved—not in the direction of the Castle. He went slowly over to a flat boulder, near the rear of the clearing, and Rosman's fixed idea was shaken for the time being when he knelt at the stone, laid down his gun, and put his hands to his face. So he remained awhile, then taking up his gun, got to his feet and appeared to drag himself towards the opening in the wood on the Glen Laggan side.

Was he going to escape ? Rosman judged the distance, pointed the revolver—and refrained. Too far ! Well, if the blackguard was not going to come to his death, Rosman would take it to him ! And Rosman was about to turn from the slit, and make his way from the darkness into the open day, when his eye was caught and held by another strange sight. The enemy was carefully examining a tree at the opening of the path—examining the lower branches and twigs of the tree. What in Hell's name was he after ?

Now he seemed to have found a twig to please him. . . . Now he was doing something to the twig and his gun—the trigger of his gun. . . . Now—

God ! Rosman understood—and again the sweat— but this time the sweat of sheer physical sickness—oozed and ran on his white face. The revolver fell from his fingers. He had desired the man's death above all things, but it is one thing to slay a man—another to behold him slay himself.

Wilfred turned and stood, as though about to step into the clearing, the gun, held by the barrels in his right hand, rigidly, its muzzle obliquely to his cheek. Thus he had to take but one step forward. . . . After-wards—it would look like an accident ! Once he gazed up at the blue sky ; then his eyes closed.

Rosman tried to shout, and no sound came. " Oh, don't let him do it ! " he went on silently. " Oh, God, it's too horrible—too—"

Wilfred's lips moved—became still.

Rosman's hand went to his eyes, only to fall. He did not want to look, yet he had to look. Once more he opened his mouth to shout—then clapped his palm to it, for in the shade, a few feet, within the opening, beyond his enemy, he saw another face, ghastly as that of the man about to die, who now raised his foot to take the last step—the face of the Laird.

In the same instant the Laird sprang, his hands shot forth, throwing man and gun apart—

Crash !

In the quivering silence that followed the explosion Colin clutched at a stout branch and clung to it, panting, sick, yet stricken less by the sudden horror of it all than by the fearful thing that had flashed into his mind.

Had Peggy—his Peggy—in her girl's thoughtlessness brought the poor soul to this ?

His gaze sank to Wilfred, who lay on the turf at his feet. At last he spoke—a single word—hoarsely—

" Why ? "

Wilfred was dazed. He heard, but his eyes met the questioner's uncomprehendingly.

Colin wet his lips. " For pity's sake, answer me ! What made you do it ? "

Presently he saw that he must wait longer for an answer. " Come now," he said, and helped the young man to his feet. " Come away to the house, Mr. Silver. There's nobody there but myself just now. Come ! "

Picking up the gun and taking Wilfred's arm, he guided him unresisting, dumb, into the wood. He did not observe the book on salmon fishing lying sprawled at the side of the path.

Nor was it noticed by Rosman, who followed, a minute later, shocked and shaken, yet a saner man than he had been for a twelvemonth. Hate was still there, but it was no longer blind. It had beheld a punishment more awful than anything of its own devising.

Colin held his peace till they were in the Railway Room, till he had put Wilfred, who was reviving, into an easy-chair and placed the gun in a corner. Then he said—

"Mr. Silver, you can say anything to me, but now I'm asking you for only one word. Why?"

"Money."

"Praise Heaven!" said Colin under his breath and wiped his face.

For a while he stood at the window, staring out and seeing nothing. Then he went over and rang the bell, remarking, in a voice not yet his own, "Maybe we would both be the better o' a wee dram."

When Rosman appeared, he nearly exclaimed, "Thank the Lord it's yourself!"

He said, carefully: "Mr. Silver has had an accident— a fall—not very serious—but you might bring the whisky."

"Very good, sir."

There was silence till the butler returned with the tray.

"Rosman," said Colin, remembering, "I thought you were going to take the afternoon off."

"Thank you, sir. I have had all the outing I wanted." Which was true enough.

"Well, well, you ought to know best. . . . You'll see that we aren't disturbed here—not on any account?"

"I'll see to it, sir. Would you like tea now, or later?"

"Oh, I had forgot about tea. In half-an-hour, Rosman."

Colin put a drink of fair strength into the hand of his guest, and patted him on the shoulder, saying : " You must have had a sore time, and I'm vexed for you. Just sit quiet for a bit. There's no hurry. Later on, if you feel you want to speak about it, good and well ; if not, good and well, just the same. But, Mr. Silver, I want you to get a grip o' two things. It's all a dead secret betwixt you and me ; and if it's possible for me to help you, I'm ready to try. I've a great regard for your father —and—there's cigarettes at your hand."

He mixed a small drink for himself and carried it unsteadily to the writing-table, where he affected to become engrossed in some correspondence. He lighted a cigarette with a shivering match. It had been terrible— terrible !—but oh, the relief to be assured that Peggy had had nothing to do with it ! Only money ! He wondered how much it might be.

Minutes passed.

Out of the stillness came a sound like a sob. Colin had dreaded something of the sort. He put his elbows on the table, his palms over his ears. But the sound came again—again—and the heart of him could not stay unresponsive.

He went over to Wilfred's chair, dropped on one knee and threw his arm about the bowed, heaving shoulders, whispering—

" Poor chap, poor chap, you're just broke to bits— and no wonder ! But surely the worst is by ; surely there's better to come ! I've no idea what your trouble is, except that it's to do wi' money. Maybe—mind you, I'm only guessing—maybe you were afraid o' some—some disgrace. But even so, I wouldn't be hard on you. We all get our temptations, but I never knew the

Q

temptations o' a young man in your position—the temptations that'll maybe come to my own boy, Ronnie, one o' these days—so, you see, I couldn't be your judge, if I wanted. . . . Come now! Turn your back on the past, just for a minute, anyway, and let us see what can be done for the present and future. Come, Mr. Silver! Whatever has happened, whatever's got to happen, you're still a—man!"

He rose and stood waiting. After a while Wilfred found control and sat up. He looked as if he had come through an illness, as in truth he had, but now he was in his right mind.

"Mr. Maclaggan, I don't know what to say to you," he faltered. "The shame—"

"We'll never heed about that." Colin took the chair opposite. "Just tell me—the fewer words the better—the—the position."

Wilfred was too far gone, either to keep silence, or to make a story of it; too far gone to prevaricate. Downcast, he made a simple statement concerning gambling at cards, speculations on the Stock Exchange, money—a large sum—borrowed to meet the losses; further losses, further borrowing, till he was fairly entangled in the net of his own weaving. And then the net had finally closed. Only more money could open it, and there was no more money to be found.

"It was on my nerves, those two months in hospital, and I think it got on my brain, too, after I came here. There was only one date in my life," he concluded, "the 15th of September."

Colin nodded. He did not ask why Wilfred had not gone to his father; perhaps he guessed something. He did not offer any moral remarks on the wickedness and

cowardice of self-destruction; he happened to have
known a poor man who had lost grip and drowned
himself, merely because he could not repay twenty
pounds. He said—

"And what might be the sum.

"Two thousand pounds."

Colin winced, then sat very still. To his mind the
word "thousand" still conveyed the notion of vastness.
At the moment, as it happened, his bank balance exceeded
two thousand, but if the fact made him feel generous, it
did not make him reckless. For what would Bob think
of him? And yet—and yet—if he only dared! What
would Bob do in his place?

He started at the sound of Wilfred's voice.

"There's another thing, Mr. Maclaggan '—and now
Wilfred faced his host. "I asked your daughter to
marry me."

Again Colin nodded.

"But," Wilfred continued slowly, "I want you to
try to believe that, with all my meanness, I loved—do
love—her; and that, when the time came for me to see
myself as I really was, even had we been engaged, I
would have given her her freedom. Perhaps"—his
head went down again—"that is impossible for you to
believe—"

"I believe you." Colin got up. He smiled faintly.
"Though I say it myself, I could fancy a man being extra
fond o' Peggy. Take a cigarette and excuse me for a
minute."

He went back to the writing-table, opened a drawer,
took up a pen. He was in a state of excitement, ill-
suppressed.

After a little while he muttered, "Dammit!"

In the body of a cheque form he had written " Two hundred thousand. . . . "

After another little while he muttered " T'hell! "

This time he had gone to the other extreme and written " Two pounds."

But he got it right with the third effort. Regarding his handiwork, he wondered what Bob would say, and thanked Heaven that Peggy was no longer supervising his financial affairs.

At last he went over and put the cheque into the young man's hands, murmuring—

" For your father's sake—and your own. Not a word! "

It was both fortunate and unfortunate that just then Rosman should have come in with tea. His entrance prevented Wilfred from breaking down again, but the cheque was only too obvious.

Colin followed his butler to the hall.

" Rosman," he stammered, " in a story I once read there was a butler who was so—so discreet and—and so trustworthy—that—" He halted, helpless.

" A true story, sir," said Rosman, and went his way.

Colin passed to the front-door and remained on the steps for fifteen minutes or so. While he guessed that the young man required time to steady his nerves, he found himself in need of solitude. He had lived rapidly during the past hour, and now he had to think quickly.

As soon as he returned to his guest, he said—

" You'll do me a favour, Mr. Silver, by not referring to that cheque, or anything connected wi' it. Once you get settled down in London, I'll be glad to hear that all's clear for you to go ahead, wi' an easy mind, to make good."

With a hand still shaky, he proceeded to pour out tea.

" Is your father at the fishing, this afternoon ? " he asked.

" He went down to the river again, immediately after lunch, I believe. I—I didn't lunch with him. But, Mr. Maclaggan, you must let me—"

" Now, now ! " In other circumstances Colin's admonishing finger might have looked funny. " What I was going to say is this :—Your father will not likely be back for a couple of hours, anyway, and so I propose that, when you get home, you lie down and shut your eyes. You need to let yourself go slack for a bit, and there would be no sense in causing your father to start wondering—you understand ? If you like, you can tell him you were over here to bid us good-bye—and that's what I'll say to my wife and Peggy, when they get home."

He placed the cup within Wilfred's reach, having taken care to fill only two-thirds of it.

" Now, Mr. Silver," he resumed, sitting down and attempting an easy manner, " here's a thing where you can help me. From your talk at different times I've gathered that you are well acquaint wi' London, where I've never been, though in my railway days I might, once or twice, have wangled a free trip. But it's likely we'll all be going there in the winter, for a month or two "— he smiled—" for our education's sake, you know ; and so I would be obliged to you for any hints about the living in the hotels, and so forth."

Wilfred made an effort to get back to everyday affairs. " You will travel to London by road, I suppose," he began—

" No, no ! I'm not going to bilk the L.N.E. when I

can help it ! Have you ever stopped at the Company's Hotel, at King's Cross ? "

By such devices he kept the talk going till the young man seemed to be in a fit condition for going home.

" I'll walk a bit o' the way," he said, handing over, rather gingerly, the gun. " We'll go by the main road —eh ? "

Wilfred's attempt to draw himself up was a failure, yet his words, when they came, were uttered with some firmness.

" It's about time I was beginning to try to face things. If you don't mind, we'll go by the Castle."

" Good lad ! " muttered Colin.

Near to the place of horror, Colin sighted and picked up the sprawling book.

" I was on my way to leave it at White House—" He stopped short.

" Mr. Maclaggan," Wilfred broke in, " you must let me say it ! You saved my life. You have given me the most wonderful chance to—"

" Whisht, man ! If any human being saved you, it was your own father, when he shook hands wi' me, yon first morning after I came to Glen Laggan. But maybe you'll take the book to him, wi' my compliments."

He grasped the young man by the arm and hurried him across the clearing.

" And now its goodbye and good luck. I'll be hearing from you, one o' these days."

An abrupt handshake ; he turned and as good as bolted.

Back in the Railway Room, his first act was to open

the letter addressed to his cousin; his second, after cogitation, to add a postscript.

"DEAR BOB,—Just after this letter was wrote I gave £2,000 to a man. It was *most terrible* urgent. I believe you would have done the same yourself, but I will not be too happy till I hear from you.—C.M."

Now he was a victim to reaction, but a quiet hour in the easy-chair and a couple of cigarettes had a settling effect. Still, he was not quite himself when Maggie and Peggy came in; at any rate, he did a thing not usual—put his arm round his daughter and kissed her.

Later, he mentioned his visitor.

"That was nice of him," said Maggie, and Peggy silently agreed, glad that she had written the note which, by the way, Rosman had not neglected to forward to White House.

XXVI

NO man, highly-placed or humble, however willing to love his neighbours, is without his detractors.

Mr. John Purdie, the postman, on his way to the House, had halted to have a word with Murdo, the lodge-keeper, whom he had encountered at the gate.

A month or so ago, the Laird had asked John, very mildly, if he could not manage to keep better time, and John was still deeply annoyed with the Laird. John was not Highland, and there had always been between him and a Murdo a certain antagonism.

"Gran' weather, Murdo," he said in his broad Clyde-side speech. "I dinna suppose your boss has catched a sawmon yet—haw, haw!"

Murdo, as John well knew, resented the ugly nigger word "boss," but it was with heavy dignity and quiet emphasis that he replied—

"The Laird will be getting a fine fish before very long. I have no doubts about it, at all, at all, for the Laird is a very meritorious gentleman."

"Ye ca' him a gentleman!"

Murdo stiffened. "That is just what I am calling him."

"Huh! Hoo can a railway porter be a gentleman?"

Murdo's mind worked slowly, but it worked in deadly fashion towards a definite object. "I will tell you some-thing," he said at last. "You Lowlanders, you do not know what a gentleman is ! If a man, in a good suit of clothes, is giving you a pound for doing nothing, you humbly salute him and say, ' Thank you, sir ; you are a gentleman ! '—and you do not care a damned button what is inside the good suit of clothes ! But I know what is a gentleman ! "

" What ? "

" A man is a gentleman when I am not asking myself if he is a gentleman. If I was asking myself if the man was a gentleman, he would not be a gentleman—"

" Ye're haverin' ! "

"—and all his good clothes and pound notes would be nothings to me whatever ! "

" Ye would be takin' his pound note, a' the same, I'll warrant ! "

Murdo's mighty frame added an inch to its stature.

" I would be taking a pound note from you, John Purdie—ay, and on the Sabbath day, too !—but that would not be making you a gentleman. Ho, indeed, no ! " Before the other could find words, he proceeded : " It is nothing to me that the Laird was a railway porter for half of his lifetime. That was only his bad fortune, and now he has come into his own—the land of his forefathers—and you will not find many people in Glen Laggan, to-day, who will be saying he is not meritorious. You are not a very strong man, John, except maybe about the legs, which are too short, and I would not advise you to be going about saying the Laird is not a gentleman, or—"

" Maybe," sneered the badly ruffled John, " ye fancy ye're a gentleman, yersel'—haw, haw ! "

Murdo's smile was really offensive in its patronising pity.

" I will not," he said, grandly, " be demeaning myself by boasting to a small postman, who is but a poor ignorant Lowlander ! I will only be telling you, John Purdie, that my forefathers were living in a beautiful handsome castle, eating salmon and venison and grouse and puddings and tarts off gold and silver plates, when your forefathers were all hairy and making their livings by climbing up trees for coconuts—and that is my advice to you ! "

" Ye've a hell o' a cheek ! " said John, struggling, as it were, against the current. " Ye—"

Stolidly, Murdo flowed on—" And it would be a very fine thing, indeed, John, if you were turning over a new leaf, and delivering the letters promptly, instead of wasting the good time of the Post Office, as well as my own, by standing here and there, talking about things you are knowing nothing about whatever ! Moreover and furthermore—"

It was, perhaps, well that at this point the Laird himself came round the bend of the avenue.

John assumed an air of briskness and saluted, while Murdo turned aside to hide a grin.

" Good day, sir," said John respectfully. " Sorry I'm a wee bit behind time, but there was an awfu' heavy mail this mornin'. Will you be takin' the letters yourself, sir, or—? "

" Thanks, John, I'll take them."

" I would ha'e been at the Hoose long afore this, sir," the postman added, handing over the bundle, " but for the—the windbaggery o' your lodge-keeper, there. He should ha'e been a politeecian ! "

Having thus vented his feelings, John presented Murdo with a sardonic smirk, and went his way.

"The Postmaster General," said Murdo in a loud voice, as he saluted the Laird, "is not so parteecular as he used to be. Well, sir, I was just waiting, all ready"—pointing to a salmon rod and gaff at the lodge door—"for Mr. Ronald."

"He'll be down immediately," said Colin. "But, Murdo, how is your wife? Mrs. Maclaggan was hearing from Jeanie, her maid, that she was not so well, and I came down to ask."

"Oh, I think she is maybe feeling a wee thing better now—and thank you, sir, for the kind inquiries. It was only—"

"Mrs. Maclaggan was wondering if she could manage a chicken and some jellies, and so forth, and maybe a drop o' port wine."

Murdo's smile was swiftly extinguished by an expression of profound solemnity.

"That is most kind and delightful of your good leddy, sir. Excuse me till I see if Dolina is well enough."

Murdo entered his house and turned into the kitchen, where a small woman of sallow countenance was sitting at the hearth, drinking very strong tea. He put a finger to his lips.

"The Laird and his leddy will be sending us some good things," he said in carefully lowered tones, partly in the Gaelic. "Cheeken and jeellies, and so forth, and port wine. It is very likely that the butler will be fetching them, so you must be looking as sick as you can when he comes. And do not you be touching the bottle of port wine till I come home! Sh! Hold your tongue! Lord," he muttered, going out, "what a blessing is the bile, when the wife has got it!"

He duly informed the Laird that the kind offer was

gratefully accepted by his poor Dolina, who, on the whole, was a meritorious woman. "And now," he went on, "Mr. Ronald was telling me he is going to Glasgow to-morrow, and this will be his last chance at the fishing this year. I am very vexed for that, sir, and I am very, very vexed he will not be here for the Games, at Garry, next week. That is a deplorable peety !"

"Ronnie has got to settle to his studies now," Colin returned, a little apologetically, remembering that his lodge-keeper was going to compete. "He will see plenty of Games in the future, I hope, but it would be only an upset to his studies, just when he had started, to come up to Glen Laggan for a day. After this month he will, maybe, be coming home for the week-end, once a month."

There had been some trouble with Ronnie over the question of the Games, but, for once in a while, Colin had impressed his authority.

"Well, well," remarked Murdo, with an air of resignation, "it is the God's truth that if we do not learn knowledge when we are young, most of us will go down to the grave in eegnorance. There was a brother of my wife's—not the musical harmonious one—nor the one that would be a cook, but had too bad a memory—and when he was a boy he had a wealthy uncle, who said to him : 'Malcolm, whether would you like to be a meenister, or a doctor, or a lawyer, or a mathematical genius ?'—and Malcolm, he said : 'My dear Uncle, I would like to be a mathematical genius.' 'Very well,' his uncle said to him, 'you will go to the University, in the great City of Glasgow, and I will be paying for everything.' So Malcolm went to the University, in the great City of Glasgow, and for the first year he was very

deeligent, learning to be a mathematical genius. But
after the first year he was not so deeligent. He was
going with the girls when he should have been studying
at his lesson books ; and, what was nearly as foolish,
he was going to the dancings and the pantomimes and
the public houses and, maybe, the waxworks. And at
the end of five years his uncle said : ' Malcolm, you are
going to the very devil, and you will never be a mathematical genius, and I wash my hands on you ! ' And do
you know, sir, what Malcolm is now ? "

" What, Murdo ? " Colin, anxious to be gone, was yet
intrigued.

" Malcolm is now a tobacconist in feenancial deeficul-
ties ! And all because he would not attend to his studies
and be a mathematical—Oh, here comes Mr. Ronald !
What a peety he did not come sooner, but I will be telling
him about Malcolm whilst we are going to the river.
Maybe it will be a warning to him."

" I'm sure it will ! " said Colin, hastily departing, with
a nod to his son.

Going up the avenue, he glanced through the envelopes. There was one which he guessed to be from
Wilfred Silver—not the first since the young man had
reached London. He opened it.

" I think you may care to know," wrote Wilfred, " that
I have decided to go abroad. The chance occurred
through the breakdown in health of the Firm's repre-
sentative in Spain, and, as I happen to know the
language, I applied for the post and was lucky. It is
quite a handsome salary, and I need not tell you what
I intend to do with part of it. The sooner I can start,
the better, and in ten days or so I shall be coming

North on a very short visit to my people. I would come now, but my Mother does not return till the beginning of the month. . . . "

" That's great—simply great ! " said Colin to himself. " I wish he hadn't referred to the money, but I'll just have to read part o' the letter to them. They'll be pleased. . . . My ! his father'll be proud. . . . I wonder if I couldn't tell Bob about it, without mentioning any name. I'm sure he would say I had done the right thing."

At the top of the steps he turned and surveyed the scene that was daily becoming more dear to him. The afternoon was very still. There was a haze, the flimsiest of veils, over dark wood and blue loch and silver river, strath and corried mountain, now purple with heather in great patches and green with birch and turf and bracken —a haze that softened the glare of the sun and cast a tenderness over the wildest places.

" Surely," he said under his breath, " surely I'm the luckiest man in the world ! "

XXVII

"I'LL be there in good time, and looking out for you," said Miss Carnachan. "Cheer up, Laird!" Colin smiled obediently. "Supposing it's very wet," he began—

"It won't be wet, at all. The glass is away up again. In the Glen, I admit, that's no guarantee of a spell of fine weather, but we can trust it for to-morrow, at least."

"Well, well," remarked Maggie, setting down her cup, "what must be, must be!"

"Really"— Miss Carnachan took a sip from her glass—"really, I'm astonished at you both! I thought you would have got used to the idea by this time."

"It's been getting worse and worse," said Colin. "Maggie had a bad dream about it, last night, and we both got up this morning, feeling very, very low. Believe me, if we hadn't given our words to attend the Games—"

"Laird, be a—a laird! At the Games, to-morrow, you and your wife are going to meet some of the nicest and kindliest people in the world—I'll see to that! And—"

"Miss Carnachan, whatever happened, Maggie and I would trust you for kindness—but the nicest people will be strangers. To Maggie and me and Peggy, too, yours'll be about the only kent face. Of course, I ken the Colonel, but they don't. I wanted Mr. Gregg and Rona to come along wi' us, but Mr. Gregg, though he said he would maybe see us there, seemed to think it wouldn't be quite the thing for the Laird to arrive supported by his factor, as he said."

"Mr. Gregg is right, of course. In case you haven't heard, I should tell you that Mrs. Silver came home this morning. I do not love Mrs. Silver—to my mind, she is the worst sort of Sassenach. Still, she has, doubtless, excellent points invisible to my naked eye, and you ought to find her extremely amiable, considering all your goodness to her husband and son. I expect the Colonel will lose no time in making you acquainted."

Miss Carnachan took another sip. "How does your daughter feel about it?"

"Peggy doesn't seem to be worrying," Maggie replied. "I think she's looking forward to it, though she would like to have had Rona's company, and was wishing your young friends could have stayed for the Games."

"They had as much as was good for them—the fortnight of their lives—thanks to our Highland laird and his family! They have already invited themselves for next year."

"They'll always be welcome here," said Colin. "But about the Games, Miss Carnachan—how would it do if we were to call for you at your house, and then—?"

"Not at all, Laird—not by any manner of means! The Laird of Glen Laggan must come to the Games like a laird—not like a damned tourist! So just put that in your pipe, my friend, and—"

"She's right, Colin," said Maggie. "We've got to stand on our own feet, or—"

Colin put up his hand. "That'll do, Maggie!" he said. "We'll face the music, if it ends us! Ay, will we!"

"That's the stuff to give the divvils!" cried the spinster, and emptied her glass. "And now let me

tell you about the nice people you're going to meet
to-morrow.''

" Just a moment," Colin put in. " Maggie, Miss
Carnachan is staying to dinner.''

" I'm not !—or, rather, I am, thanking God and you
both very much ! " said Miss Carnachan, hoping there
would not be any grouse.

" It's you for the cheery ! " said Colin, when the laugh
was over, but he said it so gratefully that his wife refrained
from giving him an admonishing look.

.   .   .   .   .   .

There was certainly no doubt about the weather for
the Games, and Glen Laggan House was full of smiles.
All the servants, excepting the cook who had appointed
the day as one of sober mourning, for the young man
who had once taken her to the Games, and then jilted
her, were going to Garry. Even Rosman was going.

" Well, well," Colin remarked at breakfast, " let's
make the best of it. Anyway, I'm glad the Colonel's
going to be there. We're greatly indebted to Miss
Carnachan, but a man's always a man ! What do you
say, Peggy ? "

" I expect, when it's over, we'll all be asking why
we worried about anything." Peggy spoke lightly,
though not brightly.

Maggie was beginning to wonder if her daughter was
regretting anything. There had been nothing in the
way of moping, but during the past three weeks Peggy
had seemed more dutiful than keen in the occupations
that had delighted her previously. Indeed, she had
spent less time on sport than in solitary rambles, in the
course of which she visited the crofters, with whom
she was now on very good terms. Poor Peggy ! She

R

had made up her mind that Glen Laggan was going to be her home for ever and ever, and the idea was not quite so satisfying as it had been a few months ago.

"It's a pity," her father observed, " you never thought of asking Charlie to come up for the Games. But maybe he's too busy.—And Ronnie might be hurt. I wonder what Charlie's doing about Bob's offer. The month'll soon be up."

Thus do the kindliest of souls, unwittingly, "rub it in " to those they love best.

"You might pass the marmalade, if you are quite finished with it," said Peggy, very politely.

About midday Colin's spirits received an uplift in the form of a telegram, or, rather, cablegram, the wording of which had been most unsatisfactory to the local postmaster, who liked to know what was going on at the " big house."

2000 *OK CARRY ON BOB.*

"Good old Bob!" thought Colin; " but how am I to explain it to Maggie? " However, wires were not uncommon nowadays, and Maggie, busy and rather distracted at the time, made no inquiries afterwards.

It had been planned that they should set out for Garry immediately after lunch, but Maggie, by her fiddling, as Colin termed the preening process, delayed the start for half an hour. The fiddling was deliberate, for she wanted to make certain that Miss Carnachan should be there first. Though neither she nor Colin could have put it in so many words, they recognised that they were approaching the most critical moment of their career at Glen Laggan. Perhaps thus far, everything had been made too easy for them ; always, in moments of difficulty, support had been at hand. Now they must stand alone ; stand, as they said in their hearts, or fall. It is just possible that, but for the presence of Peggy, apparently so cool and calm, their courage might have given way at the last moment.

Maggie came downstairs to a house emptied of its servants. Even the chauffeur had gone forward, for Colin had deemed it would look less " swanky " if Peggy drove.

" Keep up your heart, Maggie woman," he whispered, as he sat down beside her in the car.

" Same to you, my man ! " she replied. " And just keep mind of what Miss Carnachan said. After all, you're the Laird ! "

The car passed through a deserted Glen Laggan— everybody at the Games—and sped along the Lochside.

" Did you ever see it so lovely ? " she said. " Surely it's worth a—a dose of medicine ! "

" Sure ! " he answered, and drew a long breath. " Someway, I think, we're going to pull through."

After that there was little talk during the sixteen miles' drive.

From a rise in the road they came in sight of the field—white tents and grand stand, gay with flags, arena alive with moving sunlit figures and surrounded by bright strips and patches of summer frocks.

" What a crowd ! " Colin muttered, weakening. " Go slow, Peggy, my dear. There's no desperate hurry."

" Don't you worry, Daddy," she answered over her shoulder. " In ten minutes from now, you and mother will be hob-nobbing with Lord and Lady—"

Bang !

" A puncture ! " cried Colin. " Praise God ! "

They were at the top of a steep brae. Peggy, though she had learned many practical things since coming to Glen Laggan, was not equal to the present emergency. Besides, the prettiest of her pretty frocks would—

" I wouldn't risk that hill for anything, with a flat tyre," she said, presently, " and, anyway, I'd hate to arrive on three wheels—"

" Out o' the question ! " her father cordially agreed, lying back and lighting a cigarette.

" What's to be done ? " Maggie asked, with a glance of mingling reproach and sympathy for her man.

" I'll just have to drive the car into the heather, and then walk to the field and find—"

At this moment a young man, bound for the Games, came up on his cycle. A few words, with a smile, from Peggy, and he was delighted to seek out the Laird's chauffeur and send him along.

" Much obliged," Colin called after him. " But there's no need to alarm the chauffeur. If he's interested in some event, tell him to wait till it's over."

" Colin," said Maggie, laughing in spite of herself, " what a man you are ! "

" Daddy," said Peggy, " I never thought you were a coward ! "

" That's my name," he returned. " But don't you see—the later we are in arriving, the more the folk'll be taken up with the sports ? "

" And maybe you'll be too late to hear Murdo's piping, and he'll never forgive you ! And the tug-of-war—the Glen Laggan team, your own people expecting their Laird to cheer them on—"

"Whisht, my girl, whisht, or you'll make me wish I was back at Queen Street!"

Half an hour later, they entered the field.

"To the right, Laird," said the man at the gate, pointing to the grand stand.

On a less "fashionable" occasion Colin might very well have walked like a proud man between his bonnie wife and pretty daughter, but for the moment they were merely his comrades in distress.

"Daddy dear," pleaded Peggy, "do try to keep a stiff upper lip."

Men have been known to jest on the way to the scaffold. "The stiffness seems all to have got into my legs," he said.

"Colin," his wife faintly inquired, "can you see Miss Carnachan?"

"No! Very likely she has been taken badly at the last minute."

"She'll be in that crowd, in front of the stand," said Peggy. "She'll see us immediately. It's all right. Let's go on."

They went on—slowly—returning the salutes of two or three Glen Laggan people.

All at once Colin brightened. "Yonder he is!"

On the outskirts of a little throng of "gentry," in front of the stand, the Colonel and his wife stood alone.

"Come on, Maggie, come on, Peggy! We'll speak to the Colonel."

"Do you think we ought, Colin? Would it not be better to wait for Miss Carnachan?"

"Not at all, not at all! Come on, before somebody else speaks to them. Quick!"

"But, Daddy, Mother and I have never spoken to the

Colonel, and none of us has met Mrs. Silver. I do think we ought—"

" Once I get a shake o' his hand—a man's hand— I'll feel fit for anything ! "

" But, Colin, is it not her place to—? "

" Tits, Maggie ! It's all right ! You leave it to me. Come on ! "

Colonel Silver was watching an event—throwing the hammer—but was apparently not absorbed in it. His gaze wandered, and presently came to rest on the advancing Maclaggans.

Very quickly he turned to his wife.

" Elfrida ! The Glen Laggan people are here ! "

Mrs. Silver glanced sharply at her husband, but answered coolly enough—

" Really ! I can almost admire their hardihood ! "

Hurriedly—" As a matter of fact, Elfrida, of late I have seen a good deal of Maclaggan himself. Perhaps I ought to have told you that, on his invitation, I have been enjoying some salmon fishing. Though I have not been in Glen Laggan House, Wilfred has been a guest there pretty frequently."

There was a brief, unpleasant silence till Mrs. Silver, with a thin, acid smile, remarked—

" It would seem that you and Wilfred have forgotten yourselves during my absence ; but, after all, that is your affair, and Wilfred's. Pray do not afflict me with details. I only hope you gave your amiable railway porter a decent tip for his—"

" Please, Elfrida ! He is really a very good fellow. It is just possible that he and his wife and daughter may speak to us." The Colonel looked over his shoulder. " They are coming this way ! "

" Be calm! They will never have the impudence, now that I am here. Why on earth did you allow yourself to get mixed up with such people?"

More quickly the Maclaggans approached, Colin, at any rate, looking fairly happy and confident. Was not the Colonel his friend?

"Elfrida!" said the Colonel in a panicky whisper, "Maclaggan is certainly going to speak—"

"Nonsense!"

"But he is! I implore you—"

In quiet, hard tones she said: "Lest you should be right, I forbid you to present him and his women to me."

"For Heaven's sake, Elfrida—"

The moment was come! With a wretched smile, he returned Colin's salutation.

"Grand day, Colonel! I was real glad to see you were here. Well, now, I would like to introduce my wife and daughter. Maggie—Peggy—this is Colonel Silver, who, you'll remember, gave me my first welcome to Glen Laggan."

Colonel Silver bowed and, murmuring incoherencies, shook hands with Maggie and Peggy. Then, with something like the appeal of a condemned man, he turned saying—

"Elfrida, let me . . ."

Without haste, her face a mask, a frozen fury in her eyes, Mrs. Silver turned her back. Deliberately she moved away, leaving her husband a stricken man.

Peggy was first to comprehend. She wavered, drew herself up, and her hand closed protectingly on her father's arm.

"Come, Daddy," she muttered.

Maggie's puzzled gaze ceased to follow Mrs. Silver;

her face flushed and paled; her mouth quivered and firmed. Then she took the other arm, whispering, "Come away, dearie."

As for Colin, bewilderment gave place to understanding, understanding to anger—for an instant, murder glared from his eyes—anger, at last, to sheer helplessness. Yet quickly his manhood came to the rescue. He released his arms. He straightened his back.

"Ay," he said, "we'll just be going."

Among the scores of people who witnessed the scene, there may have been a few who rejoiced. But in most of us, whatever our grade and breeding, there is, thank God, a noble and generous indignation that rises superior to self and prejudice at the sight of deliberate cruelty.

Lord Glenaffrie, the year's Chieftain of the Games, a die-hard for his class, turned quickly to his lady.

"Muriel, did you see? Brutal! Hang it, I won't stand for that sort of thing!"

"Horrible! The beastly cat!"

"I say! Let's go right away and introduce ourselves."

Her ladyship glanced at the retreating figures. She was wiser. "No use now, Harry. Look too obvious, even to them. Let them go, poor things. I'll make a point of calling on her next week—on Tuesday. And, by the Lord, when that Silver woman comes this way, I'll cut her!"

Miss Carnachan, cursing herself for having got caught in a political argument, which had held her attention till the moment of the Laird's addressing the Colonel, detached herself from the group, hobbled across the intervening space, and planted her stick and herself in front of Mrs. Silver.

There was a greyish tinge in the tan on the furrowed

countenance ; there were sparks in the brown eyes ; for a moment she looked as though she were about to spit. Yet her voice came fairly steadily, and the words were clear and incisive enough for many to hear.

" You unmannerly Sassenach ! You may flatter yourself, with your pinchbeck pride and rolled-gold importance, you have crushed those honest people ; but let me tell you, you have only lowered yourself to the mud, and raised them higher than you will ever be ! Devil take me if you haven't made them the fashion ! Put that in your pipe, and be damned to you ! "

She ceased, turned aside, as though the shattered woman had ceased to exist, and made after the Maclaggans.

Only for a few yards, however. " They'll be blaming me," she suddenly thought. Hopeless to offer comfort or encouragement now. And there she stood, a discomfited, dejected little creature, till the friends, whose cause she had so greatly desired to advance, passed unhurriedly from the field.

The man at the gate, whose keen eyes had witnessed the affront, stood bare-headed. He spoke, but so indistinctly that only three words can be recorded here— " Yon blasted woman ! "

Mrs. Silver was to be called uglier things than that before the afternoon was far spent. Within half an hour, every person in the field was aware, clearly or otherwise, of the affront to the new Laird, his wife and daughter.

Peggy found the car, got into the driving seat, and started the engine. Colin helped Maggie to her seat and, without glancing at her, took his place at her side.

They had covered a couple of miles when Maggie's hand, groping, found his and held it close. But neither

her eyes nor his turned from staring straight ahead, and they came, at last, to the steps of Glen Laggan House, without a word having been uttered.

In the hall, Colin found voice, though a strange one.

" I'm sorry, Maggie. I'm sorry, Peggy. I ken I've ruined everything. But what's done can't be undone. I don't need to tell you that this finishes us for Glen Laggan. The sooner we're away, the better. What do you say, Maggie ? You, Peggy ? "

" Just what you say, Colin."

" Poor Daddy—but you're right."

" Well, then, go up and get off your things, and when you've thought it over, come and tell me how soon you think you can be packed up and ready. Pity it's a Saturday. Maybe you can have everything settled for Monday. I'll have a good many things to do myself, though I wish to God we could go now—this very minute ! "

Thus far he had held himself up pretty well, but left alone he sagged at the shoulders. For the next ten minutes he remained motionless in front of the great burnished steel and brass fire-place, now empty and coldly gleaming. Less than four months ago, it had offered its golden glow of welcome. His thoughts were bitter, but he blamed neither Miss Carnachan nor the Colonel—only himself. By his pig-headed folly he had made a public exhibition of his wife and daughter. Only one thing to be thankful for—Ronnie had not been there to see and suffer.

Rosman, who had gone to the Games in light tweeds, entered the hall, in his familiar dark suit.

" Pardon me, sir, but shall I take tea to the Railway Room ? "

Colin nodded. Maggie and Peggy would be the better of a cup.

" Shall I fetch you a whisky and soda now, sir ? "

Colin shook his head, but next moment said : " I believe I could take a glass o' the Burgundy, Rosman. I—I'm feeling sort o' cold. Queer, when the weather's so warm."

" I will light the fire in the Railway Room."

" Ay, you might do that. But wait, Rosman ! Tell me—what brought you back from Garry ? "

" Mr. Gregg kindly gave me a seat in his car. We came on just behind you."

" Mr. Gregg back, too ! . . . Well, I dare say I'll be wanting him shortly."

" Miss Gregg came with him. I have a message for Miss Maclaggan, that Miss Gregg is ready to come over, if wanted. . . . Excuse me, sir ; I will light the fire."

Colin experienced a moment of comfort. Loyalty remained . . .

Presently he went along to the Railway Room. A little later, the butler brought the wine, " with the chill off." Colin, forgetting that Rosman was an abstainer, would fain have invited him to take a glass to himself. The comradeship of any honest man would have been welcome then. He said—

" I may as well tell you now, Rosman, that we are leaving this place—as soon as possible."

" Very—" The formal phrase died on Rosman's lips. His look became that of blank dismay.

" I'll be obliged if you'll tell the servants, when they come back, to-night. You can say from me that they'll all be treated fairly—every one o' them. For yourself, Rosman, my cousin, as you know, has a regard for you—

and so have I. Don't you worry. I—I think that's all just now."

Rosman appeared about to speak, checked himself, and went out. On his return with the tea-tray, the Laird, glowering at the fire, seemed unaware of his presence. The wine had not been tasted.

XXVIII

BEFORE long, Maggie came in. Colin's brown eyes seemed laden with weariness.

"Maggie," he said heavily, "I've done to you what I never thought I could have done to you in this world. I've let you down. I—I ask your pardon."

"Whisht, man! Miss Carnachan meant it for the best; but it was a mistake, us going to—"

"Never heed Miss Carnachan. There's nobody to blame but me. I just ruined everything."

"Don't talk about ruin! Come!" She put the glass of wine in his hand. "Do you want to speak about it now?" She poured out tea for herself.

"We've got to speak about it now."

"But is there any need to be hasty?"

"Every need! . . . We must get out o' this! What's Peggy saying about it?"

"Nothing."

"Poor wee Peggy! Is—she breaking her heart?"

"Peggy'll not let herself do that. She feels it, of course, but—"

"Dear," he said under his breath, "I'm heart-sorry for you and Peggy—Ronnie, too."

"Listen, dearie. You haven't had time to think over it. If—"

"I did nothing but think over it, all the road home from Garry. Time? It was like five years!"

" Still—" She broke off. " Well "—after a pause—
" there's only one thing I can say, Colin. If you ask me
to do it—if you want me to do it—I'm willing to try to
carry on."

" And do you think I would ever ask you to do that ?
No—not if Glen Laggan was the half o' Scotland and the
money a million a year. Don't you see, woman ? The
thing that happened yonder, to-day, might happen again
—any day—it would happen again, sure ! There wasn't
a soul in yon field that doesn't ken all about it by now—
Mr. Gregg and Rosman were back here, five minutes
after us ! There's not a soul that will forget. I could
face a lot o' things, Maggie, but never that ! It doesn't
matter for me—"

" Nor me."

" Oh, yes, it matters for you—but it would be
remembered against Ronnie and Peggy for ever and
ever ! Every year the Games would remind folk of
it. . . . So you see, Maggie, I *have* thought over it.
There's nothing for it but to clear out. Can you be ready
by Monday ? "

" If you say so, Colin."

There was silence till he said—

" Maggie, will it hurt you terrible to leave it
all ? "

Her smooth, white throat made a swallowing motion.
She shook her head, saying—

" Yon woman—yon woman—I wanted to kill her
then—kill her with my hands—but now I only want to
get a hundred miles away from her ! She finished Glen
Laggan for me. . . . Ah, well, we've had our bit dream,
you and me. The thing that hurts most is that we can't
hold the fort, as we used to say, for Peggy and Ronnie.

Now I think Peggy wants to give up, but I wonder how Ronnie'll take it."

"Ronnie'll understand, though he's young. I would spare the lad if I could, but his life's before him, and it'll soon be less than a dream to him, poor chap. . . . Drink your tea, Maggie!"

"Take your wine!"

Another silence, broken this time by Maggie. "What about the servants?"

"I've told Rosman. He'll tell them."

"And Bob?"

"I'll write to-night, but I'll get Gregg to wire. Gregg has a code. I'm vexed for Bob, but he'll not be hard on us—I've no fears o' that—though I'd sooner go back to Queen Street than bide here. But you can trust Bob to let you and the bairns down easy, whatever he thinks o' me." Colin threw out his hands. "Oh, dear, I never thought I would ask for the knock-out I asked for this day! What a dashed fool—"

"Man, man, don't be putting it all on yourself!" Maggie got up and laid her arm round his shoulders. "Remember, dearie, you never wanted Glen Laggan for yourself—for your own honour and glory. And none of us is the worse of Glen Laggan. We're all the better of it. Try to think of it that way."

He crushed her hand—the hand that had become so fine and soft. "You're a wonder, Maggie! And you ought to be black ashamed o' me."

"Now, now, you're havering." She produced a smile. "Take your wine, and I'll away upstairs and—and make a start at things."

She left him, sipping the wine. She made a start by lying on her bed and crying her heart out; but after that she was her own mistress, and it may be said that thenceforth, in dealing with domestic matters, her dignity did not desert her.

Colin sent a summons to Mr. Gregg, who promptly came over, considerably perturbed, expecting to find an angry, disgruntled laird, whom it would be his business to soothe and cheer.

Colin had himself in hand. "Take a seat, Gregg. Take a cigarette. I'm obliged to you for coming back from Garry to stand by me. I've got to tell you that we're leaving here on Monday—for good."

Mr. Gregg gaped behind his big moustache.

"And, as you've helped me in the past, I want you to help me now."

"But—great Heavens!—Mr. Maclaggan, you don't —you can't—mean it!"

"Ay, I do mean it, Gregg. And, seeing you're here, when you ought to be at Garry, I don't need to ask you to guess the reason. You'll say I'm running away, and you'll be right; but, I tell you, honestly, I've come up against something I can't face!"

Mr. Gregg considered before he spoke.

"I'll not pretend that I don't guess. I know, for I saw the thing, myself, worse luck! An abominable piece of rudeness—most heartily condemned by everybody, I assure you—but Mr. Maclaggan, don't, for any sake, make it a tragedy!"

"It's because I don't want a tragedy that I'm giving up now."

"But you can't have thought the matter out! Surely, you are not going to be driven from your estate and home by the ill-natured exhibition—I'll allow it was perfectly vicious—of a woman who, the Lord knows why, has got puffed up with her own conceit. Take time, Laird, take time to think—"

"Man, I've had plenty o' time. When the engine jumps the points, you think quick."

"But —Mrs. Maclaggan and Miss Peggy—what about them?"

"They agree wi' me." Colin smiled faintly. "We're maybe an old-fashioned family, Gregg, but we can't help that. We stick together!"

"It's a fearful blow—a disaster! And you have held your own so splendidly till now." The factor in his distress was a new man to the Laird. "Mr. Maclaggan, I beg of you to reconsider—to decide nothing till—"

Colin's hand went up. "Say no more! No man ever had a better friend than you've been to me—I'm well aware I've often been a trial to you—and neither my cousin nor myself will forget it. And now I need your help more than ever. There's a lot to be done. In the first place, I want you to wire to my cousin. I leave the words to you. Let him know that we're leaving on Monday. Say I'm writing fully. I would propose that Rosman—till you get other instructions—carries on the house, servants and all. I don't want them to suffer, and, besides, my cousin may want to let the house as it stands. Of course, the house and all goes back to him now. Will you do that for me?"

"If you say it, I must, but —"

"There's no 'buts.' Now we'll go to the office and see what's to be done there. I'm real sorry to have spoiled the Games for you, though I'm thankful to have you by me now. Come away!"

In his downfall Colin was more the master than ever he had been in his highest hours of confidence.

Dinner, a simple meal, was an hour late that night; otherwise, everything proceeded as usual. Maggie and Peggy spent a good deal of time upstairs, arranging their belongings for packing. Their hearts were heavy, their voices dull, but they had shed their tears, and there were no more breakdowns.

At half-past nine, to the sounds of a coffee-grinder suddenly clogged with too many beans, Miss Carnachan arrived. For the first time, she came up the steps as though it were a serious exertion.

To Rosman, at the door, she said—

" I didn't intend to trouble them till to-morrow, though I cut Lord Glenaffrie's dinner party to-night; but, an hour ago, I heard an incredible rumour, and—"

" I'm afraid you heard the truth, Miss Carnachan. They are leaving on Monday."

" But only for---? "

" For good, I'm afraid."

" Hell take that woman ! Can't something be done ? "

" They seem to have made up their minds to go. Packing is going on. Will you come in ? "

" Do you think Mrs. Maclaggan will receive me ? "

" I will tell her you are here."

Leaving her in the small drawing-room, he went upstairs.

" Miss Carnachan has called, ma'am."

Maggie went down to the Railway Room. Her husband was labouring over his letter to Bob. It was a horrid task, and Colin was not, after all, of the stuff of martyrs.

" Curse it all ! Can I not get peace ? " he cried distractedly. " See her, if you like. Tell her we bear her no ill-will, but we're done wi' Glen Laggan and all connected wi' it."

Maggie heaved a sigh and went to the drawing-room. If she had harboured a hard thought, it melted at the sight of the little spinster, all her briskness and blitheness gone.

"No, no," she said, in answer to the other's question, "we're blaming nobody, except ourselves. Colin and I ought to have known better. But we've had our lesson. Glen Laggan is not the place for us. We're not welcome here."

"Now, Mrs. Maclaggan," Miss Carnachan said, with a glimmer of the old spirit, "that's just damned nonsense! Listen! Suppose the creature were to apologise —mind, I'm not saying she will; but I've bent some stiffer necks than my own in my time—suppose she were to apologise, would it make a difference?"

There was something almost youthful in the saucy way Maggie threw up her head.

"Not if she was going on her knees, Miss Carnachan!"

"In a way, I dare say, you're right. I never forgive, myself," the little woman said sadly. "May I see the Laird?"

"You'll kindly excuse him, please. He has got a terrible lot of things to do and think about."

Miss Carnachan made a small gesture of defeat. "And so have you. Well, I'll go." She moved to the door. "Tell the Laird that this has made me ten years older. Tell him, too, I still believe in him as the right man in the right place, at Glen Laggan."

Maggie went with her to the car.

"You've been our best friend here," she said, "and we'll never forget."

Miss Carnachan, with a heave that seemed miraculous

S*

from so puny a person, set the engine rumbling, and clambered on board.

" The worst of being an old woman is that one can't go to the devil and get tight, or something ! " she said crossly ; then softly, " Good night, my dear, and God bless you all."

.   .   .   .   .   .

It was near to midnight when Maggie and Peggy went into the Railway Room, where Colin was still adding painfully-filled sheets to his letter to Cousin Bob.

" I'm sorry to disturb you," Maggie said, " but what about Ronnie ? We must let him know what we're doing."

" Ay, Ronnie must be told. There's no post till Monday, so we'll have to 'phone—to-morrow."

" I was thinking you might 'phone to Charlie, and ask him to break it to Ronnie—and do it to-night."

" To-night ? What for, Maggie ? '

" Ronnie'll be in his bed, but Charlie'll likely be up. You would almost surely get Charlie alone. You could ask him to tell Ronnie, in the meantime, simply that we've had to give up Glen Laggan, and we'll all be in Glasgow on Monday evening, and, as soon as we find a place for the night, we'll 'phone."

" Ay, that seems wise enough, but—oh dear, dear !— I don't seem to have the brains left to give a clear message to anybody—and if Ronnie did happen to be there—aw, poor wee Ronnie !—I would wish myself dead ! " Colin drew his hand across his hot forehead and untidy hair. " Peggy, my girl, just you ring up Charlie, and tell him what you think best."

" Yes, Peggy," said her mother. " Help your Daddy. I'm no use at the 'phone."

For a moment or two Peggy looked like refusing ; then another heavy sigh from her father seemed to decide her.

" Righto," she said curtly, and ignoring the 'phone on the writing-table, betook herself to the sound-proof box in an angle of the hall.

Charlie, his parents gone to bed, was at the writing-table when the bell trilled. Impatiently he took up the receiver. Presently—

" What ! Peggy !—is it yourself ? "

" Yes, Charlie. Are you alone ? "

" Quite ! All off to bed."

" Ronnie, too ? "

" Ronnie went off at eleven. Is there anything wrong, Peggy ? Anything I can do ? "

" Yes. . . . Charlie ! "

" I'm listening ! "

" Charlie, I've got to tell you that Daddy is giving up Glen Laggan."

" What ? . . . Yes, yes, I heard you, but I couldn't believe I heard right. Giving up Glen Laggan ! "

" I can't tell you the reason just now. It's not a very —not a very happy one."

" I'm sorry, Peggy. . . . And is it to be soon ? "

" Monday."

" Monday—first ? "

" Yes. We'll be coming to Glasgow on that day. We've made no plans yet, but I suppose we'll get lodgings, or go to an hotel, till we see what's going to happen. Of course Daddy is letting Cousin Bob know at once."

" It'll be an awful blow to him. Peggy, must it be ? "

" It must, Charlie. But, please, don't let's talk about

it. I'm really 'phoning for Mother. She thought you wouldn't mind breaking it to Ronnie. Will you ? "

" I'd do anything your mother asked. But poor Ronnie —since he came to us he has talked of hardly anything but Glen Laggan and—"

" Don't, Charlie ! "

" Sorry ! I didn't mean to hurt you. What am I to tell him ? "

" Only that we've found we have to give up Glen Laggan, and Mother will explain when she sees him on Monday night. We'll 'phone him as soon as we reach Glasgow. That's all."

" I understand. It will be time enough to tell him to-morrow night, or even on Monday—what do you think ? "

" We'll leave it to you—and thanks awfully."

" Don't thank me for nothing. I wish it hadn't to be. Peggy, is there nothing I can do to help ? You must all have an awful lot to do at Glen Laggan, if you're leaving on Monday. Suppose—without mentioning it to Ronnie —suppose I took a run up, to-morrow ? "

A pause.

" Peggy ! Don't be thinking I want to butt in—"

" I wasn't thinking that. I was just wondering. . . . I don't know what you could do here, Charlie, except, maybe "— (a poor littl elaugh)—" keep us all from getting weepy. . . . Would you really care to come ? "

" Sure ! . . . But, Peggy, I want to ask you a question —a straight question. Are you engaged to Mr. Silver ? "

" No. Why do you ask ?—No, wait ! Tell me—that Sunday—did you go to the Castle ? Rosman, the butler, said—"

" Yes, I did ! That's why I asked the question. . . .
Peggy, was it the—the first time ? You know what I
mean."

" Yes—the first and the last."

A silence.

" Peggy ! "

" What ? "

" You've never been out of my heart for a minute, all
those months. Peggy, could you think to take me
back ? I would try to be more—more amusing."

" I don't want to be amused. Besides, it was *you* who
put *me* away ! "

" Oh ! . . . Well, Peggy—Peggy—could you think to
come back to me ? "

Another silence.

" I think—I wish I had never been away from you—
dear Charlie."

" Peggy, call me that again ! "

" You call me something else, first."

" What ? "

" Oh, you know ! "

" Peggy dear ! "

" Dear Charlie ! "

At last he replaced the receiver. A little while he
stood, smiling, then picked up the almost finished letter
to Mr. Robert Maclaggan, Buenos Aires, and began to
tear it into strips.

A sound made him pause. His father, looking very
sleepy, stood in the doorway.

" I thought I heard you speaking, Charlie. Anything
wrong ? "

" Just a 'phone from Glen Laggan. Sit down for a
minute, Father. I've something to tell you."

Mr. Fortune did not move. "My lad," he cried, "you've got her, after all! Shake hands!"

"Wait! It's true that Peggy's going to marry me, but she'll not be the daughter of Maclaggan, of Glen Laggan. I don't know why—it's not money, I'm sure—but her father has given it up."

"Given up Glen Laggan! Well, I'm jiggered! But he's too soft. It was too big for him. I guess that was it. It wants a man like me to tackle a job like that. Catch me letting go!"

"But what about shaking hands?" Charlie stepped forward.

"Oh, if you're pleased, I'm pleased," said his father, swallowing his chagrin.

Charlie kept hold of the big hand. "Father," he said steadily, "I'll ask you a straight question. If the words 'Glen Laggan' were really worth Thirty Thousand Pounds to you, is the word 'Peggy' worth nothing at all?"

For a space Mr. Fortune stared, nay, glared; then, all at once, he burst out with a great guffaw and wrung his son's hand.

"You scoundrel, you've got me soft!" he cried. "The money's yours!"

.   .   .   .   .   .

At one o'clock, Rosman knocked and entered the Railway Room. Colin raised very tired eyes from the task just finished, saying—

"Are you not off duty yet? There's nothing wanted now."

"May I say a few words, sir?"

"Of course! Sit down."

"Thank you, sir." Rosman closed the door, and remained standing. "Sir, I have to tell you that I happen to know what you did for Mr. Silver."

Colin sat up. "Rosman," he said sternly, "I'm trusting you!"

"Yes, sir—but I am not referring to the cheque. I chanced to see all that happened at the Castle. I was in the building."

Colin winced. At last he said: "If that's so, why are you telling me now?"

"Because, sir, it has only now occurred to me that if the truth were whispered—and I say it ought to be shouted!—in Glen Laggan, to-morrow morning—"

"Stop! . . . Rosman, I believe you mean well by me, but I gave my word to be secret. A bargain's a bargain, and there's no more to be said. Come, man! I want your promise—and your hand on it."

After the slightest of shrugs, Rosman gave both. At the door he halted. "If I may say it, sir, you are a great man," he said quietly, bowed, and went out.

"A great man—me!" muttered the Laird, with a laugh that was half a sob. "God, why did I ever leave the Railway?"

When he had enclosed the letter and locked it away, he moved to the door. He switched off the light—and switched it on again. He surveyed the room, its pleasant colours and comforts, the prints on the wall, the books, the great map on the ceiling, by which he had made many a dream journey.

"But we've been happy here, very happy," he sighed, and, with a quick movement, left the room to darkness.

Maggie had gone to bed. At first he thought she was asleep, but as he drew near, the blue eyes opened, the lips parted in a smile, frail, wavering, exceeding tender.

It was the smile that broke his control. At the bedside he fell on his knees, and buried his face in her breast.

" Oh, Maggie woman—Maggie woman ! "

XXIX

ON Monday morning the train from the South brought a solitary passenger to Glen Laggan. As he alighted, Wilfred Silver nodded to the stationmaster, who was standing by a quantity of baggage not often seen on the little platform.

"Who is going away, Alan?"

The stationmaster, whose manner was less affable than usual, replied—

"The Laird and his family will be going away in the afternoon—"

"The Laird!"

"And they will not be coming back any more."

"Not—! What has happened?"

"I am thinking you should be asking that question at home, Mr Silver.—Excuse me! I must be looking after the train."

Deeply disquieted, Wilfred pushed on to White House. In the garden he met his mother.

"Wilfred!" she exclaimed in astonishment. "We did not expect you till to-morrow."

He kissed her, saying: "I found I could get away last night, but there was no means of letting you know. . . . Never mind that just now. Mother, at the station I heard that the Maclaggans are leaving Glen Laggan. Can you tell me why?"

Mrs. Silver stiffened.

"Yes, I think I can, Wilfred," she said, with a bleak smile. "At the Games, on Saturday, they approached your father, evidently expecting him to present them to me, and—well, as your father ought to have foreseen, I was unable to accept the—h'm—honour!"

"You mean—you are telling me you—?"

"I kept my place and put them in theirs. In other words, I ignored—Wilfred, what is the matter? You're ill! You ought not to have taken the night journey. You—"

"Oh, Mother, be quiet! It's too hideous!" Wilfred's gesture was that of despair. "Where's Father? I must speak to him at once—you, too! Come to the house—quickly!"

There is always a price, though the demand be not immediate. Hastily it may have been assumed that Wilfred Silver had escaped the cost of his follies pretty cheaply, but now he was going to pay, and cause others to pay, most bitterly.

. . . . . .

About half-past four, that afternoon, Colin came down the broad staircase, in either hand a suit-case. Rosman ran forward.

"Sir, you should not be doing that!"

Colin smiled oddly. "Maybe it's just as well to be getting into training, Rosman. The time's getting on."

They were due to leave Glen Laggan at 5 o'clock, travelling by road. After all, Colin was going to "bilk the L.N.E." The thought of having to face old comrades by arriving at Queen Street Station had been too much for him. He had chosen the hour of departure so that they should enter Glasgow after dark.

"I was coming to tell you, sir," Rosman said, laying

aside the suit-cases, " that Murdo McMurrich wishes to speak to you."

" Murdo ! In the office ? "

" Mr. Gregg is in the office, very busy—"

" Well, put Murdo in the Railway Room."

" Miss Maclaggan and Mr. Fortune are there—"

" Ay. I had forgot ! "

Charlie was still at Glen Laggan. Time enough for him, they had all agreed, to break the truth to poor Ronnie, say, half-an-hour before his mother should ring him up in Glasgow.

" Besides, sir," Rosman went on, " Murdo is not by himself. There are, I should guess, some thirty men with him."

" Thirty ! . . . Oh, I see. Decent souls, come to say goodbye. . . . But I can't face—speak to them—at the moment. Put them all into the big drawing-room, and give them a good refreshment. Say I'll come as soon as possible." He turned and went upstairs.

In the beautiful white room she was so soon to abandon Maggie had unpacked her dressing-case, in order to pack it again, just to pass the time. She was looking at her little store of jewels—so useless now.

Colin sat down wearily.

" There's about thirty good chaps arrived to say goodbye. It—it's not easy, Maggie."

" Poor Colin ! Still, it's a great compliment."

" Would you care to come in wi' me ? "

She considered and shook her head. " I doubt I would just make a big fool of myself."

" I'll promise to make a bigger one," he said, with melancholy humour.

At the end of five minutes, he went down alone.

Rosman, looking a trifle excited, was waiting at the foot of the staircase.

"Sir, Colonel and Mrs. Silver have called. I have put them in the small drawing-room."

Colin's expression was that of a man overwrought. "What do they want?" Yet he knew it could be only one thing—an apology. Maybe Miss Carnachan had—

"If I may take a liberty," said Rosman, "I would strongly advise you, sir, to receive them. They did not ask for Mrs. Maclaggan."

"Very well," said Colin, at last. "I suppose I must."

He was crossing the hall when the factor, a telegram in his hand, came from the corridor.

"One moment, please!" Overtaking the Laird, he said, rather carefully: "This wire has just come—addressed to you personally—possibly it may be from Buenos Aires."

"Dear, dear!" Colin tore the envelope. He read—

STICK IT MAN STICK IT.

"Good old Bob! . . . But it just can't be."

With a shake of the head, he passed on to the small drawing-room, while Mr. Gregg, who had arranged with a friend in Glasgow to send the telegram, went drearily back to the office, realising that his last shot had missed, that all was as good as finished.

Colin entered, closed the door—and put his back to it. He needed the support.

Was the sick man, yonder, the Colonel, who, whatever his cares, had always carried strength in his bearing, health in his countenance? Was that poor, crushed-looking creature the haughty dame who, but two days ago, had turned her back on his Maggie?

The Colonel spoke. "Mr. Maclaggan, our son has told us everything—everything."

Awhile Colin stared, bewildered; then the full significance of the words—their significance to the father and mother before him—blazed upon his intelligence.

"Oh, God," he said in a hushed voice, "that's just awful!"

"I see you understand what it means to us," the Colonel continued. "We would have come sooner, had my wife been less—less broken down. We have come now to offer you our gratitude, though you may well despise it, as you must despise us. We have come to say that, were it possible, we would give all we have to undo what was done on Saturday." He tightened his sustaining hold on his wife's arm. "And we have come, very humbly, to beg that you will, even at the last minute, decide to remain at Glen Laggan—"

Colin's hand went up.

"Pray allow me to finish," said the Colonel. "Within the next few days, we shall be leaving this place. White House will be offered for sale—"

"Stop, stop! Surely that's not—"

"We have been considering making the change for some time, and—and I think that is all I can say. . . . Elfrida!" he said gently.

Without raising her head, she spoke, in little more than a whisper—

"Sir, will you tell your wife that you have seen a proud woman brought very low—that she is sorry beyond words, and will be sorry to the end of her days?"

"I'll tell Maggie. . . . Be sure, ma'am, she'll forgive."

" Let us go," said the Colonel.

Colin opened the door and, not knowing what else to do, stood aside. Slowly they passed out into the hall. After a moment he followed.

Half-way up the staircase stood Maggie. He hurried to her.

" Maggie," he said in a low voice, " they're sorry—sorry's not the word. I can't break a bargain ; I can only tell you that I once did something to help their Wilfred—and now they've found out, and they're down—down in the—dust. And they're going away—for good. I doubt it's money."

It may be that Maggie did not fully comprehend his words. Her gaze was on the two figures now passing the door held open by the butler—particularly on the figure of the woman. Was ever a figure so dejected, so expressive of humiliation ?

" Colin, if they're sorry," she said, suddenly, " I can't let them go like that."

She overtook them at the foot of the steps.

" If you like," she stammered, " I'll shake hands."

She came back to the staircase, looking ashamed of herself.

" Maggie," said her husband, " you're the greatest ever ! "

" Whisht, Colin ! It's terrible to see folk looking as if they had been whipped. I want to forget about it."

" Same here ! But what brought you downstairs ? You haven't got your things on, and it's coming near the hour."

" I changed my mind. I felt I wanted to shake hands with the men. I—I think I can thole it. It'll be something to remember afterwards. You haven't been into them yet—have you?"

"Not yet. I told Rosman to serve them wi' refreshments."

The butler was still at the door, and Colin called him over.

"You've served the refreshments?"

"Yes, sir." Rosman hesitated before he said: "Perhaps I ought to—to warn you, sir—that the men are not here to bid you farewell."

"Are they not? Then what brought them? I sent round word by Mr. Gregg that nobody was going to suffer. I'd better see Mr. Gregg—"

"It's a deputation, sir, including the postmaster, head gardener, stationmaster and the older crofters, led by Murdo McMurrich, who has prepared a speech. The preparation of the speech, I gathered, accounts for the deputation's arrival so late in the day."

"But what do they want?" asked Maggie.

"Ma'am," Rosman answered, a hint of emotion in his utterance, "they want what all of us who have tried to serve you want—the Laird to remain in his place here, at Glen Laggan." With a little bow, he turned and left the hall.

Colin took his wife's arm and led her into the room of that recent tragic interview.

"What am I to do? It's getting cruel hard. First the Colonel, and now Murdo and the men—and look at this!" He showed the telegram. "Good old Bob! My letter isn't posted yet. And then there's Ronnie and—"

"Colin"—she put her hands on his shoulders—"*could* you stick it, as Bob says?"

" Maggie—Maggie, would you back me up ? "

" I would ! Indeed, I would ! "

" Then, by Heavens, we'll carry on ! Glen Laggan's ours. We'll hold it ! And, God helping me, I'll never let you down again ! . . . Is that right, Maggie woman ? "

Her hands slid round his neck. " What a man ! " she said, almost humorously.

Within the minute, however, she must needs rush off to the Railway Room, to tell her daughter.

" Peggy, we're not going ! Your Daddy has decided to carry on ! "

Peggy, ready for the road, sprang up from the arm of Charlie, who rose slowly.

" Not really, Mother ! "

" Yes, really, ducky ! The Colonel and Mrs. Silver have been here—all's forgiven ; there's a desperate wire from Cousin Bob ; and now there's about a hundred men in the big drawing-room, come to ask your father to bide ! Are you not delighted ? "

" Mother, I'm nearly dead with delight ! Charlie, isn't it lovely ? "

Maggie hurried out to rejoin her man.

" Peggy," said Charlie in consternation, " I thought you weren't so keen on Glen Laggan."

" Maybe I wasn't so keen before—Saturday night. Now everything's perfect ! "

" Do you mean that ? Are you sure you're not regretting anything—me, for instance ? "

Peggy might have her flighty moments, but this was not one of them.

" Dear Charlie," she said, " don't be silly ! "

" Well," said Colin—a new Colin—" I suppose we

must go in and face up to all those good chaps. Only I wish to goodness Murdo had left out the speech. It'll be a sermon. I expect he'll be telling us an anecdote about one of his wife's brothers—she must have twenty at least—"

A clock struck five.

From the corridor Mr. Gregg, in his hand a bunch of documents, appeared.

From the door Rosman announced, " The car, sir ! "

" Righto ! " said Colin, absently. " Come on, Maggie."

They approached the big drawing-room.

" May I have a word with you, Mr. Maclaggan ? " the factor called.

" Certainly, Gregg. And, Gregg, I've got to tell you that—"

" Miss Carnachan ! " Rosman announced.

She stumbled, rather than hobbled, into the hall. She gasped—

" Thank God, I'm in time ! I couldn't think of you going, without my getting a handshake. But the damned old caravan did the dirty again. I've walked—run— three miles—"

Colin and Maggie hurried forward. " Come away in," said Colin, taking her by one arm, while Maggie took the other. " Rosman ! A whisky and soda for Miss Carnachan ! "

" Very good, sir," Rosman answered, but sadly. His last order. . . .

" And, Rosman—"

" Sir ? " He stopped, half-way across the hall.

"—Miss Carnachan is staying to dinner."

" Sir ? "

" I'm saying, Miss Carnachan is staying to dinner."

Dinner ? For a moment Rosman looked as though he wanted to scratch his head. Then—illumination !

" Oh, very good, sir—*very* good ! " he blurted, and bolted.

Silently Mr. Gregg slipped away, but, once round the corner, went bounding to the office, to 'phone the news to Rona, and, after that, to destroy a cablegram addressed to Buenos Aires.

As for Miss Carnachan, freeing herself, she wheeled and stared at the two happy faces. She drew a long breath.

" And so," she said, softly, " I backed a winner, after all ! "